The Firs
By Gab

Table of Contents

Prologue: Revelry in Death

Chapter 1: As Above...

Chapter 2: Fraternity of Blood

Chapter 3: An Amaryllis by any Other Name

Chapter 4: Empty Candles

Chapter 5: The Pity of Polonius

Chapter 6: In the Land Reminiscent of Home

Chapter 7: Under Pressure

Chapter 8: A Weaved Web

Chapter 9: The Glory of Euphemia

Chapter 10: Emergence of Ekayana

Chapter 11: The End of Eligius

Chapter 12: Ghosts of the Past

Chapter 13: Calm Sea of Sand

Chapter 14: The Heir of Hipponax

Chapter 15: Heaven and Earth

Chapter 16: Ex Memoriam

Table of Contents cont.

Chapter 17: The Gates of Heaven

Chapter 18: Sacrificing Saint Michael

Chapter 19: Enter, Erebus

Chapter 20: Sickening Sights

Chapter 21: Laplace's Demon

Chapter 22: Borne Back Ceaselessly

Chapter 23: Hubris of Holliday

Chapter 24: DB Cooper's Captive.

Chapter 25: A History of Heresy

Chapter 26: Iscariot's Mercy

Chapter 27: Regencide of Romanova

Chapter 28: Ash on the Ashtabula River

Chapter 29: The Truth of Theseus

Chapter 30: Mechanical Monstrosity

Chapter 31: Buccaneer O' The Bootstrap

Chapter 32: The Penultimate Battle

Chapter 33: Progressus Ultimum

Chapter 34: Postultimum

Chapter 35: The Zealot and The China shop Bull

Table of Contents cont.

Chapter 36: Heartache of a Sanguine Amaryllis

Chapter 37: ...So Below

Epilogue: The Hardest of Hearts...

Afterword: G

Afterword: S

Prologue: Revelry in Death

It's the middle of the night and I'm driving. I turn 17 in a few months. *I'm starting to think this wasn't a good idea.* I took my mom's car out for a joy ride with my friends, and we've been driving around for hours at this point. My friend Alex is sitting in the passenger seat. He looks pretty nervous. I kind of feel bad for forcing him to come. My other two friends, Kevin and CJ, are sitting in the back. CJ's talking at Kevin, and Kevin is just staring out the window.

"Hey, Kev! You good over there? You're starting to make me worried," CJ asks, still talking at Kevin.

"I'm fine," Kevin replies, a lack of emotion in his voice. Kevin had always acted kind of distant when it came to me. I mean I considered him a friend, but I'm not sure he sees it that way. To him, I'm probably more of a friend of a friend. Alex and CJ know him a lot better than I do.

"Cat, are you really sure this was a good idea?" Alex questions, starting to bite his nails. *My actual full name is Cathryn, but I go by Cat.*

"Oh, come on Alex, when's the last time I had a good idea?" I joke, trying to lighten the mood. I can barely see in front of the car. *Is that an intersection?... Ah well, who cares?* Just as I'm passing through the intersection, I turn my head to the left to see an old man, *who was most likely drunk*, driving a large blue pickup truck heading straight for us. And about as soon as I saw him, he t-boned the car, sending it flying off the side of the road and into the woods.

Chapter 1: As Above...

I open my eyes... the light filtering through the leaves of a tree shines down onto my face. I feel the soft grass brushing against the nape of my neck as a calm breeze flows around me making the leaves above me move around. I get up and look around. *I guess I'm at the edge of a forest, but...* The forest in front of me seems to go on and on, a softly lit hall of trees. Turning around I look out of the forest and see a hill going down into what looks like a small 19th-century town surrounded by a large stone brick wall. Laying on the ground next to me is my friend Alex. It looks like he's out cold. *Wait... something's off... Why am I here? What about the car? And it was the middle of the night...* I try to push away the thoughts clouding my mind and kneel on the ground and start shaking Alex by the shoulders to wake him up.

"Alex!" I exclaim in my attempt to wake him, "Alex wake up!"

After yelling at him while shaking him he finally wakes up. He opens his eyes swiftly, covering them with his hand in an attempt to block the sunlight. He looks around at his surroundings with his eyebrows slightly furrowed and an uneasy look in his eyes.

"Cat?" he says, slowly getting up, "What's going on? Where are we?"

"I'm not too sure myself," I say, shrugging my shoulders.

"Where's CJ?" Alex asks, looking around. *CJ, another friend of mine I'd met along with Alex due to us being put in the same English class in middle school. We've been friends for years, but someone else is missing...* I look behind to see CJ on the ground unconscious.

"He's right behind me Alex. Could you go and wake him up for me?" I say.

"Yeah, sure," Alex replies, a confused look still plastered across his face. He gets up and walks over to CJ and starts shaking him. *Something's still not right...*

"Hey CJ!" Alex exclaims, as he continues to shake CJ by the shoulders, "CJ wake up!"

CJ wakes up and looks around, a look of unease on his face,

"What's going on?"

"Not really sure, CJ," Alex shrugs his shoulders.

"Where's Kevin?" CJ asks, a look of concern replacing the unease. *Kevin?... Wait... Kevin!* It all came back to me. Kevin, another one of my good friends I had also met in that same English class, though Alex and CJ had known him longer and better than me.

"Where is he?!" CJ yells at Alex before looking up at me, his concern and fear clearly displayed on his face.

"I have no idea CJ I just woke up too," Alex looks worried, trying to rationalize with CJ. "Seriously though Cat what's going on? Weren't we just in the car? I mean where are we 'cause this place sure as hell doesn't look like New England," Alex asks, trying to get some sort of answer out of me. *I don't really know how far we got on that night ride. We left when it was still light out and last, I can remember it was the middle of the night... We could be all the way out in New York!*

"Look, I don't know, okay, I'm just as in the dark about this whole situation as you are," I say, trying to calm him down.

"Well, why don't we start searching for him? He has to be around here somewhere," CJ suggests.

"Agreed," Alex and I say in unison. We get up and walk down the hill to the entrance of the town. There's a gap in the wall, one guard on each side wearing some sort of old fashion military uniform. There's a large sign hanging over the gap and it says... Well, actually, I don't know what it says at all it's in some sort of foreign script maybe,

"-Russian?"

"No, that's definitely not Cyrillic, I know Russian," CJ replies, trying to analyze the sign, "Maybe Hebrew?"

"Yeah, that's not Hebrew," Alex says. One of the two guards lets out an exasperated sigh,

"It's in Abramonic and it says Tirentod, a nice little town in this world we call Sotaqt. You all must not be from around here. It's probably best that you head to the town hall."

"Sota what?" I say.

"Soh-**Tah**-quit. You guys must really not be from around here if you don't know that."

"You could say that," I say, not exactly sure where here is. *I've never heard of a language called Abramonic before. This is all so strange... I guess we're not in New York.* We walk into town and immediately someone catches my eye. There's a woman standing at what looks like a fruit stand. Now, that seems perfectly normal, but the thing that's strange is that she has what looks like cat ears on top of her head, and a cat tail sticking out from under her skirt the color of which matches her hair. Something strange is certainly going on.

"Excuse me, I don't mean to bother you, but where is the town hall? We're new here and we were told it would be best to go there," I ask, trying to follow the guard's directions.

"Those sure are some strange clothes you're wearing. Wait, could it be! It's been years since. I mean there was that one time recently though... Ah, never mind. Anyway, the town hall is a little way down the street and to the right. You can't miss it, there's a huge clock on the front," the woman with the cat ears explains.

"Thank you," I say.

"No problem," she responds. We all walk down the street and just like she said, there's a large building with a clock tower. We head inside and walk over to the front desk.

"Hello, we were told to come here by the guards at the entrance," I say, to the person sitting at the front desk. She looks up from her paperwork and looks us over,

"Of course, please come this way."

We follow her into a room where there are two couches facing each other, one occupied by an elderly woman.

"Please sit," she requests. We all sit down on the couch facing her and she continues, "I'm sure you are all very confused and have many questions, but please wait first I must register your synats."

"Synats?" CJ says, sounding very confused.

"Synats are a special power that every person who enters this world Sotaqt we call it, whether it be in birth or from another world gets. They are unique to each person and are represented by two words on which your powers are based. The first word is based on death and the second life. In other words, the first word gives you a peek into your fate and the second describes you as a person. Starting with CJ I think it is your synat is Glass Ego, next Alex your synat is Force Sight, and last Cat your synat is Burning Song," she explains, "You may be wondering how I know all this and that's due to my synat Aged wisdom."

"Synats? Power? What are you even talking about?" Alex asks.

"I'm sorry, but we're out of time. I'm going to have to ask you to go," the old lady says. We leave the room still with many questions unanswered. *Maybe we can ask Kevin about it once we find him.*

"I think we should look for Kevin now, no?" I say.

"Yeah, that's probably what we should have done first," CJ says, obviously annoyed by the lack of information we got, giving us more questions than answers. Out of the corner of my eye, I see that woman with cat ears again.

"Excuse me. Sorry to bother you again, but have you seen someone about my height, blond and wearing dark clothes?" Alex asks.

"Actually, I did. I think he's standing by the church," she says.

"Thank you," I say, starting to walk away, "Wait. Where exactly is the church?"

"Down the street to the left," she says, with a smile.

"Thank you," I say. We walk down the street and to the left and sure enough, there's a building that looks exactly like what you'd expect a stone church to look like. The building is on the other side of the town from the entrance and leaning against the wall is,

"Kev! Hey, where have you been?! We've been looking for you!" CJ says, his mood finally improving.

"Kevin, how's it going?" Alex says.

"Where have I been!? Where have you been?! I haven't seen you in a month! Not since... not since... not since the crash," Kevin exclaims, tears forming in his eyes.

"A month? Kev, we just got here less than an hour ago," CJ says, clearly a little confused.

"Less than an hour ago?... but... Don't you guys remember we crashed?" Kevin says.

"Crash? Kevin, you can't mean..." I say, rejecting the reality of what happened.

"The car crash! We died! We're all dead!" Kevin exclaims. It all came back to me: the joy ride, the conversations in the car, and then the crash.

"Dead? Come on Kev you must be joking. Right?" CJ says, a look of disbelief on his face. Kevin looks CJ straight in the eyes with a dead serious look,

"You're dead CJ. I'm dead. We're all dead."

"Well, if we're dead then, where are we? Some sort of afterlife?" Alex asks.

"No, I don't think so. This is some other world. Like an alternate universe or something. And from what I gather people coming from earth is a relatively common occurrence, though it seems to happen in some places more than others," Kevin explains.

"Another world? That's pretty far out, but I do remember the car crash, and as weird as it is that seems like a pretty good explanation," Alex says, "So, do you think we'll be able to go back? To Earth I mean."

"My guess is most likely not." There's a moment of silence. A solemn realization that we are stuck in this 'other' world. Alex attempts to break the tension, "Also we were told about these things called synats, but the explanation wasn't exactly super descriptive. Do you know anything?"

"Oh, synats are basically powers you gain when you come here, though the people born in this world also have them. I'm sure you got told your synat. It's not something you'll get immediately, but you'll eventually have a decent amount of control over it. Your powers are based on your two words, or in other words, your powers are anything you can think of related to your two words."

"So, we have superpowers?"

"Yeah, for example, Cat what's your synat?"

"If I remember correctly, she said it was, 'Burning song'."

"Alright so 'Burning Song' hmm," he pauses to think for a second, "Got it! You could use your voice to control and create flames."

"Oh, mine is 'Force Sight'. Hmm, what exactly would be a combination of the two?"

"Well, Alex, your powers don't necessarily need to come from a combination of the two words. They can be from just one or the other as well as both.

"Oh, so I could create a force field or see in the dark or something?"

"Exactly. I mean some are better than others, but the playing field is still equal in a certain sense."

"So, how exactly do we learn to use these 'synats'?" Alex asks.

"It's kind of hard to explain. It will probably happen in the spur of the moment and then you'll be able to use it from there. It's not really something you learn to use."

"I guess that kind of makes sense. So, Kev, what's your synat?" Alex asks.

"Oh, my synat? It's-" Suddenly, Kevin is cut off by the sound of an explosion and the wall falling down on top of him.

"No... I never got to... to-" Kevin attempts to say, before going silent. Alex stretches his arms and an invisible force pushes the falling stones and half-burnt candles from the wall around CJ and me.

"Kevin!" CJ cries out.

"Hmph, my master said you would put up more of a fight," A man in some sort of dark red robe says.

"Who are you?!" I yell.

"That's not for you to know. The only thing you do need to know is that I'm here to kill you," the man says, followed by a crazed laugh. Without realizing I start to vocalize and the flame from the church's incense burner flies out and enlarges, engulfing the attacker. I finally realize what's going on. *Huh, so this is what Kevin was talking about earlier.*

"Agggh! Damn you," the attacker yells, in agony. He creates an explosion underneath Alex sending him into the air.

"Cat! Look out he's trying to create shrapne-" CJ is cut off by Alex coming down out of the air and landing on top of him. The attacker creates an explosion inside one of the stone bricks from the broken church wall creating shrapnel. CJ looks over at me and stretches his hand out. Well, I guess this is it. I accept my fate, but when the shrapnel hits me it shatters and does next to no damage. *Huh? But the shrapnel... It just shattered?* The attacker runs over and tries to create another explosion, but before he can CJ yells out,

"Stop!"

This seemed to, surprisingly, make him pause for just long enough for CJ and Alex to get up and grab onto the attacker, stopping him dead in his tracks.

"Hah. Hah. HAHAHAHAHAHAHAHAHAH!" the attacker suddenly starts laughing.

"Cat! Alex! Let go, he's going to blow himself up!" CJ exclaims. I jump back and my eyes shift up to the wall, a hooded figure points their finger at the attacker, and then in an instant, he vaporizes, and just like the attacker and the hooded figure disappear. What was that? I land on the ground pretty hard. Damn, I think I'm gonna pass out! Alex is on the ground a few feet from me says faintly,

"Did we win?" Before falling unconscious. CJ is probably also unconscious.

I see a slim, but muscular figure above me in black robes with a white pattern. His hair is jet black and he seems to be around 6 feet tall. My vision begins to blur before fading into black.

Chapter 2: Fraternity of Blood

Light; whizzing around the universe at the fastest possible speed. Going all over at the speed limit of the universe, and despite all this speed it still takes years to centuries to millennia for light to reach its destination. The universe is vast yet even at the fastest speed it would still take you longer than the known age of the universe just to travel across the part we can see, not even taking into account the size of the universe in its entirety. And even if you were to take such a journey your destination would move farther and farther away faster than you could get there leaving you alone in the emptiness of space with your only companion being the light traveling beside you. Light also happened to be the companion that greeted me when I opened my eyes.

"Where am I?" I say looking at the stone ceiling above me, the sunlight filtering in through a large stained-glass window. I think back, remembering the fight I had had with my friends against the person who had... who had... *killed Kevin. Huh? Killed? That's stupid Kevin's not dead.* I remember that I was knocked out at some point during the fight.

"You were injured so I brought you and your friends into the church to heal," says a man who looked to be about my age in clothes usually worn by a priest who is sitting beside the bed I am currently resting in.

"Who are you?" I ask, my synat's passive ability activating without my knowledge, which boosts my charisma a little.

"I am called Father Veau, but you may refer to me as Argent," the priest introduces himself, getting up and sitting next to me in the bed.

"Thank you, Argent. I'm sure I'd be in much worse shape if it weren't for you," I say, thinking back to the beating I took in the fight yesterday. I look down to see that I am wearing some sort of black robes, my scarf lying on the small table next to the bed.

"Your clothes were burnt during the fight yesterday, so I lent you some of my old robes," Argent smiles faintly at me.

"Kevin. Argent, where's Kevin?" I say, grasping at some faint hope that he was still alive and that this man, Argent, might have been able to save him. The wind of my panicked movement ends up putting out the candle beside me.

"Kevin? Hmm... you must be talking about that boy with the blond hair..." Argent pauses seemingly to collect his thoughts trying to figure out what to say.

"Yes, that's him. What happened?" I say, still grasping at that faint hope.

"I'm sorry to say, but your friend... Kevin is dead. I tried to the best of my abilities, but he was already dead by the time I found him. I..." Argent stops, seemingly at a loss at what to say.

"He's dead..." I say. The last shard of my hope dropped and shattered on the ground. I can't even think. The reality of the situation hits. My best friend is dead.

"I'm so sorry. Were you close?" Argent asks, a look of concern on his face.

"He was one of my best friends..." *Maybe even a little bit more than just that.* I finish the sentence in my head. *No... he can't be dead. It's not even possible. I*

"Your friend... We can have a gravestone for him. It will take a day or two to make the preparations to get it, but..." Argent pauses again, unsure of what to say, "I will save the questions for later." I soon fall unconscious with the weight of reality bearing down upon me. Just like light, my destination is so far away, and I can only move so fast; it is only then when I realize that my destination is moving farther and farther away faster than I can get there, Leaving me all alone in the emptiness with light as my only companion. My consciousness soon returns to me.

"Oh, you're awake. Are you okay?" Argent says, with that same look of concern as earlier.

"I'm fine," I say, in a dead, flat tone.

"Are you sure? I mean you-," I cut Argent off,

"I'm fine."

"Now that I think about it, I have yet to hear your name," Argent says.

"It's CJ," I answer.

"Ah, CJ. If you don't mind me asking, where are you from?" Argent asks.

"Well, it's kind of hard to explain. This may sound a little crazy, but I guess you could say I'm from another world," I say, trying to think of the best way to phrase it.

"Other world?" Argent says, a look of confusion on his face.

"Well, I came from a world without synats and died and ended up here," I explain. *He surely thinks I'm crazy now.*

"You returned from the dead unto our land... a deo, ipse venit..." Argent looks as if he may faint.

"Are you okay?" I ask, concerned. I try to shift my thoughts towards the current situation and away from what happened yesterday.

"You are he, the savior," Argent gets off the bed to kneel at the foot, "to save us from the King of Assassins."

"Uh, I... huh?" *I mean I don't want to impersonate a religious figure, but from the way he's acting, I might not be able to get him to shake the idea.* I decide to go along with it; Also, he does seem to have healing abilities that may prove useful in the future.

"My faithful servant, I am the man of which you speak, though after all of the years in the other world and my death I have lost memory of my previous self," I say, my synat's ability helping me to get Argent to believe what I'm saying. Before Argent is able to respond Alex cuts in alerting everyone to the fact, he is awake.

"Do you know who sent that man?" Alex asks, looking over at Argent and me.

"Well, I think the 'master' he referred to was most likely The Assassin King. Reports say he's blond, a bit aged, and of a similar height and build to your friend... Kevin I mean. Though those 'reports' are really nothing more than just rumors. I doubt anyone has seen him and lived," Argent says, as a heavy silence weighs upon the church, "Ahem, anyway, he commands a group of devoted followers who are all skilled assassins. He's been terrorizing Sotaqt for the past ten years. No one knows what his goal is, except for maybe destabilizing the current world order, but other than that it's anybody's guess."

"The Assassin King. Huh..." I say, my empty sadness quickly turning into a rage, "Damn him. I swear on my life I'll kill him and avenge Kevin." I calm down and start to collect myself. "Sorry, it's just..." I say, trailing off.

"It's okay Master CJ The Assassin King has hurt all of us in one way or another. He is a scourge on the world," Argent says, in a solemn tone. *Master?*

"Argent earlier I heard the person at the town hall, and you talk about something called 'Sotaqt'. What is that?" Alex asks.

"Oh, it's the name of the world we live in," Argent says. He sounds surprised like it was something that was common knowledge. *Though I guess it would be common knowledge to anyone living here.*

"What else do you know about him? The Assassin King?" I ask.

"Well, the only other thing I know that I haven't already told you is that he has a very rare three-word synat. Other than that, I fear I am in the dark," Argent explains.

"Three words? Do you know what they are?" Alex asks, struggling to keep his cool tone. Alex may have seemed to take things better than I have on the surface, but just one look at his face tells me he's writhing on the inside. A mix of sadness and anger swirling around in his head. I'm thankful for him trying to stay cool because if he had been like I was early I probably would be in a much worse state than I am now.

"No. I'm afraid I am unaware," Argent says.

"Well, if that's all you know then that's all you know. I think we should wake up Cat," Alex suggests.

"Yes, good idea. I do need you to come with me to get some food, as I assume you will be staying here," Argent says.

"Well, yeah, it's not like we have anywhere else to stay," Alex joked, trying to brighten the mood a little. Argent walks over to where Cat is laid in a stiff-looking bed and wakes her up.

"Hey what's going on?" She asks, looking around, "Oh you guys are already awake. What happened? Did we win?" A solemn air fills the room along with an accompanying silence. "What happened, are you guys okay?" Cat asks, looking concerned.

"The thing is Cat... Well... It's Kevin he-he's dead," Alex says, looking down in a mix of grief and vicarious shame.

"Oh, I'm so sorry I didn't know," Cat says, looking down with a look of shock on her face. She puts her hands on our shoulders.

"Sorry to interrupt, but we need to go soon before the streets get too crowded," Argent says.

"No, it's fine," I say. We walk out of the church and see people working to fix the part of the city wall that was blown up yesterday. One of the men who seem to be in charge looks over at us and walks up.

"Father Veau, you're here. Do you know what happened?" the man asks.

"Yesterday one of The Assassin King agents attacked. He must've had some sort of explosive synat," Argent says.

"The Assassin King. Really? We haven't had an attack in months and even then... Anyway, do you know why?" The man asks.

"He seemed to be targeting these people over here," Argent says, pointing over to us.

"What did they do to attract that kind of attention from The Assassin King?" they say, giving us a suspicious look.

"I'm not really sure. In fact, they seem to be from Earth. I'm pretty confused myself. It just doesn't make any sense," Argent says.

"From Earth huh... Are you sure? I mean there was that kid a few months ago and their clothes are pretty strange... Well, I believe in your sacred wisdom Father Veau. When you have the time though you should probably report the attack to the town hall," They say, dropping their suspicions.

"Of course. We will as soon as we can," Argent says politely, "Alright we have to go to the food stand now."

"Alright," I look back at the broken wall and the pile of rocks that served as an early grave for Kevin. *A second grave I suppose, considering the crash*. I brush off the morbid thought as we start walking down the street.

"So, Argent, who was that guy?" Alex asks.

"He was the head of the local construction group. It's run by the town hall," Argent explains.

"Ah, that makes sense," Alex nods.

"Argent, we didn't get a good explanation. Do you know where synats come from?" Cat asks.

"Well, many will say they came from The Red Death as a kind of mutation. Others say it came from The Great War as a reward for our victory. Some say that the air is unclean, and it is our reward for surviving it. However, the true answer is that Azathoth, the one true God, gave it to us in paradise and let us keep it after paradise was destroyed by the great spider, Adamnev, as Master CJ can tell us," Argent explains, gesturing for my confirmation.

"Oh, I... uh... well." I'm not really sure what to say.

"Forgive me Young Master CJ. I forgot that you had lost your memory. I will keep that in mind," Argent apologizes, bowing slightly.

"Yes of course," I sigh, relieved.

"Ah, we're almost ther-" Argent gets cut off by a loud scream coming from down the street. I turn to see a fruit stand and Argent along with it flying in our direction, thrown by a girl who looks to be about our age and who appears to be covered in a thin layer of blood and shallow cuts. I duck down and cover my face with my arms bracing for the impact. *It's been less than a day and I've already been attacked twice, did I break a mirror or something?*

Chapter 3: An Amaryllis by any Other Name

I hear a loud scream coming from down the street. Looking to my right there's what looks like a fruit stand and Argent flying straight towards me. I stick out my hand in response. Some sort of invisible barrier surrounds me, Cat and CJ protecting us from the fruit stand and Argent. Once the dust settles, I'm relieved to see that, while a little roughed up, Argent is alright. *What was that? It was almost like there was some sort of force field.*

"Hey guys, you alright?" I ask.

"Physically at least," CJ jokes.

"I think I'm good," Cat confirms.

"Who was that?" I ask. Argent gets up from the ground and explains,

"It's probably another one of The Assassins King's agents. We should end this quickly, Master CJ."

"Agreed," CJ complies.

I look back over at the girl who had chucked the fruit stand at us. She seemed to be covered in small cuts and looked to be about our age if not a little older. *She might even be taller than me... Based on how far she threw it, her synat is probably strength related.* Before I'm able to finish my thought, she comes running towards us. She tries to punch me, but before she lands her hit, I put up another force field. *I guess I must have some sort of passive ability.* Her fist hits my force field and goes through it or maybe it's more like she shattered it because when her fist hits me it feels like more of a tap than a punch. I jump back to avoid getting hit again. *It seems that my force fields have their limit or she's just strong, which is a little scary.*

"Everybody be on your guard. I may have been able to protect us up until now, but I can only put up a force field a few more times," I say, "Anybody got any ideas?"

Argent comes over and whispers something into my ear.

"Are you sure that will work?" I ask. Argent nods in response. The girl is now Running straight at us again. She tries to hit me, but using my synat I redirect the force of her punch back through her hand and make her hit herself in the head which knocks her unconscious. Getting a bit of a closer look, her slightly muscular physique is noticeable.

"Is it already over?" Cat questions.

"Yeah, she looks like she's out cold," I comment.

"Well, that was suspiciously fast. Almost as if she was holding back?" CJ questions.

"Yeah, that was very quick," I say, I then notice something, "Hey guys do you see that!"

"What? Oh, she has a hairband, what's weird about that... Wait no you're right, that's only something that could be from Earth!" Cat exclaimed.

"But why would someone from Earth be working for The Assassin King?" I ask.

"I don't know. Maybe she was recruited?" CJ says.

"I don't know. What do you think we should do?" I ask.

"I think we should take her to the medical lodge and see if we can get any information out of her," Cat says.

"Like torture her?" CJ suggests.

"No! We have to see what she says first. She might tell us what we want to know without any resistance. We can't just go straight to torture. Besides, even if she didn't talk torture is off the table." Cat says.

"So, what if she talks? She just tried to kill us! It doesn't matter if she talks or not!" CJ exclaims. *CJ...*

"No, I think Cat's right. There must be more to it," I say, "If she is from Earth then there's certainly a lot of questions to be asked."

I pick up the girl and we go to the medical lodge which luckily was nearby. We walk into what looks like a fairly large room with a multitude of beds housing a large number of patients. We run over to the nearest nurse in sight.

"Oh my, that looks quite bad what happened?" The nurse says.

"Well, this girl here is covered in small cuts and is unconscious," I say.

"Alright, we'll take her to the priority care section," she says, "Lay her down on this stretcher here."

I lay her down on the stretcher and they wheel her off to the priority care section.

"If you want to wait here, we have a few benches outside the building. If something important happens concerning the patient you brought in, one of the nurses will inform you," a nurse says. We go outside and sit down on the benches.

"So, who's gonna pay the medical bill?" I ask.

"Hey, Argent, could you cover the expense?" CJ asks Argent, smirking.

"Of course, Master CJ," Argent says. We wait there for a few hours before one of the nurses comes out and says,

"The patient's wounds are healed, but she is not awake yet. The doctor said that it will be about a day or so until she's conscious. So, we recommend you go home. Once she's awake we'll call you in." We head back to the church. Once we get there CJ asks Argent,

"Argent, do you think we could stay in the church?"

"Of course, Master CJ," Argent says, "We only have enough rooms for 3 people. If you want, I can sleep in the storage shed outside."

"Just put Cat in the storage shed," CJ says.

"Um..." I say.

"I'm joking, Argent and I can just share a room," CJ says.

"If you want, I can sleep on the floor Master CJ," Argent says.

"No, it's fine Argent," CJ says.

"But, Master CJ," Argent says.

"It's fine Argent," CJ says. I go to my room. It's not very big, but it's not tiny either. I get into bed and fall asleep. *I look around and I'm in a hospital room. Wait, how am I back on Earth? Somebody is sitting in the hospital bed; they look pretty beat up. I look a little closer. Wait... Is that Kevin!*

"Kevin!" I yell. It seems like he can't hear me. A doctor and nurse walk in with Kevin's mom. Kevin's mom gasps when she sees Kevin.

"There's not much more we can do Mrs. Vaus. I'll be frank, your son isn't long for this world; he'll only be around for a few more days at most. If there is anything, we can do for you Mrs. Vaus please let us know. I'm deeply sorry about your son. I'll leave you two alone but do remember that there are some papers you will have to fill out. We truly hope the best for you Mrs. Vaus," The doctor says. Kevin's mom signs

some sort of form and before I can see what happens I wake up. I look out the window and the sun's already up. I leave my room and go to the dining hall, seeing that only Cat was there so far. Before I can greet her, I hear a noise coming from the room Argent and CJ had been staying in.

"Ow!" CJ exclaims.

"I am very sorry Master CJ!" Argent apologizes.

"It's not your fault Argent," CJ says. I walk into the room to see that CJ had fallen out of the bed.

"Hello, is this Alex?" A voice seeming to come from inside my head.

"What?! Who is this?!" I ask.

"Oh, sorry for not telling you I'm one of the nurses at the medical lodge. My synat allows me to telepathically communicate," the nurse says.

"Oh, okay," I say.

"Well, anyway the patient you brought in is awake now," the nurse says.

"Really?! We'll be there soon," I say.

"Hey, guys! Stop messing around, the girl from yesterday is awake," I yell. CJ gets up off the ground and we all run to the medical lodge and head in.

"Where is the room of the patient we brought in?" I ask

"The left hallway room 3," The reception desk lady says. We walk down to the room. I walk in through the door and see the girl from yesterday. *She's actually pretty attractive without all the cuts and blood.*

"Do you know anything about The Assassin King?" I ask.

"The Assassin King? That bastard!" She exclaims, "Oh, sorry for not introducing myself, my name's

Amaryll." *She seems quite reasonable, unlike the girl we fought yesterday.*

"So, why did you attack us yesterday?" I ask

"Well, I was under the control of The Assassin King," Amaryll says.

"Under control? What do you mean?"

"Part of The Assassin King's synat is the ability to control people. It's thanks to you that I'm not under his control anymore, knocking me out must've done the trick."

"So, you won't try to kill us now?"

"Of course not. You're the one that saved me after all."

"So, then how did you get under his control?"

"Well, not too unlike you all, I came here from Earth a year ago with a group of my friends, but shortly after we got here one of The Assassin King's agents killed all of my friends. I barely escaped. So, after that, I gathered some information and I went to The Assassin King's lair to kill him, but once I got there he said that he let me find him on purpose so he could make me one of his agents. After that my memory is very cloudy, but just recently I was gaining more and more control of myself," Amaryll says. *So that's why it felt like she was holding back.*

"Actually, I have one request."

"What is it?"

"Well, you're trying to find The Assassin King, right? So, I was wondering if I could join you? My synat 'Bleeding Rage' allows me to become physically stronger the more pain I am in," she looks up at me.

"Well, our goals align and the more the merrier so sure," I say.

"Really?! Thank you!" She exclaims.

Chapter 4: Empty Candles

Sometime into the conversation a nurse walked in. I couldn't help but be slightly fixated on her. She was absolutely beautiful. She walked over to us.

"Here, take this," She said, placing a folded piece of paper into my hands, "I want to join you guys. My synat can help, 'Frozen Passion' lets me control ice, and I can use it to heal as well." There's an awkward silence in the room. "Oh, sorry for not introducing myself, I'm Azalea, I'm guessing you're Cat," she says. Hearing her say my name made me blush. I open up the piece of paper and strangely enough it's in my handwriting. My bashfulness turns straight into confusion. I unfold the piece of paper that says, *2 years from now a person named Amaryll will be put into the care of the medical lodge you work at. When this happens go to her room and ask to join the group of people that are there.*

"Where did you get this?" I ask, very confused. *This was very obviously written by me, but I've never met this person and I just came to this world yesterday...*

"2 years ago, someone saved my life. They handed me this after they had brought me to safety and nursed me back to health," She explains.

"Do you know who?" I ask.

"No, I never saw their face," Azalea answers, "all I saw was their black cloak and hood."

"What do you guys think?" I turn to the others, posing the possibility before them.

"Well, if she has some sort of powers it might be useful in taking out The Assassin King," CJ says.

"Healing is useful too," Alex says, "Alright we'll let you join, but wouldn't you like to hear what we plan to do first?"

"Well, I guess so," Azalea says.

"We plan to find The Assassin King and kill him," CJ seems to have a fire behind his eyes, but be it of rage or passion I couldn't tell.

"The Assassin King... If that's what you plan to do then I'm totally on board," Azalea declares, a confident look on her face. Amaryll gets out of the bed, allowing us to begin our trek out of the medical lodge and towards the church.

"Oh, I didn't notice before, but is that you Father Veau?" Azalea questions.

"It is. Though if we are to be traveling with each other then perhaps Argent would be more appropriate," he comments.

"All right," she smiles, "I knew it was you. I mean I've only seen you a few times when I was at the church."

"Really? I don't remember seeing you there." Argent looks mildly surprised by that; Azalea isn't the kind of person you'd expect to be particularly religious.

"I understand. I mean so many people come in and out of the church it's no surprise you wouldn't remember me. I don't go there very often either."

"Oh, why were you there?" Alex asks.

"Well, the former schoolteacher, Mrs. Jorggen or something, wanted to have her kid in the church, and I was called in as a midwife," she explains.

"Ah, well that explains it," Alex says.

"I like your blue hair," I shift the subject. Her hair is pale, almost iridescent blue, like the color of glacial ice at sunrise.

"Really? Thanks! I got it from my father," Azalea says, smiling.

"Got it from?... You mean it's naturally blue?!" I exclaim.

"Yeah, it's natural. Is that so strange?" Azalea tilts her head inquisitively.

"Apparently not..."

"I don't mean to pry, but why exactly are you guys going after The Assassin King?" Azalea questions.

"No, it's fine," Alex says. "It was our friend. Yesterday we were attacked by one of The Assassin King's agents. The agent blew up part of the Town wall and it fell on top of our friend. Actually, now that I'm thinking about it. Argent, is the gravestone ready?"

"We will have to look. If it has then finished, then it should already be in the graveyard behind the church." Argent explains. We finally get back to the church and Argent leads us to the graveyard behind it.

"Ah, it's already here," Argent says. Looking out in front of me I see a gravestone that is very polished, and it looks new. Something is written on it in a script I can't read, it looks vaguely Latinesque.

"Is it this one, Argent?" CJ quivers.

"Yes."

"What does it say?" Alex asks.

"It says, 'Kevin Vaus birth: unknown death: Eauure 18th, 10,223AT. May his soul lie in the six dreaming forests of Azathoth'," Argent lays a candle on either side of his grave, lighting them both.

CJ falls onto his knees, tears forming in his eyes as his hands move to his face, cupping it.

"Why Kevin? W-Why..." CJ cries out, the tears dripping down and staining the dirt below him. Alex kneels putting his hand on CJ's shoulder to comfort him. Tears start to form in Alex's eyes as well, the despair of this tragedy seeming nigh-contagious. The church bells from behind began to ring their sorrowful notes. It was a bright and sunny day, a clear azure sky void of any clouds, but for these two it might as well have been the darkest day of their lives; truly, the gods are indifferent to the many hells of the earth. Even though the sky was clear and the sun was out it was still raining, They sat there for a while staring at that piece of stone, their expressions, their eyes, and their composure displaying only one thing, *I'll avenge you, Kevin.* They both stand up, a look of determination on their faces. The determination of the two was visibly different, however. In Alex, he seemed almost possessed by justice itself, that wrongs must be righted. In CJ however, there was only bloodlust; I could see it in his eyes, if CJ finds The Assassin King, he will assuredly make a sea of his blood.

"Master CJ, are you okay?"

"Yes," he answers, though that answer was obviously false. We walk out of the graveyard and into the church.

"So, what do we do now?" I ask.

"Well, we need to prepare for our departure." Alex tries to clear his mind.

"Agreed, we missed out on getting supplies earlier when we were attacked," Argent nods, "I think it would be best to go back out to get some."

"Alright sounds good," I look at CJ, seeing that he seems to have calmed down mostly. We get up and begin walking to the town market. "Argent?"

"Yes, Master CJ?"

"You said the month on the gravestone was Eauure. When exactly is that?"

"Ah, yes I was wondering if I should tell you about that. You see in a year of 365 days there are fourteen months, Jannur, Deuxeer, Trigg, Eauure, Pyyree, Sixx, ChannCea, Sainnte, Ninneh, Cuberr, Faleeve, Maldeey, Unlouk, and last Zagreste. There is an extra day in the year on every other blue moon. The exact number of days in each months varies with Trigg having the lowest number of days at 20 and Unlouk and ChannCea having the most at 30."

"Ah, that makes sense. That aside, Alex, Cat, can I ask you something really quick?" CJ asks, walking behind one of the market stalls. Argent tries to follow, prompting CJ to say "privately." Alex and I look at one another before I shrug, walking behind the stall with him.

"What is it?" Alex asks, visibly confused.

"Listen, when we catch The Assassin King, don't kill him," CJ demands.

"Why?" I ask, *isn't CJ the one who wants him dead?*

"I want to make him suffer as I have, as Kevin has. I'm gonna find out who he cares about, and before I rip out his goddamn throat, I'm gonna make him watch them all suffer the same fate Kevin had," CJ's face was blank and serious, his teeth gritted together.

CJ didn't seem angry in the common sense, his words were conscious and cerebral, driven by logic over raw emotion.

"CJ... Y-yeah, got it," Alex steps backward, evidently overwhelmed by seeing CJ acting like this. I felt the same, and intending to evade responding to that, I suggest,

"Let's meet back up with Argent and stuff, we should make sure that he isn't spending everything."

"Sure, I bet he doesn't spend much though," CJ's previous demeanor disappeared, returning to his usual calmer persona. We return to the others to hear Argent exclaim

"Oh, I almost forgot. We have to report the attack to the town hall."

"Yeah, I do remember the construction worker mentioning that," I comment, still mildly unnerved from what CJ said before.

Chapter 5: The Pity of Polonius

The phrase 'God is dead' is a morbid one, but it is true, nonetheless. The secret of God being dead; if nobody can judge us in the great beyond, we must judge one another on earth. I remain resolute and heavy-set in my judgement of The Assassin King. The town hall is a large structure with a grandfather clock softly ticking on the north wall. The clock has a broken hour hand, seeming snapped in half.

"We're here to report an attack," Azalea said, standing directly in front of the desk.

"Of course, sweetheart, fill out this form," the woman answers, handing out six forms to all of us.

"I can't read this," I say.

"Oh, foreigners, I do dislike your kind," she comments, chuckling.

"Excuse me? Do you know who I am?" I try to intimidate her by upping my charisma with my synat.

"See, using that line always gives me an excuse to do this. The Assassin King has eyes everywhere," she smiles as she presses the 'security' button under her desk, summoning three large cat-men brandishing what looks like large sticks. I attempt to use my synat to convince them to stop, but no words come from my mouth as one of the sticks glows.

"Oh, I don't know hi-" Alex objects before being hit with one of the sticks. It seems none of our synats are working, leaving us fully open to being knocked out with big sticks. When I awake, I am in what looks like a prison cell; I share my cell with Argent and Alex while

Cat, Azalea, and Amaryll cohabitate the cell to our left. One of the cat-men walked through the hallway in which the cells lined the wall, looking over at us with a grin. The man stops, looking at us from left to right,

"Heh, you seriously thought investigating me would be that easy? The Assassin King is smarter than that, as am I," he smirks, brandishing the big stick.

"Investigating? Ah, so you're the spy, how arrogant to reveal that." I point out.

"Oh, it's not like you'll be able to tell anyone," he chuckles.

"Are you going to kill us?" Amaryll asks.

"And it'll look like an accident," he slams the stick against the wall, cracking the bricks and allowing water to begin streaming in from the other side.

"Let us out, we'll drown!" Alex pleads as the man walks away, sealing the metal vault-like door behind him. The water begins to pool, growing larger as I shake the bars of my cell.

"Those sticks must sap synats somehow!" Cat says, trying to reach her arm out for the stick which was left behind by the cat man.

"Ex aqua gravis, precor. Hinc mihi virtus sepulcrum Lazari. Grando omnem virtutem Dei," Argent prays. The thing about slowly approaching death is that it takes just long enough to realize that your struggles are fruitless but not enough time to figure out a plan until it's too late. However, the thing about water slowly leaking through a hole is that if there is enough water behind the hole then it begins to flow much faster by widening the hole. Finally, a fun fact about prison cells and bricks, neither of them are meant to survive a flood; sadly, neither is a person, but sticks often snap too. The flow of the water suddenly speeds up after several bricks fall out of the wall, flooding the room and snapping the glowing stick. Enter water, exit air, take the exit, we're off to the reservoir. From the hole in the wall, the group begins to swim out, slipping through a bend formed in the bars of the cells. The first one to reach the surface is me,

"Thank...god," I sigh, catching my breath.

"My prayers were heard!" Argent exclaims.

"No, you moron, it was me kicking the stick," Cat counters.

"It was me shaking the bars," Amaryll says.

"You're all wrong, it was me punching the wall," Azalea retorts. There is a soft clamoring among us as we swim to the shore of what seems to be an underground lake.

"Where is this? The jail is under the town hall, so what is this?" Argent ponders as I look up, seeing a mirror on the top of the cave. I squint my eyes to see closer and see that the mirror ripples, I throw a rock into the water to make new ripples and don't see them appear in the mirror.

"I think there is a lake above us," I say. *Possibly the work of someone else's synat.*

"Young master, not to be rude, but just because you separated the oceans above and below does not mean anyone can," Argent tries to explain, looking up before realizing I'm right.

"Floating water?" Cat questions.

"I've never seen anything like it!" Alex exclaims.

"So, if we go through there maybe we'll get into registration?" Amaryll asks.

"Maybe, but how do we get up there?" I ask.

"I could try and use my force fields to make some kind of platform to walk up," Alex suggests, creating a flat platform below all of us.

"But we can't see that, could you try lifting the force field?" Azalea asks. Alex closes his eyes and the platform begins going upwards, plunging us into the breathable water. We swim up and see that the old woman isn't there.

"So, that random guard was the spy, but how did he know about us?" Cat questions.

"Perhaps he stole the file," I offer.

"And got it to another agent within a few hours of our arrival?" Alex counters as the breathable water turns solid under us, giving us a floor to stand on.

"Two," Cat corrects. I put my hand to the now solid water, feeling it's cold and smooth texture, reminding me of cold glass and giving me a shudder.

"What if the agent was here anyway and he just had to see the file then talk to them?" Azalea asks.

"Still, within a few hours," Alex counters.

"Plus, I got my order for if the first guy failed a few weeks ago," Amaryll points out.

"How? We weren't here yet?" Alex asks, sounding confused.

"I don't know," Amaryll shrugs. I walk to the couch that the old woman sat in before, searching for any kind of compartment for files. All I found was an engraving that says,

"A reader of synats sits upon the throne/ sight is a power they're yet to hone/ a mirror reflects all, but bone/ the actor is the man always alone." As I examine the engraving the old woman steps in.

"How did you survive?!?" the woman shouts, looking confused and panicked.

"How did you know we were meant to die?" Alex asks. The woman looks surprised for a moment before attaining a blank expression.

"Got me," they say, morphing into a person in a traditional stage magician's outfit.

"The spy!" Cat shouts, opening her mouth to sing as the fire begins to catch on their cape. The spy takes off their cape.

"Yes, I am the spy, The Assassin King saw my synat of Mirror Image and realized how strong I could be," they chuckle, giving an arrogant bow before turning into Cat, hitting a high note to set Cat's hand on fire. Cat screams and smothers the fire with her other arm. I shout,

"Guards! Help!" Hoping to resolve my guilt and have them stop the spy. The guards run in as Amaryll winds up for a punch by beating herself slightly to get cuts along her midriff. Before the guards ran in, the spy turned back into the old woman.

"Help me!" they shout. The guards run forwards,

"Get down! She has a strong synat!" one shouts, tackling the spy into the floor that turned liquid on impact to stop the guard and the spy from getting hurt. Thinking quickly, I step on the water above the two to turn it solid again before using the 'glass' part of my synat to make the floor crack just enough to trap it as solid and make it mostly opaque. For a short moment, I could see the fear in the spy's eyes between the cracks before the spy disappeared, only the guard's helmet that had fallen off in the incident was still visible now. I couldn't see because I was too busy with the spy but when I turned around the other guard was standing over Alex, his stick glowing. For a short moment I feared we would be overpowered again, but suddenly a spotlight fell from above, literally, the light fell and landed on the guard, crushing him. I look up to see the same hooded figure from our fight with the first assassin standing next to where the light was, holding a shard of metal that looked to have been used to cut the rope holding the light. Cat begins to sing and creates a flame to cremate the guard's body in order to destroy the evidence.

Chapter 6: In the Land Reminiscent of Home

We go over to the back of the room and find a back door that leads to an alleyway. We ran out of the door and to the church. As we're running back, I look over at Azalea and I notice that she has pointed ears. *Is she an Elf? I'll have to ask later.* We keep running and we go into the back door of the church and I ask,

"Hey, Azalea."

"Yeah?" she replies.

"So, when we were running, I saw that you had pointed ears. Are you like an elf or something?"

"Well, yeah."

"Oh, cool! I didn't know," Cat exclaims, "Why didn't you tell us before?"

"Well, I thought you guys would just be able to tell." She then mumbles to herself, "I guess they really are from another world."

"Hey Argent, did you know?" CJ asks.

"Well, of course, Young Master CJ, I knew right from the beginning. Though it is okay that you did not as you are after all from the other world."

"So, what exactly do we do now?" I ask.

"We should probably try to get more information on The Assassin King," Cat suggests.

"I have a way we might be able to get some," Azalea says.

"How?" I ask.

"Well, my dad is part of the EIA in the United Elven Federation. I might be able to get him to tell us something," Azalea says.

"EIA? United Elven Federation?" CJ says.

"Well, Master CJ the U.E.F. is the country that shares the border to the east and to the south with the United Settlements of the People, which is the country we're in at the moment. I don't know about the EIA, forgive me for my nescience Young Master," Argent explains.

"You are forgiven..." CJ says.

"Well, It makes sense you wouldn't know about them. They're very secretive," Azalea pauses for a second to think, "E.I.A. stands for Elven Intelligence Agency they gather intelligence from all across Sotaqt for U.E.F."

"Sotaqt?" I say. *I feel like I heard that somewhere before. Did I forget or something?*

"Guess you guys really are from another world. It's the name of the world we live on," Azalea says. *We certainly are. It's a little hard not to feel out of place when you don't even know the name of the planet, you're on. I definitely want to learn more, but that will probably be a slow process especially at our current level of knowledge.*

"So, Azalea, about earlier," Cat says.

"Yeah?"

"You're an elf, right?" Cat asks.

"Uh, yeah."

"So, are you really old or something?" Cat questions.

"Well, I'm 119, but for an elf, that's pretty young. In human years that's probably about seventeen."

"Oh," Cat says. *Well, that was certainly unexpected, not exactly sure what to think about that.*

"On another note, we should head to the U.E.F. Right?"

"Yeah, but where exactly is that?" Cat asks.

"Well, actually it's not too far east of here. It's only about a day's journey," Azalea says.

"Well, we're basically fugitives now so we should get going soon," I say.

"Argent, get the supplies ready," CJ says.

"Of course, Young Master CJ."

"Hey, my love, can we borrow the carriage?" CJ jokes.

"Why of course young master," Argent says before pausing. "I am always glad to receive your affection young master, but your methods are quite... unorthodox." he stumbled for a moment to find the correct word. We go over to the storage shed and help bring over all the supplies to the carriage.

"Alright, that should be the last one," Cat says.

"Well, let's head out," I say. It had gotten pretty late and it was already starting to get dark. *I'm surprised the peacekeepers haven't found us yet.* We all hop into the carriage and are on our way.

"So, how exactly do we get to this place?" Argent asks.

"If you just go onto the eastern road into the forest, we should get there in around a day's time," Azalea explains.

"Thank you," Argent replies.

"So, Amaryll you're from Earth, right?" I ask.

"Uh, yeah," She says.

"So, where are you from?" I ask. *If she is from Earth, I am a little curious. I mean by her accent she doesn't sound like she's from Texas or something and she's definitely speaking English so...*

"I'm from Vancouver. Where are you guys from?" She asks.

"We're all from this town not too far from Worcester, Mass called Ruthersfield," Cat says.

"Mass?" Amaryll says.

"Massachusetts."

"Oh." I look outside the carriage and realize it has already gotten pretty dark outside. I start to drift off to sleep.

"Alex! Hey Wake up!"

Cat is yelling at me and shaking my shoulders, waking me up.

"What's going on?" I ask. I look and it's still dark outside. *I guess I wasn't asleep for long*.

"There are bandits outside," Cat says, "They shot one of the wheels and we can't move."

"Don't worry. Let me handle this," Azalea says. The bandits come out of the surrounding trees and rush towards the carriage. I then hear Azalea say,

"Gaia potentiam, fortitudinem tuam placátus impénde."

A green magic circle appears on the ground and vines come out and grab the bandits holding them in the air. One of them tries to light the vines on fire, but Cat quickly puts that idea out by using the fire to knock the bandit out.

"We should try to get some information out of them," I say.

"If they don't comply, I could turn their kneecaps to bread," CJ says.

"That won't be necessary, Young Master CJ. Please allow my assistance in the matter. My synat is perfect for this; it has the ability to make anyone tell the truth in a 20 ft radius," Argent says.

"That is pretty useful," I say.

"Alright, let's start the interrogation," Azalea says, "Who sent you?"

"The Assassin King," The bandit says.

"Alright, tell us where The Assassin King is," she says.

"We don't know. One of his servants came to us and asked to kill you guys and they left the money with us," The bandit says.

"What did they look like?" she asks.

"I don't know, they were wearing a cloak and I couldn't see their face," the bandit says.

"Damn!" Azalea says, "These guys are useless."

The vines turn to a mist of glowing particles before disappearing; this causes the bandits to fall to the ground.

"I suggest you run," Azalea says, glaring. The bandits all run away in fear.

"Azalea how did you do that, you know with the vines?" Cat asks.

"Well, being half wood elf, I have a certain affinity for earth magic, most species have some other power other than their synat. Recent research in the UEF has shown that there is some connection between these powers and synats, but they still don't know how and why," Azalea says.

"Really?!" Cat exclaims, "That's pretty cool!" Azalea blushes a little from the complement.

"So, how exactly are we going to fix the wheel?" I ask.

"Well, actually I brought an extra wheel just in case," Argent says. *Good thing otherwise we'd be a little stuck.* I hold the carriage up so Argent can put on the new wheel. After everything is set up we all get back in the carriage and are on our way.

"So, Azalea when we met you said you had a debt to pay. What exactly did you mean by that, just curious?" Cat asks.

"Well, about two year ago I was traveling out of town with my brother to collect herbs for the medical lodge when one of The Assassin King's goons tried to attack us and they ended up killing my brother and they almost killed me too, but then a hooded figure swooped in and saved me. Then she handed me a note that said to look for you guys," Azalea explains.

"I'm sorry for your loss..." Cat says, "But how would they know about us when we only got here a few days ago?"

"I'm not sure," Azalea says. *Maybe it has something to do with that strange letter in Cat's handwriting?* It's still the middle of the night; I fall asleep again.

"Hey, Alex! Wake up! We're here," Amaryll exclaims while shaking me. I'm a little flustered by her being so close. I look outside and see a huge gate in the forest. A guard walks up to the carriage and starts talking to Argent,

"Do you mind if we check the carriage?" the guard asks.

"Go ahead," Argent says. He looks into the carriage where all of us are and says,

"Azalea, is that you?"

"Yeah Jalkud it's me," Azalea says.

"These friends of yours?" he asks.

"Yeah," she says.

"Alright, then you're cleared," he says. He then yells over to the people by the gates, "They're good. Open them up."

The guards open up the gates and we pass through. I look up and there are houses up in the trees connected by bridges and walkways.

"Where's your house?" Argent says looking up.

"It's not far, just keep going straight and then take a right," Azalea says. We keep going until Azalea tells us to stop. We all get out of the carriage and I say,

"So, how exactly do we get up there?" Cat asks.

"Don't worry I got it covered," Azalea says, "Gaia nos commodare, et potentiam tuam erigi."

A huge vine comes out of the ground from under us and lifts us up to the walkway around Azalea's house. We step off onto the walkway and the vine turns into those green glowing particles again.

"Well, everybody we're here," Azalea says.

Chapter 7: Under Pressure

Damn. This is how I meet her parents? I was hoping for something less important to spark it but this is fine I guess.

"Oh, Azalea, you're home!" Azalea's mother smiled wearing a white apron with a red stain over her left breast; "It's been so long since we've seen you. Oh, and you also brought friends, how sweet!"

"Nice to meet you, I'm Mrs. Leitner," she says, putting out her hand to shake mine. I freeze for a second before saying,

"Nice to meet you too, my name's Cat." I shake her hand back, surprised by her grip. She greets CJ next, extending her arm to grip him; CJ returns the gesture, adding in a gesture of his thumb poking the top joint of her pointer finger and his three fingers pressed to her palm. Mrs. Leitner then moves to shake Argent's hand, followed by Alex and finally Amaryll. We all walk into the house and Mrs. Leitner invites us to sit down at the dinner table. She then calls upstairs to her husband, telling him to come down. He comes downstairs and starts talking to Azalea,

"Oh! Azalea you're here and you brought a girlfriend," he chuckles, bumping Azalea with his elbow.

"Oh, come on Dad," Azalea says. *Oh, well I guess that works out...* I take a second to process.

"Yes!" I exclaim. Everyone stops talking and stares at me.

"Sorry, it's nothing," I say, starting to blush from embarrassment. An awkward silence persists for a second before the conversation starts up again.

"Well, anyway. You know why we're here. Right, Dad?" Azalea says shifting into a more serious tone.

"Yes of course," He pauses for a moment to sit down at the table, "as I'm sure my daughter has already told you that I work for the E.I.A. and about our son, so I'm definitely willing to help you in any way I can."

"We need to know where The Assassin King is," Alex says.

"We have to keep this on the low because if we don't the E.I.A. agents may catch on and arrest you guys. But also, I do know where he was last," Mr. Leitner says, changing into a more serious tone of voice.

"So, where is he?" I ask, lowering my voice to a whisper.

"He was last seen in the capital of the Republic of the Western Lands 2 miles east of the central palace," Mr. Leitner responds, also in a whisper. Suddenly a loud knocking on the door interrupts our conversation.

"Open up its E.I.A, domestic branch," a booming voice exclaims from outside the door.

"Go to the downstairs room, there's a room behind the bookshelf you can hide in!" Mr. Leitner says, still in a whisper. We all run down the stairs and Azalea pulls back the bookshelf and opens the door behind it and we all enter the room closing the bookshelf and door behind us. We hear the voices of Mr. Leitner and the E.I.A. agent.

"Hello Agent Leitner, would you mind letting me in?" the E.I.A. agent says.

"Oh, Director Holimion it's you!" Mr. Leitner pauses in shock for a moment seeing his boss who usually doesn't leave his office often and is perceived by fellow E.I.A. agents as very elusive, "Oh, and of course come in."

"Agent Leitner I'm going to get straight to the point. I know you told outsiders classified information and if you don't tell me where they are your family will be under the care of the Special Care Unit," Director Holimion says, sternly, exerting the pressure of his iron will onto Mr. Leitner. *Special care unit? What the hell? Is that some sort of torture division they have in EIA?*, "Oh and don't worry as long as you hand them over we'll spare your family and look over this incident; luckily for you, they happened to be wanted criminals in The United Settlements of the People, and we'll be greatly rewarded for turning them over."

"Of course, sir they're in the room behind the bookshelf," Mr. Leitner says, under total submission knowing there's nothing he can do despite wanting to help. *What the hell?! Did this guy just sell us out?* We hear the footsteps of someone coming down the stairs and then walking up to the bookshelf. We hear the sound of the bookshelf sliding to the side. The door opens up and for a brief moment and I get a look at this Director Holimion's face, his features are slim and he looks to be in his late twenties, *though as he is an elf he's probably much older,* he has long flowing silver hair and piercing gold eyes, he also seems to have a strange birthmark on his collar bone with three dots in a triangular pattern. Within less than a second of the door being open Azalea runs into Holimion knocking him over onto the ground before gesturing to leave the room. We run up the stairs and into the main room of the house and just as Azalea is reaching for the door she stops dead in her tracks as though a high pressure is being exerted on her preventing even the slightest movement. I try to run up to the door, but that same pressure is put onto me as a feeling of hopelessness washes over me. I see Alex and CJ frozen as well, Holimion walks up the stairs and wags his finger at Azalea.

"Tch tch, we can't have you escaping. After all, you are also a wanted criminal, Azalea Leitner!" Holimion exclaims, brushing some dust off the front of his suit jacket.

"But sir you sai-" Mr. Leitner tries to say before Holimion cuts him off,

"Silence Agent Leitner! You're lucky to keep your job, let alone your wife." Holimion pauses for a moment before turning his gaze over to me and the rest of our group.

"I guess I have yet to introduce myself," he goes into a slight bow putting his right arm in front of his torso before continuing, "I am Mindartis Holimion the chief director of the E.I.A. and as you won't be alive for much longer I will tell you this... My synat is 'Pressure Authority'!"

"Hmph, damn arrogant High elf bastards. Always thinking you're better than everyone else," Azalea says, barely able to move her lips.

"How dare you! You, a lower elf let alone a mixed breed, speak to me in such a manner!" Holimion pauses a second to collect himself and continues to speak in a calm yet serious manner, "Death is not a harsh enough punishment for you. As soon as we leave this place you're going straight to the Special Care unit for reeducation." Azalea ignoring him moves her eyes back towards us and says weakly,

"Don't worry guys you'll be fine I'm sure." A bright flash comes from Azalea. After the light fades the air in the room turns cold. Looking around I see Azalea on the floor unconscious.

"Hah! You fool this is what you g-" Holimion suddenly stops mid-sentence and seems to be frozen in place. I realize I can move again.

"Hey, guys you all okay?" I ask.

"Yeah it seems like I can move again," Alex says. I look over near Azalea. There's a letter on the floor I pick up and put it in my pocket.

"I think we should get out of here," CJ suggests.

"Yeah, but before we leave, we should beat this guy's ass," Alex says, punching his right fist into his left hand.

"Agreed," I say. Alex uses his synat to multiply the physical impact of his punches. Alex punches Holimion with a right hook square on the side of the face. Strangely enough, even after taking several punches, Holimion didn't seem to move at all though you could very easily tell the bones in his face were broken. Suddenly the cold air from earlier seems to dissipate as Holimion flies into the wall as though being hit by a train.

"What just happened?" I ask. Mr. Leitner who was seemingly frozen earlier responds to my question,

"Azalea should be able to tell you about that, the rest is in that letter you picked up. You have to leave now though Holimion will be up soon and assault on a High elf is high treason in the UEF."

I pick up Azalea and we run out of the house and Alex makes a forcefield stairway down to the carriage. We hop into the carriage and are on our way out. I take out the letter and open it up it says:

Dear Azalea and her friends,
 As you are heading to the Republic of the Western Lands, I'm sure you will need a way of getting there. There is a 'friend' of mine who runs an inn near the docks in Merizon. You can stay there for the night and then he will get you onto a cargo ship leaving for the Republic of the Western Land, where hopefully you can get that damned Assassin King.

Sincerely,
Mr. Leitner

"Hey, guys!" I exclaim.
"Yeah?" they respond.
"We're going to Merizon!" I say.
"Where exactly is that?" Alex says.
"It's northeast of here, on the mouth of the Cœurve river. It's under joint UEF-USP control," Argent says, sticking his head into the carriage, "I've been there on official church business before."

I look over at Azalea who is starting to regain consciousness.

"Azalea! You're awake! Are you okay?" I say, glad to see that she is okay. Azalea responds quickly waking up,

"Yeah, I'm fine. I'm more worried about you, Cat."

I blush from hearing Azalea worry about me like that. She suddenly puts both of her hands onto my cheeks and looks me over to check if I'm okay almost as if she's my mother.

"The rest of you guys okay?" Azalea says, giving concerned looks to everyone in the carriage.

"Yeah, we're all okay, but what was that thing you did earlier with the flash of light, and then that Holimion guy was frozen," Amaryll says, looking over at Azalea with a confused look on her face.

"Well, as I said earlier my synat is Frozen Passion which allows me to do things like healing and freeze things, shoot icicles out of my hands, but what I did there was an ability I call Frozen Instant which stops time momentarily, but it knocks me out in the process," Azalea responds.

"Really you can stop time!" I say, shocked.

"That explains why he didn't move when I punched him and the reason he flew into the wall was because all the energy was stored in him and when time resumed he flew into the wall," Alex remarks. "Wait actually that could have been my ability to store energy."

"That's probably it, as my ability only stops people's perception of time. Thing is that I can only use it once per day. I'm pretty sure if I tried to use it more than once a day I'd die. It puts too much strain on my body," Azalea explains.

"Well, if it puts some much strain on you it's probably better that you not use it for a while then," I say, concerned.

"Hopefully I won't have to use it again," Azalea says, chuckling a little which turns into a cough.

"Azalea are you okay?!" I say, now even more concerned.

"Don't worry I'll be fine after some rest at the inn," she says, coughing again. Argent pokes his head into the carriage again and says,

"We're almost there."

I look out the window and see the city. There are buildings made of stone bricks along with the roads making the ride more comfortable. There are also stone archways with lanterns hanging from them illuminating the night streets, the archways connecting with the stone walls that make up the sides of the roads with staircases leading up to each of the homes. Suddenly the carriage stops and Argent yells out,

"We're here!" We hop out of the carriage and I take a look at the inn. There's some sort of sign hanging over the doorway in some sort of script I can't read, *though it probably just says the name of the inn,* just like all the houses in the city it's built of light-colored stone brick. Looking down the street to the ocean, there seems to be a dock with several large early steamships. I open up the door and I notice Azalea's eyes light up as soon as she sees the person at the desk.

"Uncle Adran!" Azalea exclaims, waving over at the person at the desk, a smile stretched across her face.

"Azalea?!" the man at the desk exclaims, a confused and surprised look on his face. Azalea runs over to him and wraps her arms around him in a tight embrace.

"It is you, Azalea. I didn't know that you'd be one of the people your dad told me about," the man says.

"Yeah it's kind of a long story," Azalea says, as she releases her grip on the man.

"So, these guys are your friends then," he says.

"This is Alex, Cat, CJ, and Amaryll they're all from earth, and lastly Argent he's a priest in a church in the USP," Azalea introduces us to her uncle pointing to each of us as she goes.

"I guess I should introduce myself now. I'm Azalea's uncle, Adran Leitner, but you guys can just call me Adran. Also, just to check you guys have the letter, right?" Adran asks.

"Yeah," I say, handing the letter over to him.

"Good to know. You can never be too careful these days," Adran remarks, "It's pretty late and you guys have a long road ahead of you, so I suggest you all take a rest. I will get you passes for the ship in the morning."

"Thanks," I say.

"No problem," He responds. He shows us to our rooms and as we're walking, I start talking with Azalea.

"You and your uncle are pretty close," I say.

"Yeah, when I was young he would come to my house to look after me and my brother when my parents were at work so we know each other pretty well," Azalea says, looking up as though she was trying to look into her mind recollecting the memory.

"Well, goodnight Cat," Azalea says, smiling.

"Goodnight," I respond. I walk into my room and as soon as my head hits the pillow, I think to myself, *it has been a pretty long day,* then I fall asleep. The next morning, I get out of bed and gather everybody downstairs in the lobby. Adran hands Azalea the passes and says,

"Just show these to the men standing next to the ramp up to the ship with the red crest. They'll let you straight in."

"Sorry for leaving so soon," Azalea says, a sad look in her eyes.

"Don't worry we'll see each other again," Adran says, with a hopeful expression on his face. He walks us out the door and before we leave Azalea hugs him and then looks him in the eyes with a strong look that says, 'see you soon.' We continue out the door and head over to the ship with the red crest walking up to the ramp for the ship. The men standing there stop us and say,

"Who are you?"

Azalea shows them the passes Adran gave us.

"Of course, welcome aboard the S.S. Faewood," the men say. We walk up the ramp and onto the ship reading ourselves for the journey ahead.

Chapter 8: A Weaved Web

I exit off the ramp of the ship to the customs and immigration bureau station, the air feeling humid and slightly windy, with mist from the river blowing onto the shore. Three days have passed since we left Merìzon.

"Country of origin, and purpose for your visit?" a man dressed in what looks like a military or possibly police uniform asks.

"U.S.P and U.E.F, searching for The Assassin King," Cat answers, gesturing to Azalea when saying 'U.E.F'.

"For future reference, bounty hunters fall under the 'business' category of visit," the man corrects, not looking up from his migration ledger.

"Bounty-" Alex starts but is silenced by my elbow to his gut,

"Sorry sir, we don't travel often," I say, using my synat to get him on my side a bit more.

"Feel free to enter, you will be taxed on any earnings that aren't missions given by the government, here is your Paper Opus," he hands each of us a small book with a picture of the Opus Rulership, Sir Gurko the Glorious.

"Thank you again, sir," I smile as we walk through the customs port, now standing in a city boulevard, two streets adjoining one another, one made of cobblestone, the other a still river.

"The intel says he was last seen at the royal palace, we ought to check there," Amaryll suggests as I glance at a wanted poster with a sub-par drawing of a young man, written in both Abramonic and Elvish,

"WANTED: The Assassin King. Dead or Alive for 12,000,000 Quills. Last seen outside the Merciful Gurko's Center of Criminal Rehabilitation. See image below." *Criminal Rehabilitation? Sounds more like a torture center than somewhere for 'rehabilitation'. It's probably some sort of dungeon.*

"I think Sir Gurko may have found out about The Assassin king, but getting more context will help," I comment.

"New Samara is arranged in circles, so the palace ought to be straight ahead," Argent suggests. We walk through a large section filled with poverty and hunger, large groups of people waiting in line for loaves of bread.

"It's a shame, I heard there was a drought recently," Azalea mutters.

"When?" Cat asks.

"The papers never say," she shrugs as we approach the gate between the outer rim and inner sanctum.

"Paper Opus check, all of you," two guards approach us, pointing their rifles at us, the bayonets shining in the sunlight.

"Paper Opus? Here," Alex pulls his Paper Opus from his pocket, handing it to the guard on his left.

"I can tell you haven't read that; you're never supposed to hand it over fully." The guard glares, bringing the bayonet closer to Alex's neck.

"A momentary lapse of judgement sir. I assure you, we've all read it fully," I try to use my synat to get Alex out of being stabbed.

"Recite the opening words to prove you aren't traitors to the party," the other guard orders, bringing his bayonet closer to my neck, not batting an eye from the citizens.

"Oh, um. We, the people of-" I begin, before the first guard cuts me off.

"Wrong! The force at the core leading our cause forwards is Sir Gurko the Merciful. The theoretical basis guiding us is his eternal glory. You're a traitor to the party, don't resist," the first guard shouts as the second whistles, calling more guards to our location.

"Is it a crime to be forgetful?" Argent reasons.

"Yes," one of the guards answers, hitting me over the head with the stock of his rifle. The world goes black as I enter a dreamless sleep. When I awaken my compatriots and I are chained to three posts, two people per post on opposite sides. I can tell by process of elimination that I am chained opposite Argent, being as Alex is chained with Amaryll and Cat is chained with Azalea.

"Where are we?" I ask, struggling against the chains, doing nothing other than creating a rattling noise.

"Merciful Gurko's Center for Criminal Rehabilitation," a voice says from below us. I look down to see an old man in expensive robes and a crown of gold and jewels, holding a scepter of similar structure and components to the crown.

"And you would be?" Alex asks.

"Sir Gurko, the Opus Rulership. I'm here to offer you a deal," he grins, his yellowish-white skin wrinkling slightly at the corners of his mouth.

"Get us down from here and we might have a deal," Cat scoffs, looking away from him.

"Yes, that along with the reward money was the end of the bargain I was going to offer," Gurko pinches the bridge of his nose with clearly visible annoyance.

"And what do we have to give you?" I ask, wondering what we have that a wealthy dictator such as himself doesn't.

"According to some of our greatest psionics experts and alchemists, you guys have some connection to The Assassin King, or at least you will eventually; I want you to kill The Assassin King," he explains, gesturing upwards when talking about the psionics experts and alchemists.

"They do?" Argent questions, sounding surprised

"Or they will," Gurko corrects, before muttering "Filthy Abramonic," under his breath, disdain on his face.

"May we speak with these psionics experts?" I ask, hoping that perhaps they could give us a more detailed explanation of this 'connection'.

"Fine, make it quick," Gurko groans, pulling a lever next to him to make the pillars extend upwards into the alchemy laboratory before freeing us, leaving only handcuffs on our wrists and a fifty foot chain on each of our ankles to keep us from running too far.

"Experiments or questions?" a person with an orange lens and some metal covering their left eye, which appears to be fake. They are wearing a white coat and carrying a small stack of papers.

"Questions, I think. Sir Gurko said that you guys found that we have a connection to The Assassin King?" Alex questions.

"Ah, The Psionics Department; I'm the general supervisor, but I can bring you to there," they begin walking while gesturing for us to follow, leading us through a door with an image of a spiral on it.

"Oh! they're here," one of the scientists in the room comments, pointing at us with a gloved hand.

"They want to know about the psionics connecting them to The Assassin King. If you guys messed up on something this big then you're definitely losing your intellectualism license," the general supervisor said before walking off, leaving us in The Psionics department.

"Could you please explain this 'connection' business? This may be worrying if Master CJ is related to such a fiend," Argent asks, clearly very worried.

"Oh, the connection isn't inherently genetic or anything. Basically, we just know that these three specifically will impact and be impacted by The Assassin King, or possibly already have," he says, gesturing at myself, Cat, and Alex.

"And how do you know this?" Alex asks, looking slightly confused by all of this.

"...sign these," the scientist hands each of us a paper with the letters 'NDA' on them in big red ink. Argent signs it first, followed by Azalea, Amaryll, myself, Cat, and finally Alex.

"Sir Gurko paid The Assassin King to kill Rebelde Escanavo, upon returning here for the full payment he was imprisoned to avoid Sir Gurko needing to pay the full price. He escaped and managed to kill Sir Gurko's only child as well as several important members of the party. Thankfully, The Assassin King bled slightly during the escape, allowing us to use said blood to find people whom he has a deep connection with, or will eventually, via psionic magic and alchemy. If we can mix this blood with someone whom he has a connection to then the second blood donor will be able to know where The Assassin King is at all times," the scientist explains, gesturing to his coworkers, who are examining a glass vial of blood with some strange technology.

"And who is going to be donating that blood?" I ask, not much a fan of the needles and syringes lining the east wall.

"You can decide amongst yourselves, it's not my problem, just one of you three." he points at me, Cat, and Alex.

"I got this, I've got experience," Cat jokes.

"Yeah, Cat's got this one," Alex seconds.

"Sounds good. Mr. Scientist, we've decided," I exclaim. The man walks back holding a syringe,

"Which one?" he asks.

"Her," I point at Cat. The man takes the syringe and jabs it into Cat's arm, removing a decent sample of blood before going back to the odd machinery, inserting the syringe into a hole inside an arm-like machine. The machine begins spinning the blood that seemingly belongs to The Assassin King before mixing in Cat's blood. The spinning speeds up until finally stopping after about 3 minutes.

"En voila!" the scientist picks up an amulet with a glass bubble filled with blood in it, "miss, this will let you track him," he hands it to Cat.

"Do I just, like, put it on?" she asks, looking confused.

"No, you lick it," he says sarcastically, rolling his eyes.

"Well, you don't need to be rude about it-" Cat puts on the amulet and suddenly stops, eyes rolling back.

"Cat, are you good?" Azalea asks.

"He's 400 miles northeast of here and 200 feet below us. He's in New Burklenn of the Dwarven Solidarity Coalition and Dwarven Mining Coalition Northern shared territory." Cat groans, her voice sounding like multiple at once, overlapping.

"The shared territory? What could he want there?" Argent is taken aback by seeing Cat like this.

"Damn! Take the amulet off, take the amulet off!" the scientist shouts, trying to take the amulet off but getting knocked backwards and burned by a ball of her fire.

"What's going on?!" Alex asks.

"The amulet must be functioning on a two-way quantum circuit! We need to get it off!" the scientist answers. Cat shoots a burst of fire at Alex, launching him into the wall.

"Her mind is blank," Argent says, seeming to be reading her mind.

"I got this," Azalea says, before stopping time and passing out in the process. Alex recovers and launches Cat into a wall while Amaryll punches her in the gut repeatedly. When time resumes Cat is groaning in pain followed by a guttural scream of rage. Cat ignites, her body covered in flame as she grabs Alex by the throat, burning him.

"Let go of me! This hurts!" Alex shouts before passing out. I make the amulet as fragile as glass, but this doesn't seem to make the effect stop. Cat throws Alex's limp body at Amaryll, knocking them both to the ground. Argent starts healing Alex slowly.

"Damn, I'm the only one who isn't down or occupied," I mutter, a feeling of dread washing over me before suddenly I turn clear, like glass. I look down at my hand to see nothing there, and it seems Cat sees just as much.

"Gotcha," I grin, walking towards Cat and ripping off her amulet, shattering it against the floor. Cat seems to snap out of her trance and looks around, seeming confused.

"Why are Alex and Azalea unconscious? And why is CJ's voice coming from nowhere?" she asks before I become visible.

"You went nuts," Amaryll scowls as the scientists stand back up.

"He knows we're tracking him. The Assassin King knows we're tracking him," the scientist mutters, looking worried.

"Damn, does he still know our location?" I ask.

"I don't intend to find out. You need to get the hell out of here, we can get you passage on a land craft," the scientist says, removing the chains on our ankles. The man brings us out of the palace and brings us to an underground tunnel, putting us on what looks like a steam locomotive with auxiliary power coming from some kind of magic cannon on the back. The machine starts up, sending us north at an extreme speed.

Chapter 9: The Glory of Euphemia

I wake up and look around. *Where am I?* Based on the noise I'm probably on a train, *or at least that's what it sounds and feels like.* I get up and stretch, looking next to me I see Azalea still unconscious after she used her 'Frozen Instant ability'. I look up to see Cat looking out of the window and into the distance, lost in thought.

"Oh! Alex, you're awake!" Cat exclaims. *I guess I startled her enough to bring her out her head,* "You okay?"

"Yeah, I'm fine. What about you?" I ask, concerned about what happened earlier.

"I'm fine. Sorry about earlier," she apologies.

"No worries. It's not really your fault anyway," I say, trying to console her.

"Well, actually-" CJ starts before I say,

"Shut it CJ."

"So, what exactly is going on?" I ask.

"We're on a train to the Dwarven North shared territory," She says.

"Ah, that makes sense. Hopefully, we can finally find The Assassin King," I say, hopeful that we can reach this journey's end soon. I look around again at the train car where there are tons of crates stacked up near the walls with a few scattered on the floor Cat and the others sitting on them. I get up to sit on one myself. Looking down on the floor of the train car I notice that Azalea is starting to wake up.

"Azalea you good?" I ask.

"Yeah, I'm okay. I should recover shortly," She's says, coughing a little. She gets up and sits next to Cat putting her arm around her back and on to her shoulder. Cat's face turns a little red in response.

"Good to see you back to normal," Azalea says to Cat.

"Yeah, well you certainly helped," Cat responds.

"I guess you're right," Azalea says.

"So, how long should it take to get there?" I ask.

"I've been on this route before around 8 to 9 hours and we've only been on the train for about an hour," Argent says.

"Oh. Well if it's going to be a while, I'm going to take a nap," I say.

"Alright we'll wake you up once we get there," Cat says. I close my eyes and quickly fall asleep. *I see a silhouette in front of me. It looks like someone who's wearing a cloak. Looking around it seems as though I'm in some sort of dark room made from stone bricks. The silhouette turns around and I see its eyes which are bright blue and hair which is golden blond, they seem to almost glow in the darkness. The silhouette turns around and leaves the room as my vision slowly fades to black.*

"Hey! Alex! Wake up!" Cat yells, shaking my shoulders. I jump a little from being woken up so suddenly.

"What is it?" I ask. Still a little groggy. It almost feels as though I'm forgetting something important.

"We're almost there," She says. I hear the screech from the train's breaks and the wheels sliding on the tracks. The sliding door on the side of the train car opens up and we get out onto the station platform and mix in with the crowd before anyone sees us. We seem to be in some sort of underground cavern with crystals glowing blue, purple and green hues scattered around the walls and ceiling. The train station carved out from the wall of the cavern. Walking out of the train station there are houses carved out of the walls similar in fashion to the station. We walk down the path in between all the houses to see someone familiar.

"Uncle Ardan!" Azalea yells out waving to him. He turns his head around in our direction.

"Azalea?" Ardan says. We walk through the crowd over to him, *luckily it would be hard to lose someone that tall in a crowd of dwarves.* Azalea runs over to him and embraces him.

"Hey," I say.

"What are you guys doing here? I thought you guys were in the Republic of the Western lands." Adran says, his eyebrows furrowed, and forehead wrinkled. Azalea explains to him what happened after we left Merizon.

"Ah, that makes sense." he says, "So, The Assassin King is here in the shared territory. I did hear a rumor saying something like that yesterday, though it's hard to believe that kind of rumor when most of the time they end up being fake."

"So, do you know somewhere we can get more information?" CJ asks.

"Yeah, the Management Office on the floor below this one. I have to go there anyway," he responds. We follow him to the end of the walkway and into mine elevator, he presses a button and we start going down. Shortly after we got in the elevator it stops and we get out. We continue to follow Adran until we get to a building that is carved out of the walls of the cavern.

"Well, we're here," Adran says, "The front desk should be able to help you. I have to fill out some paperwork, but if you need me, I'll be in one of the waiting rooms."

"Thanks," I say.

"Yeah, no problem," Adran responds. We walk up to the front desk and Azalea asks,

"We are searching for The Assassin King and we heard he was somewhere in the shared territory. Do you have any Information on him?"

"The Assassin King! In the shared territory! There is no such thing going on!" she exclaims, before saying in a whisper, "Come with me." We follow her down a hallway into a room with two couches and sound-proof walls.

"I'm sorry about that, it's just we don't want to cause a public panic," the dwarf from the front desks says.

"I understand," Azalea says, "but does that mean there is information you can give us?"

"Yes," she says, "We're under orders to accept any help on the matter as long as they keep it a secret."

"We can. I agree that it's better not to cause a panic as it would make things harder," Azalea says.

"If that's the case then I will tell you all we know," she says, "There have been several reported sightings of him in the area and rumors that he has set up a temporary base in the lowest level of the shared territory that was abandoned a number of years ago."

"So, how exactly do we get to the lowest level," I ask.

"There is an elevator in the back of this building that goes down there used for maintenance. Meet me at the front desk once you're ready," she says. We go over to the waiting room where Ardan is filling out paperwork.

"Oh! It's you guys. Great timing. I just finished the paperwork. What is it?" he asks. I tell him about the information we got.

"Really... He really is in the shared territory. I guess the rumors are right sometimes," he says, "Well, I should come with you. My synat 'Silent Traveler' lets a group of people along with myself get around unseen and unheard."

"Great!" Azalea exclaims, "Come with us." We all go to the front desk and the lady leads us to the elevator and we get on. I press the button and we go down. After about 20 minutes we finally get to the bottom.

"I can't see a thing," Argent says. The cavern is very dimly lit by a few glowing crystals scattered across the walls and ceiling.

"Hold on, I have an idea," I say.

"So, what is it?" Cat asks.

"Well, the second word of my synat is sight so, I think I might be able to see in the dark," I say.

"So, can you or not," she says.

"Well, let me see," I say. I focus on the darkness and then it's like I'm looking through infra-red goggles.

"It worked!" I exclaim.

"Good," Cat says. I look around and there seems to be some sort of abandoned factory.

"Adran, can you activate your ability?" I ask.

"Yeah, sure," He says, "We will all be able to hear and see each other, but no one else will." I guide everyone over to the entrance of the factory. Once there we sneak in through a broken window and drop down onto the factory floor. It looks like there is some sort of forge, large pots that must held liquid metal, and ingot casts. *They must've produced some sort of special metal here from the ore mined in the Dwarven mining federation.* I see some stairs lead down below the factory floor.

"Follow me," I whisper. We all slowly walk over to the stairs and pause for a moment before we begin to descend. There is a door at the bottom of the staircase. I open it and I am blinded for a second by the lights in the room before my vision returns to normal. There is a figure standing in the room, almost a silhouette due to the bright light from behind. The lights dim and the figure turns around. Now that the lights are dimmed, I can see that the figure was actually a person. He is wearing a white suit with gold accents and has medium length iridescent silver hair, the hallmark of a high elves along with his pointed ears.

"Where's The Assassin King?!" Azalea exclaims.

"Tch tch tch, you just missed him. He's probably halfway to Heizengaard by now. Oops I shouldn't have said that... Though you all will be dead so I'm sure Number 01 will forgive me," the high elf says.

"Damn! We were so close," I say.

"If you're not The Assassin King then who are you?!" Cat questions.

"You're right, my name is... Well actually you don't need to know that," He pauses for a moment to bow, "I am The Assassin King's second in command, but you may call me Number 02. I handle all of the trivial matters The Assassin King is too pure to dirty his hands with."

"Well, if you're second in command then I guess I will have to beat you up too!" Azalea says.

"Ah, no, sorry but I can't have you interfering with Number 01's plans," Number 02 says wagging his finger. The same pressure from before freezes me in place. I can see out of the corner of my eye I can see that everyone else is frozen as well.

"I can't move!" Azalea exclaims, "You damn high elf! What did you do?"

"Well, I guess I can tell you this much. All high elves synats have the word authority in them and so we all have this same ability. It's quite useful actually," Number 02 explains,

"You see it is very important that Number 01's plans are not interrupted. He has something magnificent planned for this world. He is planting the seeds for it as we speak. It will truly be a new world though the details of it I will leave up to your imaginations."

"I'm sorry everyone, but my time here is up. I'm sure Number 01 is far enough away, but before I leave, I shall take care of all of you to make sure you don't interfere any further." He walks past us and walks up the stairs. Suddenly I hear the sound of explosions coming from above us along with low rumbling. The ceiling begins to crack and a small piece of it falls to the floor. Just as the ceiling starts to collapse, I'm able to move again and with less than a second left before we are all crushed I put up the largest force field I can. Looking to the side I realize in horror that Cat is not underneath the force field as she was the farthest away from me and my force fields can only get so large. *I'm sorry Cat. Please forgive me.* I think to myself tearing up just as the ceiling hits the floor. The pressure from all the debris is so much that I can only hold the force field for just a few more seconds. *I'm sorry everyone. I guess I can't save you.* In a flash of light all the debris above us vaporizes. While I'm still lying on the floor stunned, I look up to see a hooded figure say in a familiar voice,

"Sorry everybody, I'm a bit late."

Chapter 10: Emergence of Ekayana

I see the ceiling falling down on me and then I'm dead. I open My eyes and see my room back on earth just the way I left it. I get up and look down seeing that I'm dressed in the same clothes I wore when I left the house that night. I walk downstairs to see my mother.

"Oh Cat!" she exclaims, "Are you okay?"

"What are you talking about? Of course, I'm okay," I say confused.

"But your friends and the car crash... It's only been 3 days," she says.

"Car crash... 3 days...?" I say to myself. *Wait didn't we all die in a car crash, but how am I still alive? And I don't remember anything after the crash so... What happened in those 3 days?*

"I understand that you're probably still in denial, but their funerals are today," my mother says. I go back up to my room to think. *So when the ceiling crushed me I died, so why am I back on earth? And what happened to everyone else? Are they still on Sotaqt? They must be, I have to save them! Still though it would be rude not to go to the funeral.* I put on the black dress I got a while ago for when I would have to go to funerals. I go back downstairs and get into the car and we drive over to the town's cemetery looking out the window at all the trees passing swiftly by not a single word being exchanged between us. My mother takes a candle to place upon the grave as some kind of guide in the afterlife; for a moment it gets blown out, before somehow returning from embers, only to be put out again. After the service I'm standing in front of two gravestones which have Alex, CJ, and Kevin's names on them. Everyone standing around me in black outfits It's almost unreal. *I have to get back to Sotaqt. They might be dead here on Earth, but back on Sotaqt they're still alive!* We drive back to my house and I go back up to my room to think. *I need to go back but... How?* I sit there trying to think of something when it suddenly clicked. *That's it! If I got there last time by dying, then I can just do it again! But how should I go about it? Fire. It has to be fire. If part of my synat was burning, then just like last time the only way I'm meant to die is by fire.* I write a note to my mother and leave it on my bed. It says:

Dear Mother,

I'm to leave you like this, but it's the only way I can save my friends. I know you probably won't be able to understand why, but just know that I'm doing this for the sake of my friends and the other world. I'm sorry for having to leave you, but this is a sacrifice I must make. The lives of others are at stake here. I know this will confuse you and you'll wonder as from your perspective my friends are dead. Though, I guess that may not be the best way of saying it. I'm sorry mom for leaving you. It may not come across this way, but I'm making a bit of a rash decision in doing this, so please forgive me. I guess this may make me come across as a little crazy, but in the end, what matters most is my friends. As they say, The blood of the covenant is thicker than the water of the womb. I have to save them. Thank you and goodbye.

Love,

Cat

I put on a black hooded cloak to hide my identity. I take some gasoline and matches to my room and wait until everyone is asleep and sneak out of my window and into the woods behind my house and walk through them for about twenty minutes. I get to a small clearing and pour the gasoline on myself. I then grab a match and light it. Almost as soon as I had lit the match the fire had spread all over my body. Bright red flames engulf me along with the sensation of being burnt. It's extremely painful, but in only a few seconds I can't feel anything anymore. Looking down, I see my hands charred black. Soon after I realize I can't see anymore. As soon as I processed what was happening the shock from seeing myself in such a condition knocked me unconscious and soon enough again, I was dead. I wake up to see the leaves of a tree above me and feel the grass below. I stand up and unlike last time there is no one else around. Looking out it seems I'm right outside of Tirentod. I look over into the forest to see someone familiar. *Azalea!* She's on the ground with a terrified look on her face and someone else on the ground next to her who seems to be dead. Someone starts to walk up to Azalea. *It's the same guy who attacked us at the church! Shouldn't he be dead?* I run out over to her and stand in between her and the assailant. He stops dead in his tracks stunned for a moment before saying,

"Get out of the way, my glorious leader needs this girl dead!"

"I'm sorry, but this "girl" isn't dying today," I exclaim. I start to vocalize, sending a blast of fire at him sending him back aways into the forest. It wasn't enough to kill him though. I see him get up and run off into the forest. Normally I would go off and chase him, but right now Azalea is more important.

"Hey are you okay?" I ask.

"I'm fine you saved me, but... but... my brother... he... he's dead," Azalea says starting to cry. *Her brother? But...*

"Don't worry I'll get that bastard, but you have to run, the farther away you are the better. Now go!" I say. She nods her head and I help her off the ground. I slip a note into her pocket and then she runs out of the forest and towards Tirentod while I run off into the woods. I searched around the forest for hours and I still wasn't able to find him. I noticed that it was pretty late, so I set up camp for the night. Luckily, I had a few things on me on earth. I had brought a compact tent, a knife, and a ferrite lighter. *Not sure why I brought a lighter. Kind of redundant.* I shrug. I set up a small campfire and set up my tent. I lay down and quickly fall asleep. I wake up the next morning and pack up. *Yesterday Azalea said that the boy on the ground had been her brother meaning... I went into the past?!* I try not to think about it too much. *So, that means I'm the hooded figure?* I now know what I must do. *Azalea said that her brother died two years ago so all I have to do is wait that time and save everyone.* I spend the next two year wandering around Sotaqt making ends meet until eventually I wander back to the forest near Tirentod. I look over at the hill that overlooks the town and see Alex, CJ and myself there. I follow them into the town and to the church where they meet up with Kevin. I sit up on top of the walls surrounding the town to watch the fight unfold. I try to stop Kevin from dying, but suddenly I realize. *If he dies, he should end up going back to earth? But then why was he dead when I got there? Maybe he went back here just like me?* I try to focus on the scene in front of me. *Wait, wasn't there a hooded figure here too that helped us out?* Just before the assailant is about to blow himself up I point my finger at him, vocalizing quietly turning him to ashes. I see my younger self look up at me before she faints along with Alex and CJ. I wait about a day before I head into the underground chambers of the town hall cutting down the spotlight before escaping in stealth. I make my way to the shared territory to prevent everyone from getting crushed. After a few days I finally got there and head to the lowest floor. I hide out in the factory waiting for everybody to get there. I see them go down the stairs and into the room with Number 02. Once I hear the explosions I run down the stairs and into the room seeing that I have already been crushed. I vaporize all of the rocks and see that everyone is okay. *I did it! I saved them just in time!* I then say,

"Sorry everybody, I'm a bit late."

I see Alex look up at me in shock,

"But, Cat you... died. My force field wasn't big enough to cover you and..."

"Don't worry about it right now, we need to get out of here fast," I say. Everyone gets up and we run up the stairs out of the factory and the elevator. I press the button and we start to ascend. As we go up I hear the sounds of the lower floor collapsing.

"Cat, how are you alive? My force field didn't cover you should've been crushed," Alex asks.

"It's kind of a long story..." I say.

"Well, it did take about 20 mins for the elevator to go down, so we have time," Adran reminds Cat.

"Well, the rocks did crunch me, but after I died I found myself back in my room on earth," Cat explains.

"Really? So, you're saying that if we die here we'll just get sent back to earth?" Alex says.

"Maybe, at least that's what happened to me, but I don't think it's worth the risk," Cat says.

"So, then maybe..." CJ begins.

"Maybe what CJ," I say.

"Do you think it's possible that Kevin is still alive?" CJ asks.

"Maybe, but he was dead when I got to earth, though..." I say.

"*Though* what," Alex says.

"Well, after I got back to earth, I went to CJ, Kevin, and your funerals, but later I thought that the only way to get back to Sotaqt was to die. So, I lit myself on fire and I ended up back here," I say.

"So, if he died again on earth then it's possible, he's back on Sotaqt," Alex suggests.

"It's possible. Though the problem is when I got to Sotaqt it was about two years before we all got here. In fact, the hooded figure who saved Azalea happened to be me," I say.

"Really! Cat you're the one that saved me!" Azalea exclaims.

"Well, yeah I saw you in the forest on the ground. I was waiting for the hooded figure to show up and when the attacker was about to hit you, I jumped in to save you," I say. Suddenly Azalea embraces me tightly, starting to tear up.

"I never got to properly thank you so. Thank you, Cat. Thank you so much. If it weren't for you, I'd be dead," Azalea says, clinging to me tighter. I'm not really sure what to say. My face begins to redden as Azalea continues to cling to me.

"So, that's the reason that Kevin got here a month before us. He must've died later than we did," CJ says.

"It all makes sense now. I remember a dream I had while Amaryll was in the medical lodge where I saw Kevin in the hospital and a doctor was saying how he only had a few days left and my synat is force sight so..."

"I guess you're right," CJ says.

"So, after I saved Azalea, I just wandered around the forest for about two years until I saw us appear on the hill. Then I helped you guys out at the church by vaporizing that guy before he could explode and then I made my way to save everybody."

"Oh, and one more thing I'm pretty sure I have another word on my synat."

"You what?!" Alex exclaims, "You do know what that means right?"

"I don't, what?" I say.

"Well, remember Argent said The Assassin King had a three-word synat," Alex says.

"So, The Assassin King is from earth and has already died once," Amaryll says.

"That's the only explanation," Alex says, "Also Cat what is your third word?"

"Well, actually it came to me when I got here the second time. It's martyrdom. So, the whole thing is Burning Song of Martyrdom," I say.

"Hmm... Interesting, do you know what your new ability is?" Alex questions.

"No, I haven't tried using it yet, but I did notice that my fire abilities got stronger. It probably has something to do with the way I died on earth," I say.

"Cat," Azalea says.

"Yeah?" I say.

"I think you got taller," she says.

"Really? I guess that does make sense. I am about eighteen," I say.

"Yeah, and you got a scar that goes over your left eye," Alex mentions.

"Really? It must be from the rocks," I say. After catching everybody up on what had happened to me the elevator had reached the management office. We walk out of the elevator and past the front desk. The lady working there calls us over.

"What happened?" She asks.

"He left right before we got there," Alex says.

"Do you know where he went?" she asks.

"His second in command did say "he's probably halfway to Heizengaard by now" or something like that," Alex says.

"Heizengaard... That's the city in The Confederacy of Unionized Orcs," she says, "I'll get you some tickets on the southeast train. There's a station in the city." She hands us the tickets and as we walk out the building Ardan says,

"Sorry, but I still have some business here. Until we meet again." He waves at us as we walk out. We make our way to the station and show our tickets to the conductor and get onto the train and take our seats. The train starts to move, but strangely enough it's moving up and not forward. Looking out the window I see that we're in some sort of mountain range.

"It's been a while since I've been on a train," Alex says looking out the window.

"Weren't we on a train yesterday?" CJ says sarcastically.

"I meant a passenger train," Alex retorts.

"I don't think I ever went on a train on Earth," I say.

"Well, it's certainly a first for me," Azalea says.

"Really?" I say.

"Yeah, as after I moved out of my parents house I went straight to working in the medical lodge in Tirentod and even as a kid I never traveled outside the UEF," Azalea explains.

"I'm not really sure if I've been on one before, my memory's kind of fuzzy," Amaryll says. Looking out of the window I see that we are in some sort of evergreen forest.

"How long do you think the train ride will be?" I ask.

"Well, Heizengaard is about the same distance away as the ride from the Republic of Western lands to the shared territory. So, it will probably be about the same amount of time, eight to nine hours," Argent says.

"Oh, so it's going to be a while," I say, yawning, "Well, I'm going to sleep. I haven't slept inside in about two years, so you know." I close my eyes and think about all that's happened these past two years wandering around aimlessly waiting for everyone to arrive wondering if I would be able to save them and finally I was able to see them again. I soon fall asleep.

Suddenly, I'm woken up by the sound of the train going over something on the tracks.

"Oh, Cat you're awake," Alex says.

"Yeah. What's going on?" I ask.

"There's Probably something on the tracks," Alex says. I look out the window again seeing the same forest as before. Suddenly, I hear a loud bump and then we are all flung right into the wall of the train car. The sound of metal wheels grinding on earth and then a loud crash of the train against a tree. I feel pretty lightheaded. Looking down I see that part of one of the train seats has impaled my leg and I'm bleeding out. My vision begins to blur as I begin to lose consciousness. I see Azalea kneeling over me, her hands over my wound, a bright cold light coming from them

"You'll be okay!" I hear Azalea say, though just barely as my hearing is muffled. Soon after I black out.

Chapter 11: The End of Eligius

A singular moment of lucidity, only a few seconds in length; my eyes open, I see Cat next to Azalea, and my eyes close again. Another short glimpse of consciousness, Cat is making a fire and explaining 'I know how to do this' while Azalea seems to be standing over me, palms outstretched. Finally, I wake up in a more lasting manner, seeing Azalea standing over me, palms outstretched with dazzling pale blue light emanating from them.

"Yeah, I learned how to make fires pretty well during my time here, this specific kind of wood- is he awake?" Cat interrupts herself to ask, crouched next to a fire with a candle-like flame blossoming from her pointer finger.

"Yup, I think he's gonna stay awake this time," Azalea answers, helping me up and revealing how us six are now huddled around a fire.

"CJ, you were definitely hit the hardest. You okay?" Alex asks, a faint blue aura coming from his neck and left arm

"Yeah, I think. What happened?" I ask, confused about the events that followed the train crashing.

"Well, when the train crashed I used by synat to protect us with a force field, but I knew that I couldn't protect everyone so I focused on the best healer, Azalea," Alex explains, followed by Argent butting in to say,

"I can heal too." Causing me to notice how the same blue aura is coming from the left side of Argent's face. *Is the blue aura caused by the healing?*

"Hence my choice of saying 'best', Argent." Alex glares slightly.

"What caused the de-railing?" I ask, still confused about it.

"No clue, maybe the tracks were damaged, maybe The Assassin King's backup plan, maybe it's just a tragic accident," Azalea answers.

"Enough chit-chat, we need to get somewhere populated to avoid The Assassin King coming in to finish the job," Cat cuts in, seeming more authoritative since her semi-death.

"On that note, we probably should get to the nearest village and report the broken rails, so they close the track," Amaryll declares, her hair blowing slightly due to the soft winds created by the fire.

"How? The nearest village is too far away, it'd take all night on foot," Argent points out.

"True, but consider," Azalea lets her gesture toward the nearby wild horses speak for her.

"And how do you intend to tame wild horses?" Argent counters, sounding annoyed by the suggestion; or maybe his injuries were the bother, hard to tell I suppose.

"I think my synat may help here," Amaryll says, "maybe by using the 'blood' part of my synat I could interpret that as bonds, y'know?"

"I don't think that'll work-" Argent starts before I get him to shut up with a glare, wanting to see if it works.

"I mean the strength of synats is their adaptability, so it might work," Amaryll begins slowly walking towards the horses.

"If she fails it'll be hilarious and if she succeeds it'll be useful," I whisper to Argent.

"Ah, I see, how wise of you," Argent whispers back, smiling slightly. Amaryll tries to tame one of the horses by putting one palm on its forehead, closing her eyes to focus. A tame red aura appears from her hand, and in that instant the horse seems calm; however, per the word 'moment', this is temporary, and the horse almost immediately bites her arm.

"Ah! Stupid horse! God damnit!" Amaryll shouts, holding her bleeding arm and jumping up and down from the pain as Argent and I softly chuckle while looking at her.

"What did I say? It's funnier to see them fail-" I start to tell Argent before being struck with awe. The horse began to writhe for a moment before becoming still. Amaryll turns around and exclaims,

"I used my blood to tame it!" jumping up and down like an overly excited child who just saw Santa at the mall. *Is Santa a thing here? Probably not.*

"Your wisdom has paid off well, young master. We got both the show and the positive results," Argent chuckles, putting one arm around my shoulder.

"Thank you Argent, much obliged," I tell Argent. I finally figure out a good way to ask what I've been wondering.

"Oh, I forgot to ask before. I saw some of my divine messages have been misinterpreted since I left for the heavens, do people still follow what I said about marriage?" I ask Argent.

"That's a broad category young master, do you mean the 'freedom of' part or the 'no earlier than 20' part?" Argent responds.

"I said 21 but close enough," I say absent minded.

"I see," Argent chuckles, "Translations are a fickle thing, the holy language is Langladon, but the verses were first transcribed in Abramonic," he explains. The horse's eyes look solid white as it stares at Amaryll head-on. We begin walking to the horses as Azalea and Amaryll mount their horses easily. I get onto my horse, an amber gypsy, before helping Argent onto the horse behind me. Argent wraps his arms around my waist to hold on, seeming to have no experience with riding bareback. Cat and Alex visibly struggle with getting onto their horses, despite Azalea and Amaryll helping them respectively. Amaryll has to make her horse get down like a camel in order for Alex to get on, which looks very unnatural. I lean back, knowing that when riding bareback it's better to spread out the area of your body that hits as the horse moves up and down in its gallop; this leaves the back of my head resting against Argent's chest, an added bonus. Amaryll whispers to her horse,

"Come on, we got to get to town," causing it to begin moving forwards, to the visible shock of Alex. Azalea simply spurs the horse with her heel to get it moving, and I just pull my horse's mane forwards gently to get it moving.

"Hey, Argent, check this out." I smirk, looking up at him before giving my horse a soft tap with my leg, making it speed up to a gallop.

"Young master, do you have experience with this type of animal?" Argent asks, gripping me tighter out of what I assume is fear.

"Yeah, my da- an old friend of mine had a few of these," I quickly stop myself, unsure if the religious figure I'm impersonating has a dad. *Can I reference family around him? I probably should read this magic bible.*

"I see, interesting," Argent comments. During the ride I see Amaryll and Alex's horse almost fall over due to what I assume is a log or something like that, I honestly couldn't tell.

After three hours of riding we finally see the light of the town, just beyond the trees. Sadly, it seems that fate had other plans, as suddenly I see a crimson fluid covering the rocks as Amaryll and Alex fall off of their horse. I stop my horse and get off to see what happened, but the moment I get close to the horse I see its head rip off as a man dressed like a mall goth leaps from its throat, grabbing onto me before seeming to disappear. I see my arms moving forwards and grabbing Argent's throat, starting to squeeze against my will. *This isn't me! I don't know what I'm doing.* I attempt, but no words come out.

"Y-young master, what are you doing?" Argent struggles against my grip, my weakness triumphed only by his. I see his face begin turning pale before becoming a soft blue, and then I seem to stop. I see the sky above me and feel my back thud to the ground as the man from inside the horse jumps out of me and into Argent.

"Oh, were you looking for these, 'young master'?" Argent smirks, putting a mocking emphasis on my title as he drops a clump of chalk-white soft little threads, "those are your tendons, don't bother trying to move."

"Who the hell are you?!" Azalea asks, sounding terrified as she points at Argent.

"Oh, little old me? I'm just a pathetic little servant, with the weakest synat known to man," Argent chuckles, seeming to be mocking the others as well as he walks to the severed head of the horse, picking it up and kissing it on the forehead before throwing it at Cat at high speed. The horse's head hits her in the chest, seeming to phase through her chest, but not fully, the ears sticking out of her like handlebars. Cat almost instantly passes out, her body falling down with the horse's neck acting as a faucet to let her blood out. With Alex unconscious from the horse crash, Cat bleeding out, myself paralyzed, and Argent being puppeteered, all that's left is Azalea and Amaryll.

"Aww, is the world's weakest synat too much for you all?" Argent giggles, crouching down and picking Cat up by the hair.

"You're still outnumbered, we have the advantage!" Azalea runs forwards trying to pummel Argent with ice. I can't react fast enough to actually see what happens before Cat's body becomes phased into Azalea's, severing Cat's left hand at the wrist. I watch the last remaining ally, Amaryll, as she watches in terror.

"So, pathetic, what easy prey," Argent giggles, picking up Cat's hand and beginning to chew on it, taking a small bite before throwing it into Alex's throat.

"You- you monster!" Amaryll steps backwards, horror visible on her face. *She's our last hope, a melee fighter against a person who can phase through flesh. I wish I could move so I could write my will.* I mentally joke with my last moments. Argent falls to the ground as I see the man phase into Amaryll, taking over her body. I see Amaryll kicking Argent into unconsciousness before walking towards me.

"It's honestly sad, you were probably the biggest threat to me, your abilities aren't physical," She explains, sitting down on my chest and pulling out a marker from inside the horse. She then phases the tendons back into my face and throat, allowing me to speak.

"Please stop, I'm sure that you'll regret this," I cough, trying to use my ultimate ability to turn the enemy's psyche against themself, like depression times ten. For a moment there is silence before Amaryll laughs,

"You idiot, these aren't my ears you're speaking into," she laughs more, using my own tendons to wrap around my throat, choking me.

"W-wait, don't kill me, I'll do a-anything-" I plead, watching the world go blurry.

"Anything?" she asks, seeming interested

"Yes! A-anything," I choke out, struggling to speak

"Aww, babe, then die~" she takes her fist and moves to punch my face, probably about to phase it into my skull. *At least it'll be painless* I think as I close my eyes. Finally, after a moment, I'm not dead. I open my eyes to see Amaryll ejecting the man from her body, leaving the man writing on the ground in pain.

"The culmination of my power, by fueling it with rage I can bring my blood to 230° Fahrenheit!" Amaryll scoffs as the man tries to crawl away.

"D-damn, I need to return to a body, she won't kill a friend!" The man leaps at Cat but is stopped by Amaryll kicking him into a tree.

"Normally I might show mercy, but what you've done is far from being forgivable," Amaryll uses a sharp stick to cut her wrist, letting her boiling blood pour out onto the boy. Before my vision disappears from the lack of air, I see the fate of the male, drowning in a puddle of his own flesh.

Chapter 12: Ghosts of the Past

I open my eyes and see Azalea over me again, her hands emitting a pale blue light. *Damn, I really have a knack for getting seriously injured. I hope it doesn't become a habit.*

"Oh! Alex, you're awake!" Azalea exclaims, finally noticing that I was conscious again, "Are you okay?"

"Yeah, I'm doing great, thanks to your healing. I'm sure we'd all be dead at this point if it weren't for you," I say, genuinely grateful.

"We'll I did kind of die so..." Cat says.

"Well, it wasn't exactly the kind of death I could have saved you from. You pretty much died instantly," Azalea retorts.

"It's not like I blame either of you for it, I was just kind of saying. Actually, in reality if I hadn't died there we'd be in worse condition than we are now," Cat points out.

"Yeah, I guess you're right..." I say, pausing to think for a second, "I mean yeah if you hadn't died there then you wouldn't have been able to save Azalea and she would've been dead before we got here. Kind of a paradox if you think about it." I realize this line of questioning could form questions we aren't prepared to answer, hence my choice to shift subject; "On another note how is everyone else doing?"

"Well, my left hand did get detached, but Azalea was able to reattach it along with healing the wound from the horse head, though I am still low on blood," Cat comments.

"Well, my healing does have its limits. I can't restore lost blood," Azalea explains, "Amaryll also lost a decent amount of blood loss, but she should be fine in a few weeks. I was able to heal CJ and Agent up pretty well too." I get up and walk over to Amaryll to see how she's doing,

"Are you doing okay?"

"Well, I am a little faint 'cause of the blood loss, but otherwise I'm doing good," Amaryll says, "Though my synat may increase the rate of blood production after serious blood loss, I'm not exactly sure." I turn around to look over to Azalea,

"So, where exactly are we?"

"I think we're not too far from the nearest town. I had to drop everything and heal everyone, so we're also not too far away from where Amaryll fought that guy," Azalea responds, "He was probably another backup measure from The Assassin King, but he could've also just been some random psycho, though the former is probably more likely."

"Man, that guy's pretty paranoid," I say, thinking about all the backup measures he had in place.

"Since everybody's awake now It's probably best if we head over to the town," Azalea suggests. We all get up and start walking.

"I'm sorry about earlier CJ," Amaryll says.

"It's fine. I mean you literally weren't in control of your own body," CJ says.

"I guess you're right," Amaryll says. After a little while we finally get to the nearby town.

"This place! I-" Amaryll says before falling unconscious.

"Amaryll!" I catch Amaryll before she hits the ground. I carry her on my back while running to the nearest inn. We get a room and I lay her down on the bed.

"Is she gonna be okay?" I ask, casting a concerned look over at Azalea.

"Well, she's fine physically, but due to her being low on blood any sudden surprise could cause her to faint; so that's probably what happened. Though as to what exactly surprised her I don't know," Azalea explains. Amaryll slowly sits up groaning and putting her hand to her forehead.

"Amaryll! Are you okay?" I exclaim.

"Yeah, I'm fine it's just when we walked into town something came back to me. It was almost like I've been here before. Maybe..." She says, pausing at the end.

"Maybe what?" I say, curious.

"Well, it's just that..." Amaryll says, pausing again.

"Just that, what Amaryll?" I ask.

"I think this is the town I woke up in after I died on earth," she says, seeming to doubt her own words.

"You think?" CJ says.

"Well, it's just that my memory is kind of foggy," Amaryll explains.

"Maybe if we take a walk around town it'll jog your memory," I suggest.

"Good idea," Cat comments. We leave the Inn and start walking around. It's a relatively small town in fact, village would be a more apt description, it's really just a small collection of Log cabins maybe ten or fifteen, the largest one being the inn we were just at. Though with it being in the middle of the woods like this it makes sense that it would be on the smaller side.

"So, remember anything?" I ask.

"Well, it's certain now, this is definitely the town I was in when I got to this world," Amaryll says, an air of confidence in her voice.

"Well, that's good. Do you think you could tell us anything?" I ask.

"I guess I'll start from the beginning then. Back on earth I was on a bus coming back from school and I was with my friend group, we all lived near each other, so we all had the same bus stop, the last stop. So, after the second to last stop it was just me, my friends, and the bus driver and right before we got to the last stop someone crashed into the back of the bus and in the process damaged the drive shaft which caused the bus to flip over and the engine to explode killing my friend and cause me to bleed out from the injury. When I woke up, I was here in this village with my friends. We walked around for a little and then we were attacked by one of The Assassin Kings agents. He killed all my friends, only leaving me behind. I was frozen with fear. I couldn't move. He took me back to The Assassin King's lair and I was put under his control. Those guys must've been able to tell what synat I had and thought I'd be useful. After I was put under control I don't remember much until I met all of you in the medical lodge," Amaryll explains.

"Huh... but you said back at the medical lodge that you ran away and then tried to find The Assassin King to get revenge and then you got put under his control," I say, pointing out the inconsistency of her two versions of the story.

"Well, I wanted to look cool and make a good first impression. I mean you guys had just knocked me out without much of a fight. I didn't want you to think I was a wimp or anything," She explains.

"Wait, so how old were you when this happened?" I ask.

"Well, on earth it was 2024 and I was born in 2017, so probably seven or eight. My memory's pretty fuzzy so I can't remember exactly when," Amaryll says. Everybody else seems a little shocked at her answer.

"You were that young! I mean you're probably like sixteen maybe seventeen, so that means you've been here for like eight to nine years and all while under The Assassin Kings control! So, when we knocked you out and he lost control of you wouldn't you revert back to your younger self?" I ask confused

"No, I don't think so I probably was able to develop, and I might have actually made memories during that time the thing is The Assassin King's synat might have some sort of failsafe, so that if anyone where to get out of his control their memories would be blocked off so they would be able to reveal any information. In fact, it's possible that if The Assassin King dies that I might be able to remember what happened during that time, though I'm not sure if I really want to remember..." Amaryll says, drifting off into thought.

"It's getting late Master CJ; don't you think we should head back to the inn?" Argent asks.

"I think you're right Argent," CJ replies.

"Yeah, let's head back for the night," I concur. We turn around and head back for the inn. Azalea and Cat head to their rooms and CJ and Argent to theirs.

"Alex, if you don't mind, do you think I could stay in a room with you?" Amaryll asks, shooting me a look of concern, "It's just I get a bad feeling from this town and just being here stirs up old memories I'd rather not think about."

"Of course, if it makes you feel better," I say. *I mean if I was in her shoes, I'd do the same thing. I'm a little nervous about it, but if it makes Amaryll feel better then I don't mind.* We head over to our room. Luckily there are two beds. She gets into her bed, and I get into mine. I blow out the candle and fall asleep.

I wake up from the light of the sun filtering into the room. I open my eyes to see Amaryll's face right in front of mine. *Why is she in my bed?! She didn't do it in the middle of the night did she? She probably did it in her sleep. Maybe she's a sleepwalker.* I get out of bed as quietly as I can to avoid waking her up and once, I was out of bed I heard a knock on the door.

"Yes?" I say, while answering the door.

"Alex there seems to be some sort of commotion going on outside. I think it's best if we check it out. Oh, and would you wake up Amaryll? It's important that she comes," Argent says. I walk back over to Amaryll,

"Amaryll! Wake up!"

"What is it?" Amaryll says, while yawning and rubbing her eyes.

"Apparently something important is going on outside," I say.

"Oh, alright give me sec," she says, slowly getting out of bed and then stretching.

"Sure," I say.

"Alright, ready to go," she says, smiling at me while sticking her arm out and giving me a thumbs up. We walk out in front of the inn meeting up with everyone, though there is someone else I don't recognize. He has a slim figure and is probably about six foot.

"Finally, you're all here. It's rude to keep someone waiting you know," he says, brushing his brown hair out of his face.

"It's you!" Amaryll exclaims, glaring at the man. Ignoring Amaryll's statement he continues,

"It's about time I introduce myself. My name is Number 03 and since you all won't be alive for too long, I guess I'll tell you my synat as well. It's Broken Rejection, anything that enters my body gets shot back out at high speed, though whether or not it happens is up to me."

"Do you know this guy Amaryll?" I ask. *Number 03? Must be one of The Assassin King's goons.*

"Yeah, I know him. He's the man who killed my friends," Amaryll says, glaring at Number 03 with rage.

"So, it is you, Amaryll! I did hear you were able to escape Number 01's control, though I was skeptical. I guess this proves it," Number 03 comments.

"Alright let's get this over with!" Amaryll exclaims. She runs over at Number 03 and throws a punch at the left side of his face. Her fist seems to sink into his face before ejecting making her fly back at high speeds. I use my synat to dampen the force of her fall.

"You alright Amaryll?" I ask.

"Yeah, I'm fine," she says, standing back up. Number 03 takes out a number of knives and sticks them into his stomach handle side in, they then proceed to shoot at Amaryll at a rate faster than anyone could possibly move. I put up a force field in front of Amaryll blocking the knives. She shoots a quick glance in my direction. She takes one of the knives and makes a small cut at the end of her index finger. She runs over to him and points the same finger directly at his head.

"Oh, and what exactly is the point of pointing fingers at this point Amaryll dear?" Number 03 taunts. Amaryll remains unfazed and ignores his taunting.

"Take this!" Amaryll yells, shooting a high-pressure stream of boiling blood out of her finger and directly into Number 03's forehead. The jet only makes it less than an inch into his head before shooting back up into the air, but what he didn't realize was that after the jet of blood Amaryll must've shot out a stream of superheated vaporized blood at his face. The vaporized blood hit his face giving him severe burns.

"Agggh! Bastard! I'll kill you!" Number 03 screams out in agony. What Number 03 also failed to remember in his agony that he had shot Amaryll's boiling blood up into the air, as just after he was hit in the face with high pressure vaporized blood at point blank range, the boiling blood fell down and hit both him and Amaryll, though she only sustained minor damage.

"Agggh!!" Number 03 cries out, holding his face to keep in the semi-liquid drips of flesh. Number 03, in all his pain and rage, didn't see Amaryll's fist coming straight for his already vulnerable face. Her attack impacted with great force dealing the final blow and indenting Number 03's face, causing what I assume used to be his brain to flow out of his tear ducts. I run over to Amaryll to make sure she isn't hurt.

"You okay?" I ask.

"Okay? I feel great. I finally avenged my friends and now they can rest in peace," She says, a look of relief on her face.

"Well, that's good and all, but you're injured," I say, concerned. She walks over to Azalea to get healed. That same pale blue light emanating from her hands she heals the cut on her finger and all the burns from the boiling blood that got shot up into the air.

"You know Amaryll," I say.

"What?" She replies.

"That was pretty damn impressive. I mean you took him out all by yourself and got out relatively unscathed," I say, singing Amaryll's praises.

"Well, not totally alone. I would've been out of the fight if it weren't for you. I mean you softened the blow when I got flung back and blocked the knives. Either of which would have either killed me out right or seriously injured me. So, don't downplay yourself so much Alex okay," Amaryll says.

"She's not wrong Alex, but in a sense neither are you. In reality the only other people who could have beat that guy would be me or Azalea," Cat comments.

"Well, I would've needed to use Frozen Instant to beat him and at the moment using would not end well for me," Azalea explains, "So, in reality Cat you're really the only other person who would have dealt with him."

"I'm glad that you think so highly of me, but I didn't really have the right to barge in. That was Amaryll's fight," Cat says, forming a stern look on her face.

"Ahem. I think it's about time we head out of here," CJ says, trying to break the tension.

"You're right. Number 02 said The Assassin King was heading to Heizengaard no?" I ask.

"Yeah, I'm pretty sure that's what he said," Azalea says. We walk into the inn to ask the innkeeper where the nearest train station is,

"Train station? I think the closest station is the one in a town just south west of here called Düvenberk. It's only a few hours by horse carriage. If you head to the end of town there's a guy who runs a carriage service.

"Thanks," I say, while we walk out the door. We head out to the edge of the town and find the guy he was talking about.

"Are you all looking for a ride?" the man sitting in the carriage's driver seat says.

"Yeah, we need to go to Düvenberk," I say.

"Düvenberk huh. Alright that'll cost yah 200 quills," the man says.

"Quills... I guess they would use that around here," Argent says to himself, "Don't worry Master CJ I will cover the cost."

"Thanks," CJ says.

"There is no need to thank me Master CJ. I am your humble servant," Argent says, brushing off CJ's hollow gratitude. Argent hands the man two silver-colored coins, though they appeared heavier than silver.

"Alright, hop in," the man says. We get into the carriage and prepare for the journey ahead.

Chapter 13: Calm Sea of Sand

I open my eyes and look out the window of the carriage and see that the sun is starting to set. *I must've fallen asleep.*

"Cat you're awake," Alex says.

"I guess so," I say.

"You pretty much slept through the whole ride. We should be in Düvenberk in a few minutes," Amaryll says, "Though today was pretty eventful so I kind of understand."

"Yeah, definitely eventful," I say, pausing to think for a moment. *These next few days will certainly be even more eventful,* "Well, then-"

I begin getting off the carriage,

"Alright we're here."

"Finally," CJ says, letting out a sigh of relief. We'll get off and look around. This town seems bigger than the last one, but not by much. The driver dropped us off right in front of the train station so luckily, we didn't have to search for it. There doesn't seem to be many people around, but that does make sense as it's late and this is still a relatively small town. The train station is small so it's no more than a small log building with an exit to the platform. We walk into the building and walk over to the desk at the right.

"Tickets please," the person at the desk says. We hand her the tickets we got in the shared territory. A look of shock spreads across her face.

"You're from that train?!" she exclaims.

"Yeah, except for maybe one or two people we're the only ones who survived," I say.

"I'm terribly sorry. Our inspection crews should have noticed something had happened to the tracks. Don't worry though your tickets are still valid. In fact the higher ups said that if we were to contact any survivors that we should inform them that they now have a lifetime rail pass that allows them to ride on any train free of charge," she says, apologizing profusely.

"Well, it's not really your fault. Actually, we think the most likely thing was that The Assassin King damaged the tracks," Alex says.

"Really? I did hear something like that, but still take these."

She hands us something similar in appearance to dog tags but with the metal piece being made out of what looked like brass with an engraving of a steam train on it.

"If you show these to the person who asks for tickets, they should let you on with no questions asked," she says.

"Thank you," I say as we walk out onto the platform. Our timing was perfect as just as we walked out the train came from the left and stopped. We get onto the train car and take our seats, I then ask the conductor,

"How long is the ride to Heizengaard from here?"

"Heizengaard? Hmm let's see I think it's only about an hour from here," the conductor says.

"Huh, guess we did most of the traveling on foot," I say.

"Well, we did take that carriage," Amaryll comments.

"Yeah, we probably did most of the traveling on that carriage," Alex adds on.

"Oh..." I say. I quickly fall asleep as it's already late in the day. I was pretty tired even though I slept through the ride.

"Cat! Wake up! We're here!" Azalea exclaims. I get up and rub my eyes with a yawn.

"You sure like to sleep a lot don'tcha," Azalea says with a sigh shaking her head.

"Oh, come on. How am I supposed to save you all if I'm not well rested?" I joke. It seems as though my joke didn't go across too well as there's an awkward silence right after. We walk out of the train car and down onto the platform. I immediately notice the drop in temperature. Looking up it looks like it's still night.

"So, Argent," I say.

"Yes?" he says, looking slightly annoyed. I ignore his current disposition towards me.

"What kind of city is Heizengaard?" I ask, out of curiosity.

"Well, it's a medium size city in the Confederacy of Unionized Orcs and it's an oasis in the middle of-" he cuts himself off, "Well, anyway you'll see soon."

"Huh?" I say. *What is he talking about?* I was about to ask what he was going to say, but when we walked out of the station it answered the question I wanted to ask. Looking around we seemed to be in some sort of desert oasis. There were palm trees lining the streets and houses made out of sandstone. Looking off into the distance it seems to be an endless expanse of sand dunes, although it was a little hard to see as it was still nighttime.

"Welcome to the Dezron Desert. The largest desert in the world," Argent says.

"So, what do we do now?" Alex asks.

"Probably find somewhere to stay for the night," CJ suggests.

"Good Idea Master CJ," Argent agrees.

"I guess so," I say, looking around I see some signs, but, "One problem though I can't read these signs at all."

"Well, they are in orcish so that would make sense," Argent says, mostly to himself, "Don't worry-"

"I can read it," Azalea says, cutting Argent off. Argent looking visibly annoyed says,

"Well, if you're such an expert then please elucidate us to what it says."

"Hmm let's see..." Azalea says, starting to mumble to herself, "Ah! There's an inn right around here. It should be right over... there!"

Azalea is looking at a tall sandstone building right on our left. Azalea looks up above the door of the building and to the sign.

"Yup, this is it," she says. We walk in and someone is at the desk. They're pretty tall and muscular so much so that they look a little cramped in this relatively small space. His skin is flat grey color and he has small tusks coming from his lower jaw similar in appearance to the tusks of a wild hog.

"So, I assume you want to stay here," the man says, his voice very gruff.

"Yes, we did just come off the train after all," Alex says.

"You can speak orcish Alex?" Azalea asks.

"Orcish? No of course not," Alex says.

"Well, you just spoke in it," she says.

"But..." Alex says, his confusion only intensifying.

"You know, back in UEF I heard that people from earth can understand the spoken languages of Sotaqt, but not the written language," Azalea explains, "I didn't notice the whole time because I've been speaking in Abramonic which is spoken along side elvish in the UEF due to close relations with the USP. And you guys are human so I thought it would be best to speak Abramonic, though I wonder if you actually know it."

"Huh that's pretty interesting I wonder why?" Alex asks.

"Well, UEF scientists think it has something to do with synats. They're not sure what exactly though," Azalea says.

"Are you guys just gonna stand there and talk or are you gonna get a room?" the man at the counter asks.

"Sorry," I say. We walk over to the counter and Argent hands some coins over to the man.

"Alright we only could get three rooms so we're pairing up again," Argent says, then speaking to himself, "Though not like that will be a problem."

Argent and CJ go off to their room and Alex and Amaryll to their's. I walk over to our room and get right into bed.

"Jeez, how are you still tired after sleeping all day," Azalea says, with a sigh, "Do you plan on sleeping through life?"

"No, I'm just particularly tired today. Maybe it's from the blood loss?" I say, shrugging my shoulders.

"Well, if that's the case then it's probably better if you rest then," Azalea says, changing her tone.

"That's what I plan to do," I say. I close my eyes and quickly fall asleep. I wake up and see that the sun has just risen and Azalea is still asleep. I walk over and tap Azalea on the shoulders in an attempt to wake her up.

"Good morning Azalea," I say.

"Good morning Cat," Azalea says, stretching.

"So, today's the day huh," I say.

"It sure is we'll finally put an end to this mess," Azalea says, a look of confidence on her face. Azalea gets out of bed and we walk out the entrance of the inn bumping into Alex and Amaryll on the way.

"Oh, you guys are already awake," I say, surprised that Alex is up this early.

"Yeah, Amaryll woke me up," Alex says.

"Ah, that makes sense," I say. Alex wasn't exactly what you would call a morning person, in fact he was quite the opposite.

"Well, today's important Alex," Amaryll says, "It was necessary for you to wake up early."

"I guess you're right. We'll need time to get prepared," Alex says, his tone switching to a more serious one.

"We should go check if CJ and Argent are awake," I say.

"No need," A voice says from behind me. I turn around to see CJ and Argent.

"Oh, you're already awake. Good it saves us the trouble of having to wake you up," I say.

"Yes, it was quite troublesome to wake Master CJ. I mean no offense of course," Argent says, sounding mildly annoyed.

"Well..." CJ tries to come up with some sort of excuse and fails.

"Alright well let's get going," I say. We walk out of the inn and onto the street. There aren't too many people out as it's still early in the morning.

"So, where exactly are we going?" CJ asks.

"That's... a good question. I don't know," I say.

"We could go and ask the owner of the inn," Alex suggests.

"Good idea," Azalea says. We walk back into the inn.

"Oh, you all are already back? Looking to stay longer?" he says.

"No, we were just wondering if you've heard anything about The Assassin King," I ask.

"The Assassin king huh... that bastard. You know, now that I think about it, I did hear something about him a day or two ago," he says.

"Really!" I say.

"Yeah, I might as well tell you. I mean you're already patrons. Here's what I heard. So, apparently The Assassin King's base is out in the desert a mile or so from the city," he says.

"That's it?" I say.

"Yup, didn't hear anything else. Though, who knows whether or not it's true. It's not like anyone around here has the balls to go and check," the man chuckles a little before continuing, "And besides we've got a whole war going on so it's not like anyone has the time either. I'd be fighting myself if it weren't for this damn leg."

The man points to his right leg where instead of the lower half there's a wooden peg.

"Well, thanks," I say.

"No problem. Anyone who pays to stay can ask all they want. I wish ya luck," he says. As we walk out the door the man waves at us. I wave back.

"So, I guess we're off to the desert," Alex says.

"Yeah," I say. We walk out to the edge of the city and start walking in the desert.

"So, the owner of the inn was talking about some sort of war going on," I say.

"He was probably talking about the orc civil war," Argent says.

"Orc civil war? I think I heard something about that recently," Azalea says.

"Recently? The Orc civil war started years ago," Argent exclaims.

"Huh. Well It didn't seem too long ago, though I am an elf so..." Azalea says.

"Hey guys!" Alex yells.

"What is it?" I say.

"I think I found something," Alex says, "I was walking, and I felt something hard under the sand."

"What is it?" CJ asks.

"Not sure. Can you guys help me brush the sand away?" Alex asks. We walk over to Alex and start brushing sand off something.

"It's some sort of metal hatch," Azalea says.

"Maybe it's the entrance to the base?" Alex says. We open it up and there's a staircase that leads down, down into the end of our journey.

Chapter 14: The Heir of Hipponax

All life, all *things*, are born from the earth; when we die, we feed the earth below us, this is the natural order of things. Then, about 3300 years ago, humanity began the path that led us to breaking this order, creating great structures of metal and death. Death itself became more timid, and death no longer served the earth, but instead served man. Walking down these sleek, futuristic stairs, surrounded by walls more artificial than anything I've ever seen, it's hard not to get a bit existential.

Click, Click, Click, Click, Click, Click

"This place looks like something out of a Sci-Fi film," Alex comments.

"What's a Sci-Fi?" Argent asks.

"Film? Like what they take Photographs on?" Azalea adds.

"Well... actually we don't have time to explain all that," Alex raises a finger as he speaks before slowly putting it down.

Click, Click, Click, Click, Click, Click

"You know, the artificial lights do kind of creep me out, I'm not really used to it," I comment, not even noticing that I'm scratching my own left cheek until I feel the vague warmth of my own blood.

"Yeah, really mental. I haven't seen one of these in years," Cat agrees, looking around anxiously.

Click, Click, Click, Click, Click, Click

"What IS this place?" Argent wonders aloud, having to speak over the clicking of our feet against the presumably metal stairs.

"It'll be a metal mausoleum if we aren't careful. These stairs don't have any kind of railings on the outside" I comment.

Click, Click, Click, Click, Click, Click

"I hate hearing my footsteps, it's so surreal," Amaryll complains.

"Agreed," Argent shudders, "and it's ever so cold down here in comparison to the desert sun."

Click, Click, Click, Click, Click, Click, Click

There is a common phrase often used in times of peril, 'It's always darkest before the dawn'; the thing people rarely realize is that this phrase is only true if there IS a dawn. A more universal version is 'it's always quietest after the cacophony', but that doesn't have the same ring to it, and that phrase goes both ways. This phrase may be better for this situation both reversed and taken literally, "it's always loudest after the silence." So, when the room seemed to come alive once more, with buzzing CPUs, spinning dials, and bright screens, it makes sense everyone was more than surprised.

"What's going on?" Azalea is taken aback, nearly falling off of the stairs.

"And so it says in The Book of B'ellum, 'before the metal men and the sticks of death, Azathoth was silent, for the cages of rubber snakes and mystical paintings were strong, yet Azathoth is stronger," Argent recites a suspiciously relevant verse under his breath as a way of calming himself down.

"Maybe we triggered something?" I propose, hopping down from the stairs into the room below us. *I may not be good with computers, but I watch a lot of true crime shows. Considering this place is really advanced tech-wise I'd estimate we have about thirty-ish seconds before whatever alarm we triggered reports our location to anyone outside this base. This place seems abandoned, so those outside are the big priority.* I put my second and fourth fingers against the screen that lit up, shattering the screen. With the screen broken, I can easily pick up anything blunt and smash the circuits, which should stop the broadcast from going out. Of course, this all relies on the assumption that this computer is the broadcasting mechanism, however it could just as easily be the detection mechanism, or entirely unrelated. *Fifteen seconds.* I look for anything that can be used to smash up a computer, finding something that looks vaguely similar to a plumbing wrench. *Ten seconds.* I pick up the wrench and smash the circuits to bits, making sure nothing is left.

"CJ, what exactly are you doing?" Alex asks, looking genuinely confused by my actions, just like the others.

"Well, it takes about fifty-three seconds for a bank vault to report a break-in to the authorities at the International Bank in Munich, this place looks really advanced, so I decreased that to thirty seconds. That meant that I had thirty seconds to smash this thing before anyone off-site became aware of our break-in," I explain, using that one book with the teenage boy and the sci-fi fairies as my only source on this claim.

"Paranoid much? This place looks like it's been abandoned since The Great War, it probably was some intel base from The Great Invaders," Azalea chuckles.

"What was The Great War?" Alex questions

"Well... actually, we don't have time for that either." Azealia's gestures mimic that of Alex almost explaining what a Sci-Fi and a film are.

"I like to call it 'prepared', but regardless, who knows if the communications are still active," I glare up at her. For a moment there was silence before I felt my left ankle restrained. I feel myself pulled back by said left ankle, my back being struck by a blunt force. I fall to the ground, seeing the chain that was formerly around my ankle unties itself.

"CJ! Behind you!" Cat shouts, but it was a bit too late.

"A bit late, miss. You may refer to me as Number 04. For the sake of honor, I will tell you my synat, 'Hopeless Chains'. Naturally, to make sure you don't run, I am using your friend here for collateral, and for that I do apologize," Number 04 introduces himself, two chains coming from each of his two palms, with his pale-yellow almost sand colored solid eyes seeming to look everywhere and nowhere at once. He is extremely tall, maybe 7 feet or so, with broad shoulders and a very muscular build. For clothing, he is wearing a flowy red cloak that goes down to his calves, but has no sleeves. His hair is a beach-blond and his skin a deep, tan color.

"Number 04, does that mean you work for The Assassin King?" Alex asks.

"Indeed, I am his personal guard." Number 04 bows, like a violinist after a performance.

"If we are to duel with honor, we need stakes," Cat suggests, "should we defeat you, you shall tell us the

location of The Assassin King as well as his synat."
Finally, you're using that tiny brain of yours!

"Hmm... I consent to these terms, but should I win, your friend's head will belong to me," Number 04 proposes. *Consider using your brain less next time! Say no Cat!*

"Hmm... deal," Cat jumps down from the stairs. *What the hell Cat?!*

"Then let us begin, may your soul enter Valkkara alongside your friend."

"And a worshiper of the Hollow God! I can't wait to see Cat turn you to a pile of ash!" Argent shouts, evidently a bit religiously invested now and much more passionate than usual. His fervor is greater even than that of his sermons.

"We will stand back to back, then we will walk ten paces before our duel begins." Number 04 chooses to ignore Argent. Number 04 detaches a chain from himself in order to attach me to the pipe before him and Cat move back to back.

"One, two, three-" Number 04 begins counting, but Cat turns on three and directs a blast of fire towards his back. Number 04 feels the heat and jumps up, landing on top of a boiler.

"Have you no honor?!" Number 04 removes the chain binding me and shoots it out towards Cat, looping the middle around her throat and making the two ends tie to two opposite pipes, both restraining and silencing her. That moment of dishonor was enough to trigger the other four to enter the fray. I was still recovering from that blow to my back, which I think must have damaged something back there.

"For lord CJ, for Abramon!" Argent shouts, his synat not having any combat uses at the moment, but he does have a lead pipe he picked up. Argent tries to hit Number 04 in the head with this pipe, but Number 04 uses the chain on his left hand to wrap around Argent's arm and throw him into the wall. I realize that with a non-combat-centric synat and my injured state, I need to get to a safer space. I crawl through a doorway and into what looks like an office room, with a plexiglass-like window to watch the battle from. In the minute it took me to reach this room and look through the window, Azalea and Amaryll had already been defeated somehow, and Number 04 had begun an onslaught against the forcefield that Alex had constructed to protect himself. *It's just chains, how is this guy so damn strong?* Then it came to me, *He was strategic in his plan, first he took me with a sneak attack because I have a synat that can be used on anyone within earshot, then he battled Cat, who he knew would cheat, and thus could use the deployed chain against her as well as justify attacking the others. From there, Argent has no combat use, so he was easy to just pick off, and neither Azalea nor Amaryll have range that can't be deflected and is longer than his chains. He took out the ranged fighters first so all that would be left are melee fighters, who his chains have the advantage against.* I was soon taken away from my thoughts by a scream, the scream of Alex getting thrown into a wall. Number 04 deployed two more chains in order to drag the five down the hall, throwing them into what seems to be a cooling unit for this base. *There isn't air in there! It's gonna be like in movies where they trap someone in a meat freezer!*

"With that taken care of, I just need to find where that last pest ran off too," I hear Number 04 say from down the hall. I realize I need to hide, moving to a supply cupboard and hiding inside, looking through the blinds.

"A deal is a deal my friend, come on out!" Number 04 repeats, dragging his chains behind him. *I didn't agree to crap! Regardless, that bastard ought to move to a different level of the base, and once he does, I can sneak out and rescue my friends.* Then, I hear something clattering at my feet. *God damnit! I must have knocked something over!*

"There you are!" The doors of my cabinet are ripped off their hinges by two chains, which then drag me out and tie me onto the table.

"L-Let go of me!" I exclaim, struggling fruitlessly against his chains.

"No no no, my friend. A deal is a deal, I won, thus your head belongs to me." Number 04 grins, pulling a dagger from inside his cloak. Number 04 brings his dagger up against by throat, getting ready to cut before I shout,

"Wait! The deal is not fulfilled." *Come on, that bought me a few seconds to think, what can I do?*

"Hmm? What aspect? I have won, and thus earned the right to your head," he tilts his head with confusion.

"I-uhh. OH. You have won my head, yes, but you have no right to my neck, and thus cannot slice it," I claim, knowing that this man's obsession with honor as well as some subtle suggestion from my synat may be enough to save my hide.

"Hmm, you are a good lawyer. Let us make a deal, I will spare you for one hour, but during that hour we shall speak, honorably, as The Hollow God intended."

"As it was intended, yes. But may you tie me to a chair instead of this table so we can be eye to eye? And may we sit in front of that cooling unit? I'm boiling in here," I request, a plan forming in my mind.

"Fair enough." Number 04 removes the chains around me except for one, which he used to swing me into a chair and re-bind me. He then dragged the chair to right in front of the door that the others were trapped behind.

"You know, the way you fought was impressive, but your strategy was even more so," I comment, intending to butter him up some.

"Really? How so?" he asks, pretending to be humble.

"You targeted me first, then Cat. This is because we are the only two with powerful ranged synats. From there you had the advantage against everyone else due to the range of your chains. In addition, by choking Cat and by hitting me in the back you were able to prevent us from speaking, which thus stopped our synats," I continue to use my synat to make him more confident.

"Ah, thank you. Usually my enemies are too dead to comment on my strategy," He chuckles.

"I do have to ask you something, however," I smile. "Do you know what separates man from beast?"

"Honor. Honor is what makes a man superior to a beast," he answers, his sandy eyes beating down on me,

"Close, but no. It is ambition that makes us human. You have trapped yourself in your chains of honor, you have refused yourself the fruits of true ambition. This is not what The Hollow God intended for us. You are subhuman, an ape at best," I begin to feel saddened. *Relax, that's part of the plan.*

"W-What do you mean? Even a dog has ambition!" Number 04 objects, standing up.

"I mean what I damn well said. You're too dumb to even realize how my synat even works. You probably thought my passive ability was just charisma, but that's where your idiocy shines. My passive ability is to make others perceive me the way I perceive myself, meaning that by making myself feel like trash..." I begin to gently weep, tears streaming down my face. By this point Number 04 is having a much worse reaction, having fallen to the ground and rolled into a ball.

"Stop feeling sorry about yourself and put your scummy life to good use! Open that goddamn door you rat-bastard!" I demand, using my free foot to kick his side, "and untie me too."

"I-I'm sorry, I've failed The Hollow God," Number 04 subconsciously recalls his chains. *Thank you, Argent, for ranting about these other religions.* I open the door to let my friends out, my tears freezing upon landing on the floor. As my friends exit the coolant unit, Number 04 looks up.

"Time for the 'hopeless' part of your synat to come true. But first, let's hear where The Assassin King is?" I ask, taking the lead pipe Argent had before and tapping Number 04 in the back of the neck.

"He's beyond the door down the hall! Please don't hurt me, I'll repent!" Number 04 begs, terrified.

"Hmm, how about no, you rat-bastard." I quickly dispatch Number 04 with a blow to the head.

"That was pretty cool dude," Alex comments, stepping over the body.

"It'll be even cooler once we kill The Assassin King. For Kevin," I say, beginning to open the door that The Assassin King should be behind. *I'm gonna make you suffer, for Kevin.*

Chapter 15: Heaven and Earth

CJ slowly opens the door in front of us. On the other side a large dimly lit room, in the back of the room a cloaked figure wearing a mask sitting on top of a throne. The mask has a white base, with a black ink smile painted on top.

"Ah, it's so nice to finally meet all of you, *even though it may be the second time*. I'm sure you're already familiar with my name, but I shall introduce myself anyway. I go by many names The Assassin King, King of Assassin's, and even the second coming of Adamnev," says, an eerily familiar soft spoken voice, "But for all you today I may as well be The Reaper." The Assassin King puts out the four candles on the arms of his throne.

"So, it is you. I'm sorry Mr. Assassin King, but today The Reapers will be us!" CJ declares, taking a stance pointing toward the cloaked figure.

"Ah, now what's the point in pointing fingers, how about we all calm down," The Assassin King chuckles. Suddenly, my body freezes up, I've lost all control over it. I'm only just able to move my eyes enough to see that everyone except Amaryll is also unable to move.

"This one seems to still be in control of herself, how bothersome," The Assassin King grumbles, still in the same soft voice.

"Seems like mind control doesn't work twice huh," Amaryll smirks.

"Wha-t's go-ing on?" I barely manage to squeeze out.

"Quite the tough one isn't you. We can't have you talking anymore," The Assassin King says, forcing my mouth closed with his synat. *Damn! I can't do anything, but watch.*

"Ha, did you think I would just make you stand there and watch the fight? That wouldn't be fair at all," The Assassin King teases, "Don't you think everyone should have some fun?"

"Damn you! You toying Bastard!" Azalea yelled, barely able to move her lips.

"What did I say earlier about talking?" The Assassin King questions, silencing Azalea as well, "Finally, now I can watch the show."

I can only watch as The Assassin King controls Cat forcing her to start to vocalize creating flames around Amaryll.

"You sadistic freak! Do you get some sort of sick sense of enjoyment doing this?" Amaryll shouts, looking each and every way as a circle of flames surrounds her.

"I do Amaryll. I very much do," The Assassin King grins, forcing Cat to slowly close the circle of flames around Amaryll. Out of The Assassin King's view Amaryll takes a small knife and pokes the ends of the fingers on her right hand. She spray's a thin sheet of blood at the wall of flames creating a temporary gap for her to jump through.

"Did you think such a simple plan would work on me?" Amaryll mocks.

"Of course not, that was just the appetizer," The Assassin King chuckles, making Cat send a blast of fire which hit Amaryll's left arm.

"Aaaaghh!" Amaryll cries out. She runs straight at Cat, delivering her right fist directly to Cat's side, knocking her unconscious.

"Tch, quite the strong one. No matter, this fight is far from over," The Assassin King says, obviously starting to get annoyed.

"Sorry Cat," Amaryll says, crouching over Cat ignoring The Assassin King.

"Hmph, let's see if this will work," The Assassin king mutters to himself. A bright pale blue comes from Azalea. The Assassin King seems to be frozen in place. *Whatever plan he had obviously didn't work out.*

"What an Idiot," Amaryll says to herself. She starts walking around knocking out CJ and Argent presumably so they will be unable to be controlled once they wake up. She begins to walk over towards me to do the same, but before she can the frozen instant ends and The Assassin King forces me to run away from her as CJ, Argent, and Azalea hit the floor.

"I can't be. Why didn't I enter the frozen instant?" The Assassin King stuttered, seemingly a little short of breath.

"You Idiot! Did you seriously think that would work? Azalea has to think someone is an ally for them to be included in frozen instant and since you weren't changing the way she was thinking and only controlling her body it only makes sense your plan didn't work," Amaryll snickers.

"But I... I... it should have..." The Assassin King stammers. While The Assassin King is distracted, Amaryll runs over towards me.

"Sorry Alex. This might hurt a little," Amaryll apologies, as she proceeds to knock me out.

I regained consciousness shortly after I lost it. Opening my eyes, I see Azalea above me. *She must've healed me so I would wake up sooner.*

"Alex are you okay?" Azalea asks, shaking me by the shoulders, "Oh good you're awake." Azalea lets out a sigh of relief.

"I'm fine. What's going on?" I ask, looking around my vision still slightly blurry. Next to me I see that CJ and Argent are already awake.

"Well, take a look for yourself," Azalea says, moving so that I can see what's going on. Cat is already up and fighting along with Amaryll. It seems that they have already whittled him down quite a bit.

"Not so strong without all your minions around," Amaryll mocks.

"Hmph, on the contrary. You will be the first to witness my secret ability," The Assassin King chuckles. The Assassin King throws a small dagger at Amaryll barely grazing her right arm.

"Some secret ability. You barely hit-" Amaryll stops, a look of despair spreads across her face. She looks down at the cut on her right arm as it starts to grow in size faster and faster until her arm is completely severed off.

"No... No... No... It can't be..." It looks as though Amaryll had totally lost it, despite the blood coming from where her right arm used to be, she had curled up into the fetal position slowly rocking back and forth. Azalea and I immediately ran to heal her. I put a force field to protect her from any further attacks while Azalea begins to reattach her arm.

"What did you do to her!" I yell, looking over at The Assassin King.

"Ha Ha-ha," The Assassin King begins to chuckle, "My synat is Accepting the Crushed Escape. It allows me to mind control people, but it also allows me to make a wound on someone grow the more they feel like they're losing. This works in tandem with my other ability which when I create a small wound on someone It makes them feel an immense sense of despair."

"Cat finish him off," I say. She nods in response and shoots more blasts of fire at him, almost knocking him out.

"Let me finish him," CJ declares, running over and grabbing The Assassin King by the collar. CJ steps in a candle in his haste.

"He's all yours," Cat says. CJ rears his fist back ready to take him out once and for all.

"First let's see who this bastard truly is. For Kevin," CJ says, punching The Assassin King in the face shattering the mask he was wearing like glass. The shards fall slowly and gracefully down onto the ground as I catch a glimpse of his face. This person who had been terrorizing Sotaqt for the past ten years and who killed one of my best friends.

"Kevin?" CJ quivers, his hand shaking slightly, "No. Kevin you. It can't be! Why!"

CJ lets go of The Assassin King letting him fall to the floor. CJ drops to his knees, tears beginning to form in his eyes. The man who had been terrorizing the entire world had been Kevin from the start. A look of shock forms on Cat's face as she sees him.

"What is it, Master CJ? What's wrong? We did. We defeated-" Argent stops out of pure shock, after running over to comfort CJ he sees the true face of The Assassin King.

"What's going on?" Azalea asks.

"That's him. That's our friend who died in Tirentod," Cat says, the reality of the situation still not fully sinking in. Azalea gasps,

"But how? Didn't he die?"

"He must've returned to earth and then died again going further back into the past, but still I don't understand why... why he would... why he would do this..." Cat tries to explain.

"It all makes sense..." I say trailing off. I think back to the dream I had about Kevin in the hospital.

"What makes sense Alex?! How does any of this make sense!" CJ cries out, holding Kevin in his arms.

"Back when Amaryll was in the medical lodge I had a dream about Kevin being in the hospital. In the dream Kevin's mother showed up to see him and a doctor came in and told her that he only had a few days left to live. I only realized now that that wasn't a dream, but my synat showed me what was happening on earth after Kevin got crushed by a wall. So after he died he ended up in a hospital and died a few days later sending him back to ten years before we arrived in Sotaqt," I explain.

"But why Alex?! Why did he do this?!" CJ cries out, "Even if we know how he got back to Sotaqt it doesn't explain why he did this!"

"Your right CJ I don't know why," I say. Azalea walks over to CJ and crouches down looking at Kevin.

"What are you doing?! He's dead?!" CJ yells.

"No CJ he's still breathing," Azalea says, slightly shocked, "If you want, I can heal him back up so you can talk to him. Just know that if I wake him up it might not be the Kevin you knew."

"Do it! I don't care what happens if I can just talk to him again," CJ says, looking intently at Kevin. Azalea puts her hands over Kevin emitting that brilliant pale blue light.

"Kevin?"

"CJ is that you?" Kevin asks, opening up his eyes.

"It is. But why Kevin? Why did you do this?" CJ asks.

"I don't have much time , but I'll explain as much as I can. I'm sure you already figured out how I got back here. So, I'll start from there. Not too long after I got back to Sotaqt this man, I'm not sure what his name was, but he took me somewhere and then he began to control me like a puppet. I remember all of it. He made me into The Assassin King. I'm almost out of time," Kevin' voice was starting to fade. He grabs onto CJ's hand in a final effort, "You must visit Furui Taimā in the capital of the Kingdom of Aochikyuu. She can tell you more. Ask her about the southern angel kingdom. Now that he knows I'm out of control He's going to kill me. I'm sorry I couldn't tell you more. G-Goodbye CJ..."

Kevin's grip loosens on CJ's hand as his body goes limp, the life slowly draining from his eyes.

"Kevin no. I can't lose you again. Don't go. Kevin. Please," CJ starts to break down, "Can't you do anything Azalea?"

"I'm sorry CJ. I can heal all sorts of injuries, but bringing some back to life is out of my reach," Azalea explains, looking down in guilt.

"Azalea. Do you think it's possible he's alive now? Back on earth?" I ask, trying to grasp at some faint hope.

"I don't think so. People who come from earth die and then come back are extremely rare. The only two instances I know about are Cat and Kevin. I've never even heard about it until it happened to Cat. It's likely that the percent chance of coming back dramatically drops off each time. I'm sorry to say Alex, but your friend is most likely dead. For real this time," Azalea explains. The reality begins to set in. That small hope being crushed under the boot of the universe. Denying me any more time with Kevin. This time he's totally and truly gone... forever. I begin to hear a low rumbling sound.

"What is that sound?" Azalea asks. Small pieces of rock and dust begin to fall from the ceiling.

"Master CJ! We have to leave this place; it's going to collapse!" Argent yells.

"But Kevin. We can't just leave his body here," CJ says.

"We have to leave, or we'll all be dead!" Argent grabs CJ pulling him off the ground. I pick up Amaryll as she's still unconscious from earlier and we run out of the room down the hallways, up the stairs and out into the desert. We run past the broken candles and a broken clock. We start to run away from the entrance and back towards the town. I hear a loud noise, most likely the sound of the base collapsing. Looking back, I see a large crater in the sand where the base used to be. We continue to run back to the town.

"So, what do we do now?" I ask, as we finally arrive back in town.

"I think we should head to the port city south of here and take a ship back to Azaronia," Argent says.

"Azaronia?" I say, confused.

"It's the continent that the USP and UEF are on. We took that ship across the ocean to the Republic of Western Lands which is on Pisonia. We are also currently in Pisonia. I was suggesting that we go back to the church in Tirentod in the USP," Argent explains.

"Ah, that makes sense, and agreed. Heading back would make the most sense," I say.

"Agreed," Cat nods. Off to the side, CJ looks like a husk of his former self, dried tears staining his shirt; I hope this isn't a permanent change.

Chapter 16: Ex Memoriam

A lot has happened in these past few months. We left Heizengaard and headed back on a steam ship out of Dezaria, a city southeast of Heizengaard. Finally, after almost a month of sailing we arrived back in Merizon.

"Ugh, it's good to be back on land again," I groan.

"Agreed. Maybe we should stay the night at Uncle Adran's inn and rest," Azalea suggests.

"Good Idea." We walk over to Adran's inn and go inside.

"Oh! Uncle Adran you're here," Azalea exclaims, running over to embrace him, "I thought you would still be in the shared territory."

"Actually, I just came back here a few days ago myself. I had just finished my work in the shared territory right after you guys left," Adran explains, "Then I headed out on ship back here. You guys look pretty worn out, why don't you stay the night here?"

"Actually, we were thinking the same thing," I chuckle. Azalea released Adran from her embrace and we walk into our rooms. Azalea and I lay down in the bed.

"Do you think he'll be okay?" Azalea asks, "CJ I mean."

"CJ... yeah, what happened in that base. It looked like it hit him pretty hard." I say, "But the thing is CJ has good friends and a strong will. I'm sure he'll recover. I have high hopes for him."

"He certainly does have good friends," Azalea mumbles to herself, smiling.

"What?"

"It's nothing," Azalea chuckles. I turn off the lamp and quickly fall asleep. We wake up and head downstairs to the entrance.

"So, how exactly are we going to get back to Tirentod?" Alex asks, still looking a bit drowsy from waking up.

"Actually, I had a feeling this would be a problem so I asked the workers who helped me at the inn to maintain the carriage and we sent the horse to rest at a stable. Yesterday, we brought her back, as I had a feeling you would be here soon. I have the carriage parked outside," Adran explain.

"Thank you. I hope Esther didn't cause you any trouble," Argent says.

"Don't worry she's a good horse."

"I guess we'll be going now," Azalea says, "We'll come back some time to visit."

"I'm looking forward to it," Adran smiles, "In fact I'll visit you guys sometime too. So, look out for me." Adran waves at us as we walked out to the carriage. We hopped in and made our way back to Tirentod, arriving at the church less than a day later. After only being there for a few days we got noticed by the town government. We were swiftly brought into the town hall. Apparently, the news had spread that The Assassin King was finally killed. In fact, there were rumors that the people who killed him were us. There must have been somebody who saw us leaving the base. We tried to tell them that we weren't the ones who killed The Assassin king, but they didn't really listen. Soon after we were taken to the largest city in the USP, Kailias. There were huge celebrations all throughout the towns we passed through. Once we finally got to Kailias we were told that we were to receive medals for the killing of The Assassin King along with the bounty that was attached to his head. There was a huge ceremony, hundreds of thousands of people must have shown up. We were given medals by the city's head councilman and received the enormous bounty which we split up evenly. It didn't feel right at all. Not only did we not kill him, but it was our friend who was under that mask. After it was all over, we got visits from emissaries from around the world asking for us to come to their country to participate in the ceremony and to receive the bounty. We wanted to reject the requests, but Argent said that it was better if we did as the money would come in handy in finding out the truth of this whole situation with Kevin. The next few months were spent traveling around the world going to celebrations and receiving the bounties. It didn't feel right at all. It was totally unreal. It was as though reality had slipped away from us After that was all over, we headed back to the Church in Tirentod.

"So, what should we do now?" Alex asks.

"Well, I think it would be best for you all to find yourselves somewhere else to live. The church is getting a little crowded," Argent complains. "Master CJ is welcome to stay of course."

"Hmm... I do agree that the church does feel a little crowded." Alex says, "Ah! I have an idea. If we split up it would be easier to get more information."

"Good Idea," CJ agrees. "I'll stay here with Argent and Alex and Amaryll can move somewhere and Cat and Azalea can go to the UEF."

"Sure," Azalea and I agree.

"That sound good to you? Alex? Amaryll?" CJ asks.

"Uh, yeah," Alex and Amaryll confirm.

"Alright, it's settled then. Tomorrow you guys we'll head out and settle down and, in a month, we'll meet back here."

The next morning Azalea and I left for the UEF. Alex and Amaryll moved into a house in Kailias, CJ and Argent stayed at the church in Tirentod. Azalea and I bought a house in Sycarro near where Azalea's parents lived, for the past few weeks we've been living there. It was a really nice house built into the tree right next to Azalea's parent's house.

"Azalea."

"Yeah?"

"I was thinking. Since we moved in and everything, don't you think we should start to collect some information?" I ask.

"Yeah you're right."

"Thing is, where do we even start?"

"Well, my dad might know a thing or two. He is in the EIA after all."

"You sure it's a good idea to ask him? I mean last time he gave us information the director of the EIA showed up and attacked us."

"Well, we did get pardoned at the ceremony in the capital. Oh, and don't worry about Holimion. He was arrested for political interference," Azalea pauses before mumbling to herself, "Though I did hear he escaped."

"Political interference?" I inquire.

"Apparently he was basically pulling the strings for the whole country. Little to say the president, Elrauch Klonsom, was not very happy, but neither were the high elves. They voted him out of power because they thought that someone who was incompetent enough to let someone else pull the string shouldn't be ruling. There's going to be an election soon."

"An election? Are you gonna vote?"

"What's the point? It's not like someone of mixed blood like me has enough votes for it to matter anyway."

"Mixed blood? Not enough votes?"

"Well, to start I'm half-moon half wood elf. Thing is, the mixing of different elven races is kind of taboo. I'm a unique case though." *A unique case? I wonder what she means?*

"What about the vote thing?"

"Oh, that. Well, the way the voting will work for this election is that the different elven races will be ranked. The higher the rank the more votes and people of mixed blood and half elves are at the bottom of the ranking, so we get the least amount of votes. Though even for the other races it's not really worth it. The high elves get a disproportionate amount more than any other. Basically, only the high elves' votes matter."

"Damn, that kind of sucks."

"Yeah. Though that's only for this election. Normally it's by wealth, but since Elrauch Klonsom has fourteen percent of the country's wealth they changed it so he wouldn't elect himself again. Someday I hope this country will reform, even though I probably won't live to see it. Elves live so long, any change in policy even a small one can take decades to go through. And that's if any change was considered, which it usually isn't. Maybe a new president will change that, though most likely not."

"Damn..." I stutter, not really sure what else to say.

"Sorry about that. I kind of went off on a tangent," Azalea apologies, blushing slightly from embarrassment.

"It's no big deal. Anyway, back on topic. What were you saying about your dad?"

"Oh yeah. Well he's in the EIA so I thought he might know something. Why don't we walk over?"

"Sure." We get off the couch we had moved in yesterday and walk across a small bridge over to Azalea's parent's house. Despite being a small bridge, it was pretty high off the ground, due to the houses here in Sycarro being built in the trees and all. We open up the door and Mrs. Leitner greets us as we walk in,

"Oh Azalea, Cat, you're here. Nice to see you. It's nice having you two so close by."

Over the past few weeks, I've gotten to know Mrs. Leitner. She helped me move and I made dinner together with her once. I actually acquired quite the cooking skill over those two years out in the forest. Mr. Leitner not so much. He was working most of the time, so I never really saw him.

"Nice to see you too Mrs. Leitner."

"Of course. Now it would be great if you guys would stop by just to say hello, but I have the feeling that's not it."

"You see right through us mom. Well part of the reason we're here is to find information about the truth behind what happened to Kevin." I had already explained what had happened with Kevin at the base outside of Heizengaard to Mrs. Leitner. Azalea continues, "We thought that dad might know something."

"Your father... huh. He might know something. He's in his room, let me get him." Mrs. Leitner begins to walk upstairs towards what I can assume to be Mr. Leitner room.

"Juli! Could you come down, Azalea and Cat are here!" Mrs. Leitner yells up to her husband.

"Azalea and her girlfriend are here?" Mr. Leitner yells. I hear the sound of a door opening and then Mr. Leitner coming down the stairs.

"Good to see you Mr. Leitner."

"Mister? Ah come on, there's no need to be so formal just call me Julius," Mr. Leitner chuckles. His hair is the same pale blue as Azalea's.

"Well, then 'Julius' what's up?"

"Not much. I was just reading through something work related. Anyway, why are you two here?"

"Thing is dad, we wanted to see if you knew anything about who made Kevin into The Assassin King and why."

"The Assassin King and your girlfriend's friend Kevin..."

"Girlfriend!" I exclaim, a little embarrassed.

"Oh, come on, you live together, it's not much of a stretch. Ow!"

"Juli please stop teasing Cat." Mrs. Leitner smiles in my direction while pinching Julius.

"Fine, fine, I'll stop. About The Assassin King though, recently I was assigned a mission that was related. Actually, if you want, I could ask if you can come."

"Really dad? That would be great!" Azalea exclaims. Julius walks up the stairs and into his room. After a few minutes he comes back downstairs.

"They gave the okay. I mean you guys are world heroes after all. It's best if we get going now. We'll head to the train station," Julius tone shifts to a more serious one, "I'll debrief you while we walk." Mrs. Leitner waves at us as we walk out the door. "Actually before I do I should mention, my synat is 'Rain Pressure'. I can pull the moisture from the air to form small droplets of water that I can shoot at my opponents with deadly capability." We follow Julius to the train station across all the small bridges between houses. Julius begins to debrief us, "There have been reports of a base being set up in the Piliverre mountains down south. We believe the people setting up the base to be remnants of The Assassin King's high command."

"You mean the numbers?" I ask.

"Yes. You know about them?"

"Yeah, Number 02 almost killed us, and we fought and killed Number 03 and Number 04," I explain.

"Well, that means we'll only have to deal with seven of them."

"Seven!" I exclaim, "There were that many?"

"Yes, there were ten of them to be exact, but since you killed Number 03, Number 04 and Number 01 or The Assassin King is dead, so there are only seven left. Anyway, our mission is to infiltrate the base, get as much intel as possible and eliminate the remaining Numbers. Oh, it seems we're here." While we were talking, we had walked all the way out to the train station. We went to the desks. Julius showed them his badge and Azalea and I showed them our passes. We boarded the train and were on our way to the Piliverre mountains and whatever dangers lurked there.

Chapter 17: The Gates of Heaven

Religion has always been an odd subject; it can easily uplift the masses, and just as easily it can blind them, perhaps those are one in the same. With my synat able to pass on my charisma, my famed reputation, and Argent's much more situational mind-affecting ability of making groups of people believe him, but easily grow disillusioned afterwards; the church is booming with followers. It's ironic to be spreading the will of a god that I don't believe in, but money is money. We used some of our portion of the reward to repair and expand the church, adding more living spaces. It's quite disheartening to see the grave of my best friend each morning when I go to water the honeysuckle and red-fuchsia poppies, even more so to know his body isn't actually there, but I will survive I suppose.

"CJ, please come inside, the next sermon starts soon!" Argent calls from inside the bell tower, ringing the bell 12 times.

"Yes honey, just a moment," I reply, picking up the empty red snail shell that somehow ended up in the poppies. The shell was perfectly clean, as if never used, or removed perfectly. I then stand up, brushing the dirt from my hands as I return into the church, taking a seat in the first pew. Argent smiles at me before starting his sermon.

"And so one day the world shall enter a Great Sleep, the material world becomes bland, and we shall form the seventh dreaming garden of Azathoth," Argent preaches to the crowd, dressed in his traditional ryasa along with the gold ring I got him for his birthday a month ago.

"Ita obediemus," the crowd speaks in unison, myself included. *may we be blessed*.

"And there, like the souls of the unfaithful, the pages grow burnt. The siege of the old vaults destroyed these pages. So, we shall beat on, boats against boats, borne ceaselessly into oblivion," he continues.

"Haec sunt mendacium," we say again. *Blessed be the believer*. I can't help but let my mind wander some, thinking about my couple of months here. I remember training my synat some, going more into the 'glass' part. I discovered I can turn invisible and change my appearance some with my synat, because glass comes in many colors, such as none. I learned the details of how Argent's synat works, and just how... convincing it makes him. Although it felt like just a moment, soon after it seemed the sermon had ended already. After the sermon Argent pulls me aside, into the confession box.

"Are you finally gonna kiss me?" I jokingly flirt, looking down at Argent.

"That's a sin, and this is a church, making it a double-sin. I'm here to discreetly discuss some information," he visibly is a bit pink.

"We're in a confession box, we can confess right after," I offer.

"Sir, I'm going to request you cease this."

"Ugh, fine. So, what is the news?" I sigh, somewhat annoyed by my failure to kiss Argent.

"Thank you, sir. As you may know, we've been losing followers at a consistent rate of one each week, I have discovered that these followers have been tricked into joining a local cult," Argent explains. It takes every bone of my body not to say 'another cult' or some smartass comment like that.

"So, what exactly do we do about it?"

"Sadly, cults are not illegal, so we must begin the holy crusade," Argent says, sounding extremely dedicated to his fabricated cause.

"I'm pretty sure crusades are illegal these days," I point out.

"Only if we get caught."

"Only if YOU get caught."

"Sir, I assumed you'd be able to help. Do you have a prior engagement?" I attempt to make up some excuse, but instead what comes out is,

"No, I have time to help." *What the hell?*

"Oh, thank you young master, I doubt I could do it without you." *That bastard used the truth field on me, the nerve!* We begin walking out into the stable area, once again taking the carriage to our destination. It seems we're going to the south part of town, near the tavern and the crystal shop.

"What are we doing out here?" I ask, eying the tavern.

"We are here to speak with an informant," Argent explains, hopping out of the carriage and giving some drunkard 10 silvers to make sure nobody steals it.

"What informant?" I ask, following Argent into the crystal shop.

"An old friend of mine, from back at the orphanage," Argent looks straight ahead as he speaks. *Orphanage?*

"Oh, does the church run the orphanage too?"

"Oh, no. I used to be an orphan until I was adopted by the former head priest," he opens the door for me into the crystal shop.

"Ah, old A-list, how are you doing these days buddy?" the owner immediately asks, greeting Argent with open arms.

"The church is treating me well, how are things at the shop?" Argent asks.

"My wife left me," the shopkeeper deadpans, before both of them begin laughing hysterically. Evidently, I was not in on the joke.

"We got to talk more often, let's keep in touch. Regardless, we sadly are not here for just a meet and greet," Argent smiles softly.

"Oh, are you looking to buy a crystal?" the shopkeeper asks.

"No. I need the map." Argent's facial expression becomes a lot more serious, as the shopkeeper's expression remains unchanged.

"Oh, a serious purchase. Naturally, you can't let the cops know about this"

"How much?" Argent takes out a pouch from inside his robes.

"40 platinum," the shopkeeper answers. *40 platinum? Isn't that like 4000 dollars on earth? What the hell are we buying?*

"30. No more, no less"

"37"

"33"

"35"

"Deal," Argent places 35 shiny platinum coins on the table, and in exchange the shopkeeper slides him an old looking map. We walk out of the shop, getting back in the carriage.

"35 platinum? Did you see our reward money and confuse it for firewood?!" I object.

"This is necessary to the plan, I apologize sir."

"What the hell does that map even do?" I cross one leg over the other and cross my arms to show impatience.

"The shopkeeper has a very useful synat ability. I don't know his synat exactly, but I know he can enchant items like maps and compasses to point to specific people so long as we can provide something like hair or blood."

"And what exactly did you use?" I question, making sure he knew I was still somewhat disappointed.

"A hair from Sister Bini's habit,"

"Sister who?" I ask.

"The one that ran off." I choose to remain silent due to how I legitimately forgot we had nuns. Following the map, we go a bit past the town walls and into the woods, reaching a spot in the forest. The trees are large oaks, with green carnations and gardenias on the ground in a circle around it. *Fairy circles? There aren't any sprites or spirits around here, I think.* A nightingale corpse was about ten feet away, looking like it had been eaten by some kind of snake. A constrictor probably, judging from the amount of struggling.

"Are you sure this is the right spot?" I ask.

"The map says we should be right on top of it," Argent says.

"Maybe we need some kind of sight synat, do you know anyone useful?"

"I can request Sister Rubral," Argent crouches down and shoves his fist into the ground while speaking in Old Abramonic. *Sister Rubral, convent sister of Tirentod, you are summoned for aid. Be swift.* There was an awkward pause for a few minutes.

"Are you sure she's coming?" I ask.

"I'll call ag-" Argent is cut off by a woman in a nun's habit erupting out of the ground, landing in front of us both.

"I'm sorry for the late arrival, there was a hollow space in the ground that forced me to detour," she explains.

"Well, then, it seems your plan has worked, Argent. The spot is quite literally under our feet," I chuckle on my own stupidity for not thinking of that.

"Is the weird hollow space your destination?" she asks, tilting her head.

"Yes, could you please help us enter it?" Argent chimes in. the nun nods her head before moving her hand, touching the tree and revealing a hidden door inside it that contains a ladder going down.

"You first, Sister Rubral," I suggest. We go down in the order of Sister Rubral, then myself, and finally Argent.

"It's really dark, how deep does this go?" I ask.

"About another seventy feet," Sister Rubral answers.

"Hey, Argent, did you tell anyone where we were going?"

"Yes sir, I told Sister Rubral to call the police if we aren't back by midnight-" It takes Argent until the end of that sentence to realize his stupidity.

"If we die, I'm beating the crap out of both of you in The Dreaming Gardens." We reach the bottom of the ladder and enter a base made mostly of metal, with lots of tech lying around like the base we found Kevin in, but in more disrepair. *I hate this, I hate this, I hate this.*

"Young master CJ, do you recognize this place?" Sister Rubral asks, evidently having seen my expression.

"Oh, no, it's just creepy."

"I know you're lying; I can feel your heartbeat through the ground," she raises an eyebrow.

"Leave the young master alone, his reason for lying is valid," Argent defends me.

"Oh really? Then let him defend himself, Brother Argent," she begins to pick up more of an attitude.

"Your actions are extremely disrespectful, Sister Rubral. Let it be reminded we both outrank you-" I interrupt Argent's passionate defense.

"Argent, I will handle this. Kid, you're speaking up for what you know is right, and I've got to respect you for that. This place is familiar to me, because I've been in a place just like it; that's where I watched my best friend die at my own hands," I tell her, being truthful to avoid being caught in a lie.

"I am sorry, I had no idea-" she begins to apologize.

"It's fine, you didn't know, but if you ever try to tell anyone about this, or bring this up at all," I lean down and put a hand on her shoulder to appear threatening, "I'll bend your back until it breaks and make you drink your own spinal fluid. Do you understand, Sister Rubral?"

"Yes sir, my lips are sealed, as is the confessional," she looks terrified. *That worked well, I ought to use fear more often.* We begin looking around for any signs of life, finding a scrap of cloth and a button. We also try checking the computers, or more so I do because I'm the only one who actually understands computers, however the only one that worked needed a password that I didn't know. It required an eight-character password, so I tried the simple ones, such as password, Password, and 12345678, however after the third failed attempt it locked us out.

"Sir, I believe this is a door!" Sister Rubral calls us over.

"What makes you say that?" I ask.

"I tried using my tremor senses to detect a hall or something, it doesn't work as well with metal, so I had to go along the wall, hence me taking so long."

"Well, then, open it," Argent gestures for her to open it.

"Yes sir," she begins forcing the door open with her synat, revealing six people on the other side. Before we can react, we are blasted with some kind of gas; as I lose consciousness, I see Sister Bini standing over me, and then it all goes black.

Chapter 18: Sacrificing Saint Michael

You know, this certainly isn't where I'd thought I would be. A few months ago, I was living that American high school experience and now I'm in another universe, living in a 19th century style city, and with a girl I met 4 months ago. I'm not complaining, of course, but really you never know where life will take you. I mean sometimes you even have to die to get there. The house Amaryll and I had moved into was average in size, not too small and not too big. It's on the edge of the city in the suburbs. It's a nice house for the technological level here. It even had running water. It only had one bedroom, so it was a little awkward at first, but after a week or so it just felt normal. Amaryll had just gone out to get a set of chairs for our dining table and would probably be back any minute. She calls out to me from the entryway of the house.

"Hey, Alex, could you help me out here!"

"Coming! Sorry!"

I get up from the bed, walk out of the bedroom, go down the stairs and walk out the front door. Amaryll and I begin to unload the chairs from the back of the carriage. I start chatting with Amaryll,

"These chairs are pretty nice. They even have cushions!"

"Well, the carpenter at the shop said it was the finest woodwork in the city." Amaryll has a slight laugh at my over enthusiasm about the chairs.

"Well, he must've been telling the truth." There was an intricate carving of what looked like a noon day sun on the chairs, with other designs across the rest of it. We take the chairs in one by one and set them up at the dining table. It had already been about three weeks since we moved in and only now do we get chairs for our dining table. I'm not sure why it took so long to find a carpenter in this area. It's only a week before we have to return to the church and we're short on any new information. We sit down at the table.

"Amaryll, you get any new information about Kevin or anything related?"

"Actually, I heard about there being some strange structure set up in an abandoned mine just east of here in the western part of the Piliverre mountains."

"Maybe it's one of the bases they had set up?"

"It might not, but I still think it's worth checking out. It's probably best if we wait until tomorrow. It's getting kind of late."

"Yeah you're right."

We go upstairs and change into bedwear. Sleeping in clothes wasn't exactly ideal, so we bought some bedwear a week or two ago. It was a queen bed the perfect size for the both of us. *A few weeks ago, this would've been pretty awkward. I guess I'm used to it now.* I shrug my shoulders.

"Alex, what are you doing?"

"Nothing. I was just thinking about something."

"Oh. Goodnight then."

"Yeah, goodnight." I turn off the gas lamp next to our bed and quickly fall asleep. *Images begin to flash through my head. They're of a dark mine shaft. Soon its large metal blast doors. The doors begin to open and inside, there's the same eerie electric lighting from the base outside of Heizengaard. That same futuristic material lining the floor, ceiling, and walls. The eerie blue glow coming from screens in the walls. As I'm walking through this hallway, I can hear the clacking of my shoes against the hard floor. A door opens up in front of me and there is a blindingly bright light with the silhouette of an elf in front.* I gasp as I wake up from the dream. "Alex, are you okay?" Amaryll asks, rolling over in the bed to face me.

"I'm fine. It's just, *it* happened again."

"What happened?"

"I had a vision in my dream of another base, like the one outside of Heizengaard, but inside a mine."

"So, the rumors I heard might be correct then."

"That's not it though. I saw a silhouette of an elf in front of a bright light."

"But that's just like when..."

"When we met Number 02, exactly."

"Does that mean he'll be there?"

"Possibly." I get out of bed and change into my clothes, Amaryll does the same. We go down the staircase and out the door. It was still early in the morning and the air was wet with cool dew. The roads were made out of cobblestone which had been smoothed down. We call over a carriage and hop in. The driver pokes his head into the carriage and asks,

"So, where are you two headed?"

"Just to the train station," Amaryll replies.

"That'll be 2 gold coins." I hand over the coins to the driver. After a few minutes we arrive at the Kailber Train Station. We hop out of the carriage and down onto the cobblestone streets.

"Amaryll did you remember to bring our special train passes?"

"Train passes... Oh yeah, you mean the ones we got in Düvenberk?"

"Yeah, those ones."

"I brought them."

"Oh, that's good." We walk up to the ticket stand and show the worker there our passes.

"Those passes... You must be Alex and Amaryll! One of The Slayers of The Assassin King. I saw you at the ceremony they held at town hall." A dreadful silence ensues. I think back to that horrible scene. Kevin lying dead in CJ's arms. Totally lifeless, his eyes glazed over. It sent a chill down my spine. The worker attempts to break the silence,

"Did I say something wrong? If so, I'm very sorry!"

"No, it's fine. Is a train heading into the west Piliverre mountains from here?"

"Yes actually, there's an abandoned mining town not far from the station there."

"A mining town that's perfect!" Amaryll exclaims.

"Actually... The train should be arriving at the platform any minute. You should hurry if you want to catch it," the worker says, looking at their watch. We run out onto the platform just as the train comes screeching to a halt. We walk over and onto the train finding our seats. Out the window you can see the west Piliverre mountains. I begin reading an informational pamphlet about the city that I had picked up earlier at the train station. They're not as tall as the main mountain chain, but they're full of natural resources that were pushed up when the southern part of Azaronia collided with the main part of the continent. There were especially large amounts of iron and coal, perfect for fueling the growth of an industrial city like Kailias. While now Kailias is a bustling metropolis with a population of over two million people, go back only thirty years it was a relatively small town with only a few thousand residents. The industrial revolution started in the dwarven countries across the ocean and came overseas to Kailias. Once the ore deposits were discovered in the western Piliverres people came flooding to the area and the small town grew and grew until it became the city we all know and love. The city was originally founded by one of the seven council members that-. My reading was abruptly cut off by Amaryll,

"Alex, we're here! Jeez, did you not hear the conductor announcing that we had stopped?"

"Oh, sorry. I kinda zoned out while I was reading."

"Well, that explains it. Hurry up, we have to get off the train!" I swiftly get up and we run over to the end of the train carriage, going out the door, and hopping down onto the platform. It looks like we're in some sort of abandoned town. There's old wooden houses that are all broken down, a lightly worn path trailing in between all the houses in the dirt. We step off the platform and onto the dirt road. All the windows on the house are shattered and you can even see furniture in the houses.

"This place is pretty creepy."

"Yeah, it's cold too," Amaryll replies, rubbing her arms. We continue walking down the dirt road through the lines of houses and other buildings. At the end of the road there's the entrance to the mine. I point this out to Amaryll,

"There's the entrance to the mine!"

"Yeah, you're right." We run over towards the entrance. Large wooden planks form the edges of the entrance of the mine. We walk into the entrance. The walls are made out of cold hard stone and it's very dark. Thankfully we brought an oil lamp which I lit, illuminating the stone hallway. Just like in the dream I had last night, there were large metal doors at the end of the mine. We walk up to them, getting a closer look. They look like blast doors. As we open them a familiar sight greeted us. The eerie glow of electric lights, the unnerving clacking that one made while walking through, and the strange futuristic material lining the place, this was certainly another base just like the one outside of Heizengaard. *It's just like in my dream.*

Click Click Click Click Click

We continue to walk down the brightly lit hallway. In front of us was what looked like the end of the hallway began to slowly move upwards. It moved up without a single sound. A bright light came blasting through the door. As my eye adjusts, I can see the silhouette of an elf. We walk into the room. The silhouette turns around and the light dims.

"My my, what a surprise to see you two here!" Number 02 exclaims.

"You really are here. I guess my vision was correct," I mumble to myself, ignoring Number 02's greeting.

"You are really quite shocking. I'd expect you to be more angry," Number 02 shrugs his shoulders, "And where are the rest of your friends? Did I kill them? Maybe after they died you became so numb to all of it you don't even have the energy to be angry. Maybe you came here so that I could kill you and end your suffering. Well, I sorry to say, but I'm on-" I cut Number 02 off,

"You do talk a lot, you know? And also, none of what you are saying is accurate at all. The rest of my friends are perfectly healthy, and we don't have any particular reason to be mad at you. I mean you did try to kill us, but we didn't even get hurt so..."

"They're all alive?! But I know I killed at least one. What was their name.... Ah yes Cat. I killed your friend Cat."

"Oh yeah, I guess you did, but she came back and it's probably a good thing in the long run so..."

"She's still alive!? But how?!"

"Well, it's kind of a long story. Anyway, the reason we're here is that we need information," Amaryll explains.

"Information? Information about what?"

"About the Assassin King. We need to know who was controlling him and why."

"The Assassin King... Oh! You must mean Number 01. About that, strangely enough I have been ordered not to kill you, but to help you acquire some information. But before any of that I will not be taking any risks." I felt that same pressure holding me in place just like when we met Number 02. He begins to mumble something to himself, "I can never understand what father is thinking." Number 02 shakes his head.

"Using your synat to hold us in place huh... Well I'm fine with it as long as we get some information."

"My synat? Oh, right I did say that this was part of my synat. I'll tell you something, this ability called Authority, is not actually part of my synat, but an ability all High elves have. We don't like telling people our synats, and even if we do it's only the death word not the life. We cover this up by saying our life word is Authority when it's really not."

"So, you mean to say that there's something else to Director Holimion and your synat."

"Director Holimion? I remember him, we put him in charge of taking over the UEF. It's a pity he failed; I'll have to punish him. Oh, it seems once again I've said too much. And to answer your question, yes," Number 02 glance down at his watch, "Ah, It's time for me to leave. Oh, and there are some files in the desk here that may be of some use to you. Farewell, I'm sure we'll meet again." Number 02 walks right in between me and Amaryll, leaving the base and the mine. After a few seconds the pressure keeping us in place disappears.

Chapter 19: Enter, Erebus

The scenery passes by swiftly. An endless expanse of verdant rolling hills and the occasional patch of trees. The Piliverre mountains ahead of us standing proudly over the landscape. Their snowcapped peaks emit a dazzling white shine in the bright noonday sun.

"It's beautiful isn't it?" Azalea asks, snapping me out of my daze.

"Huh! What?" Azalea chuckles a little at my surprised reaction,

"I was just mentioning how beautiful the scenery is."

"Yeah, it is," I think to myself. *Wouldn't it be funny if I said something like,* "but, it's not as beautiful as you, my lady." Azalea bursts out laughing,

"How knightly of you Cat."

"Wait, did I seriously say that out loud?!"

"You certainly did," Azalea says, struggling to get words out through her laughter. I cover my face in embarrassment. *I'm such an idiot. How could I say that out loud?!*

"You two are certainly a lively bunch," Julius says, chuckling.

"Oh, come on dad, stop teasing her."

"You're one to talk to, Azalea."

"Well, you're not exactly wrong." Azalea shrugs her shoulders. I go back to looking out the window of the train at the landscape. A few hours pass and It's seems that we're closing in on our destination; a small village at the foot of the mountain range. We'll stop there and then switch trains to get to the mine where the base supposedly is. A few minutes pass and I hear the conductor announcing that we had reached our destination. We get out of our seats and walk down onto the platform.

"Follow me," Julius says. We walk through the town to an average looking house. We enter to find that it was completely empty. Julius crouches down and lifts up a large hatch in the floor revealing a staircase going down. We walk all the way down the stairs entering a large room with many smaller ones attached, a large number of people walking around through the rooms.

"This is the EIA's southern HQ. Pretty impressive, no?" Julius says, a smug look of pride on his face. One of the people running around the place comes over to greet us.

"Oh! Agent Leitner you've arrived! Please come right this way." The young elf leads us through the room and out to what looks like a train station.

"What is this place?"

"It's part of the EIA's underground railroad network. We'll take it to the mine."

"Oh, so this mine is deep in the mountain then?"

"Correct." We get on the train taking our seats. A few hours pass and the conductor announces that we have arrived at the mine. We hop out of the train and down into a large open cavern. I start a low hum creating a small flame above the palm of my hand, to brighten things up. Walking down the stone hallways it almost seems as though they go on forever. According to Julius these were old iron mines from about 10,030AT. They were abandoned after the iron in the area ran dry. After walking around in the maze-like tunnels, we stumbled upon what look like large blast doors.

"What are these?" I ask.

"Most likely the doors to the base we're after. I've never been to one of these bases before, but this is certainly like what I've been told," Julius explains, "This metal isn't like anything I've seen before. There's something strange about it. It's unnerving."

We attempt to pull these large doors with no success. I begin to vocalize, increasing the temperature of the flame that had been floating over my palm. I put my hand up to the doors and cut out a hole large enough to get through. Azalea uses her synat to cool off the metal enough so that we could walk through safely. A familiar scene comes into view. That same futuristic and almost translucent material, the strange glow coming from cables in the floor and screens on the walls, and that unearthly white light coming from the ceiling. It was Deja vu. The resemblance to the place where Kevin had died was obvious.

"It's exactly how they described it. How unnerving," Julius says, a slight shiver coming over him. We walk through the brightly illuminated hallways.

Click, Click, Click, Click, Click.

Even the sound of our shoes on the floor. Everything was the same.

Click, Click, Click, Click, Click.

We continue walking until we reach a split in the hallway.

"I'll take the path to the left and you two take the path to the right."

Azalea and I nod in response. The straight hallway slowly turns into a maze of inter-connected halls. After only a few minutes of walking around we had already gotten lost.

"Hey, Azalea I think we're-"

"Quite lost. Quite lost indeed," a voice from behind me says. I quickly turn around to see that there is no one there.

"Where'd they go?"

"Why, I'm right here." A man begins to emerge from my shadow. His hair white and his skin a darkish grey with a slight violet hue. I jump back away from him.

"A dark elf!" Azalea exclaims.

"How observant you are."

"Who are you?" I ask.

"Me? I guess you could call me Number 05."

"Another one of the numbers!"

"Another? Ah, so you've met a few of my brothers. I suppose you are part of the group that disposed of Number 03 and Number 04. I actually have to thank you. Working under those two was hell. They were so disagreeable. It's a shame I'll have to kill you." Number 05 drops down into his own shadow disappearing without a trace. Suddenly, I feel like I'm falling into the floor. Azalea swiftly grabs me before I fall all the way into my own shadow.

"AAAAAAGH!" I scream out in pain. It feels as though the lower half of my legs are being pierced by multiple sharp spikes. Azalea quickly pulls me out. I attempt to stand up, but end up falling to the ground. I look down at my legs to see several holes around two inches in diameter punched through my calves, ankles, and feet. Azalea immediately starts working to heal the wounds. Number 05 pops back up out of the floor, panting seemingly out of breath.

"You... have... quite... the... quick... reaction... time," Number 05 says, pausing to take a breath in between each word. He takes a deep breath and sinks back into his own shadow disappearing into the floor. A set of spikes come out of the ground inching closer and closer. They appear to be made out of shadow, completely pitch black in color. Azalea grabs me and slides to the side of the hallway. The spikes continue to move in a straight line, poking in and out of the ground, oblivious to our movements. Azalea finishes healing my wounds and I get back on my feet . The spikes stop and Number 04 emerges from them back onto the floor panting and acting as though he was out of breath. As soon as he does, I vocalize sending a blast of fire towards him. My blast of fire skims his left arm right before he completely drops back into his shadow. Thin disks of shadow start to fly at us from the floor. We dodge to the side just as Azalea puts up an ice shield. Despite the thick layer of ice in their path the disks seem to pass through the ice as though it was not there. They fly through the air passing just a fraction of an inch around Azalea and I. Before the disks hit the wall, they seem to dissolve into the air. Number 05 emerges from the ground again, seemingly still out of breath.

"This... may... be... harder... than... I... thought," He says, gasping for air. He takes one more deep breath before plunging back into his shadow.

"Those disks. They passed right through the ice I created like it was nothing. The ice wasn't even damaged... It's almost as though he can control what they go through..."

"You give me too much credit-" Number 05 says, poking his head out of the floor. As soon as I see him I vocalize, sending another blast of fire his way. He swiftly dodges, dropping back down into his shadow. He pops his head out of the floor again,

"As I was saying, I can only-" I send blast of fire at his head, only for him to drop down into his shadow and then pop back up somewhere else continuing to speak,

"Damage living orga-" I send another blast of fire his way. He dodges moving across the floor, continuing his speech,

"-nisims. So of course, it would pass straight through your ice, regardless of how thick it was." I begin to vocalize again, but before I can he pins me to the wall using tendrils of shadow.

"I suggest you stop any attempt at an attack, or your friend here will soon be absorbed into the great god of gods."

"Damn you!" Azalea exclaims, sending a large spear of ice at him. He easily dodges and proceeds to pin Azalea up against the wall with those same tendrils of shadow.

"I've had enough of this. You two are far too annoying to continue playing with. Behold my maiden of shadow," I feel myself beginning to fall into the floor, "I'll-"

"-end this here," Number 02 says, appearing seemingly out of nowhere finishing Number 05's sentence as he slams a large metal pike straight through the back of his head, killing him instantly. His grey matter splattering on the floor.

"Huh!?"

"My my, how interesting to see you two here. I wasn't even two days ago when I saw your friends... What were their names? Ah yes! Alex and Amaryll."

"What did you do to them?!" A scowl forms across my face.

"Now now, don't get things twisted. I didn't touch a hair on their pretty little heads. We merely had a little chat in the base in the Western Piliverres. You could even say we worked together," Number 02 pauses before bowing in an apologetic manner, "Oh, and please excuse Number 05's behavior, he was out of line. I directly ordered him not to kill you or your friends if they were to show up. But of course, his arrogance got the best of him. Not that I'm surprised of course. I should have done something prior to prevent this."

He paces around the hallway, supposedly trying to think of what to say. While he's distracted I begin to vocalize in an attempt to shoot a blast of fire at him, but before any sound comes out of my mouth I feel that same oppressive pressure all over my body preventing any movement.

"Tsk tsk. I don't intend to harm you, but if you're going to be like this then I have to take preventative measures. I'm doing this for my safety and nothing else. I have been ordered not to kill or injure you in any way, shape, or form. I'm sure the reason you've come here is to get some information. No? There is a room connected to this hallway. You should find something helpful in there. Now it's time for me to leave." He begins to walk down the hall, but before he goes out of sight Azalea asks,

"But why? Aren't you supposed to be our enemy? Why help us?"

"You know... I've asked the same question myself. The inner workings of father's mind is a mystery to me. Oops, it seems once again I've said too much. I bid you farewell."

He walks the rest of the way down the hallway and out of sight. After a few minutes the pressure holding Azalea and I in place is released allowing us to move again. We rush to the room he mentioned. It's mostly empty except for a table in the middle with a file laying on top of it. We grab the file and run back to the place we split up with Julius with. Once we get there, we see him lying on the ground unconscious with injuries all over his body.

"What happened to him?!" Azalea exclaims.

"I don't know. I'll pick him up and let's get out of here." I pick him up and as we're walking back to the train station Azalea begins to heal him. We get on the train, which had been waiting there for us, taking our seats. After a few minutes Azalea finishes healing Julius and he slowly begins to wake up.

"Dad Are you okay?"

"I'm fine thanks to you Azalea. Are you two alright?"

"We're fine dad. What happened?"

"I ran into Number 06 through to Number 10 and we had quite the brawl, but in the end, I won out. I got back to the place we had split up and fainted from my injuries."

"Did you get any information out of them?" I ask.

"No, I couldn't. Did you guys find anything?"

"We did get this file, but I think it's best to look at it once we regroup with everyone else. You should get some rest dad. I may have healed your wounds, but you did lose a fair amount of blood so try to relax." We get to the station at southern EIA HQ and leave Julius to rest there. We take the train back to Sycarro and take a carriage out to Tirentod ready to share findings with the rest of the group.

Chapter 20: Sickening Sights

Darkness, in combination with uncomfortable pressure on my wrists and back, is a negative combination. The darkness is easily fixed by the opening of my eyes, however the pressure on my wrists and back would require a knife and mobility of my limbs. I can see visually that I am tied to Sister Rubral and Argent by a rope binding our arms together behind us. Above us I can see several individuals, one of which is Sister Bini.

"Sister, I compel you to let us free," Argent demands. Sister Bini looks down with solid white eyes before simply saying,

"I have been ordered not to." Naturally, this was shocking, both literally and figuratively due to the static electricity that can be felt whenever physically near Sister Bini.

"You see, Sister Bini follows the true savior now, the father of the godfather, Number 01, The Assassin King," one of the other individuals says, seeming to be the only one without whitened-out eyes.

"You worship a dead guy, how legitimately pathetic," I comment, scoffing in an attempt to anger him into doing something rash.

"Ironic you say that, soon all followers of Abramon will worship a dead god," The individual says, looking down at me, "you will die before sunrise." Before I can ask how exactly we will die, it is answered visually. The group leaves, and soon after we see what they meant; we see from outside a window in the room, a woman from before putting her hand in a pipe, and soon after we see purple gas entering our room.

Almost immediately Sister Rubral has the bright idea of blocking the pipe with dirt. This idea was not as smart as she thought, being as that was our only source of air.

"Congrats dumbass, make sure to take shallow breaths now that you've damn well smothered us," I tell Sister Rubral, "we have at most ten hours of air in this room."

"So, we should leave this room," Argent suggests.

"And how do you propose we do that?" I ask.

"The walls aren't metal, only that pipe was. The door is one way and they are watching through the window over there," Sister Rubral chimes in, pointing at a wall.

"Okay, that's useful info. Odds are they can't hear us, but they can see us. The window is there. The walls are nonmetal, and most likely non earthen because Sister Rubral cannot move them. We do not know what room this is-" I stop. *This is like the freezer room number 4 tried to lock the others in.* "Sister, how many are watching us?" I ask.

"Five"

"YES! Okay, that means one of them, the leader, isn't with them. I know where he is. We just need to break out," I cheer.

"Yeah, now how do we break out?" Sister Rubral asks.

"Oh yeah, sorry. Hmm, what if we tried to convince them to open the door?" I suggest.

"And how do we do that?" Argent asks.

"We could convince them we escaped so they check inside" I offer. *Like in movies.*

"How?" Sister Rubral asks.

"Sister, is there dirt on our clothes or anything?"
"Yes, why?"

"I need you to make a swarm of dirt in the air, then you both need to get as close to me as you can. I will try to hide you by making us invisible," I explain, unsure if this will work.

"Okay. on three?" Sister Rubral asks.

"One." I begin.

"Two," says Argent.

"Three." Sister Rubral makes a cloud of dust to obscure the vision of the guards as I grab her and Argent and try to make us all invisible. When the dust settles it is visible only, I am not.

"They are moving," Sister Rubral mutters. The door opens and Sister Bini walks through. She immediately starts shooting electricity around the room, spread out to try and hit me in case I was still here. *20-meter rule, I just need to close the distance.* I run towards Sister Bini. *I can't hurt her too bad.* My solution? I hit her on the head really hard. The strategic oversight here is that the other four were right outside the door.

"Congrats, you just exposed your position. None of you have good combat synats for this situation. You shall now perish," the others speak in unison.

"May I have my last words?" I ask. *Okay, did they check my pockets?*

"Nope! You will die by flame," they say in unison again. Two of the individuals on the sides extend their hands to prepare the killing blow.

"Whelp, it seems this is the end of the line," I say, closing my eyes. Suddenly there was a loud bang, meaning my plan had worked. I had emptied four bullets from the revolver that the cultists had failed to steal.

"Sister Rubral, please take Sister Bini and leave for the church. Do not alert the police," I order. Sister Rubral nods, picking up Sister Bini, muttering something affectionately, kissing Sister Bini's forehead, and leaving.

"Did you know they were a thing?" Argent asks.

"No, did you?"

"No." A burst of purple gas shoots out towards us, the same as what knocked us out the first time.

"Oh, you're alive," I point the gun at the girl who summons the gas and pulls the trigger, leaving her brain splattered on the floor. *Five bullets.*

"So, where is the room where the other guy is?" Argent asks.

"Right that way-" I point down the hall before seeing a specter of Kevin standing before me.

"Killing me wasn't enough, was it? You need to kill my followers too?" Kevin says, walking towards me.

"Y-you're dead! How are you here?" I step backwards in shock

"Young master! What's wrong!" Argent exclaims.

"Do you not see! I-it's Kevin!" I point at Kevin, stepping back and tripping over one of the bodies.

"You kill everyone you come across; you are not a hero, you are a serial killer with state funding," Kevin continues, standing over me.

"No! I'm a good man! It was in self-defense!" I plead, trying to keep him away.

"Self-defense? What about Number 04? What about her just now?" Kevin points at the woman who summoned the toxic gas. "The few you do spare either run or join you out of fear! You're a greedy monster!"

"Please! Leave me be! I'm sorry!" I begin crying I think, closing my eyes in the hopes Kevin leaves. For a moment there is silence before I open my eyes to see that Kevin is gone.

"Young master, are you okay?" I see Argent looking down at me with concern.

"Y-yes, sorry, just a memory of a friend since gone," I say, standing back up slowly.

"I see. Are you ready?"

"Yes, let's get this over with." We begin walking towards the door, opening it up to see the guy from before, sitting down with three glasses of wine.

"Ah, welcome. I saw you killed my assistants; would you like to sit down and talk?" the man asks, gesturing to a seat at the table.

"It's poisoned," I call his bluff.

"I will check, young master." Argent uses his synat to check for poisons, something I did not know he could do. The drink glows white for a moment. "It is not poisoned."

"Exactly. I wish to simply hold a polite dialogue," he takes a sip of his wine.

"Take a sip of my glass, then I'll trust you," I instruct.

"Very well," he takes a sip of my wine, and Argent's too. I see him swallow.

"Hmm. What would you like to discuss?" I ask, taking a sip of my wine. Argent does not partake.

"We all serve something higher, do we not? Perhaps that?" he proposes.

"Elaborate?"

"Argent serves his god. You serve your own guilt. I serve the blessed father and the founding godfather. Your guilt has led you to kill our blessed father, making the founding godfather into the father. One has passed, and Two has become One," the man monologues.

"What do you mean 'The Founding Godfather'?" I ask.

"Oh yes. You know him as 'Number 02'. He founded this beautiful world of ours, showed us the one true god. You killed god, and he replaced god."

"I see. Do you wish harm upon us?" Argent asks.

"Yes, but I have no intent to act upon this wish," he answers, "he will," he points at me. Suddenly, my arm moves against my will, grabbing at Argent's throat.

"Young master! Stop!" Argent exclaims, trying to pry my hand off. *What the hell???*

"Be not afraid. We are both men of our own gods, so I can assure you that god has not turned against you. My synat, 'Bloody Plague-bearer', allows me to control the body of anyone who drinks my blood, which was mixed with the wine. I can even do this." suddenly a rash appears on my arms, producing a burning feeling.

"I am sorry, young master," Argent grabs the rashes and twists, producing an extreme enough pain to force my subconscious brain to let go. *I think I'm screaming.*

"I suppose that was cocky of me," the man says, taking another sip of his wine as I try to punch Argent. Surprisingly, Argent catches the punch and manages to throw me at the wall with shocking strength. *I think something is broken.* Argent kicks me in the chest to prevent me from getting up before grabbing the revolver from my belt.

"You idiot, CJ used all five shots already. I'll just stab you with this and it'll be all over," the man takes out a dagger and cuts himself with it to get blood on it.

"No, he didn't? We didn't shoot Sister Bini, that's 4 servants," Argent protests.

"Yes, but he shot Miss Haber twice, remember?" he says, referring to the lady with the gas synat.

"I'm not going to fall for a trick that simple, he wouldn't waste a bullet like that."

"I can see through the eyes of my thralls dumbass; I know he used two bullets on her." *Argent is getting him to lower his guard! How smart.*

"You're bluffing, I know that," Argent puts his finger on the trigger.

"Oh my god, you're actually this dumb," the man suddenly lunges at Argent with the knife. There is a loud bang and the smell of smoke, I instinctively close my eyes, and when I open them back up, I have the ability to move again.

"H-how? You used all five bullets-" The man holds the wound on his chest.

"No, he didn't," Argent refutes, *wait, Argent genuinely didn't know how many bullets I used?*

"Believe it or not, you're both bloody idiots. The gun was custom made, six shots," I smirk intentionally, walking over to the man. *Five-cylinder revolvers being more common in this world*, "now, tell me how many of your creed remain?" I put a foot on his wound and dig in my heel.

"I-I refuse to tell you anything!"

"Then you will die screaming." I crouch down, putting one of my fingers in the wound and stirring it around, "I happen to know a good deal about human anatomy. You have a nerve cluster right around here."

"You wouldn't, you're meant to be the 'heroes' or whatever," he mocks, thinking I'm bluffing.

"Yes, I am; a hero is just the person who wins," I intentionally laugh to get the psychological edge on him before hooking the nerve with my finger and pulling.

"Stop! We were weakened by the father's death! We were told to capture you and bring you to the base below the ice and stone, where something wicked has finally grown."

"What does that mean?" I demand, pulling harder.

"I don't know! I don't know!" he pleads.

"You act like I believe that" I begin to squeeze the nerves with my two fingers.

"I-I'll see you in hell," the man bites off his own tongue to stop himself from saying more before bleeding out.

"God damnit!" I get enraged by this stupid riddle, ripping out the nerve ending and shoving it down his throat before walking away.

"Are you okay, young master?" Argent asks.

"No. I will be, once this job is done."

Chapter 21: Laplace's Demon

As soon as we are able to move again, we rush outside to see where Number 02 had gone. The sight that greets us when we exit the mine is certainly not what we had expected.

"So, you were able to escape?" Number 02 asks, a look of distaste on his face.

"Those lower elves were fools to think they could contain someone of my status." Standing directly opposite to Number 02 was none other than Mindartis Holimion the ex-Director of the Elven Intelligence Agency and current fugitive in the UEF.

"It's just one fool after another and tomorrow I have to deal with..." Number 02 mumbles to himself. Mindartis continues ignoring Number 02,

"Normally I'd have some qualms with fighting another high elf, but this is a special case. Someone like you raised outside of the warm bosom of the heartland is equal in status to the lowest half-elf."

"Status...? You fail to comprehend the position you are currently in Mindartis. Kicked out of the EIA, considered a criminal, and you failed to achieve the mission assigned to you. And calling me low in status when only a few months ago you were taking orders directly from me. Who are you trying to fool? From your perspective what does it matter if a couple of humans from earth believe you're of higher status than you really are? Obviously, you know I know the truth. So why go through the trouble of saying all that. Does the opinion of two humans really matter that much to you?"

"No, I-I..."

"How can you say that you are better than me when you hold the opinion of mere humans in high regard? You just can't accept the reality that you are just a little parasite leaching off the status of others. Only in a position of power due to the help of other people." Number 02 shrugs his shoulders in disinterest after laying out his argument.

"Shu-uu-tt up..." Mindartis struggles to get his words out after Number 02 saw straight through him, totally stunned and in a daze from having his fragile ego shattered. Number 02 turns around to face us,

"Sorry if I said anything that might have offended you. I was merely using that speech as a form of psychological manipulation against Mindartis."

"Oh no it's fine. We understand," I say, shaking my head a little shocked to hear Number 02 apologizing.

"I'm glad you understand. You see, this situation is quite troublesome. Mindartis's continued existence would be a nuisance to us both. I know we aren't on the best of terms but, would you mind lending me a hand? To take care of him?"

"Sure. I don't have a problem if it's Holomion we're dealing with. What about you Amaryll?"

"I don't have a problem with it. I mean I would be lying if I said I wasn't suspicious of him, but for now this seems like this is the best option."

"Then we're in agreement then," Number 02 says, "Since we'll be fighting him, I should tell you Mindartis's synat. It's 'Hopeless Future'. It allows him to see the most likely negative outcomes of an action and avoid them. Though due keep in mind he most likely knows some form of magic." Mindaritis brings himself back from the brink of a total mental breakdown.

"Do you really think I would believe the words of an outsider?" Mindartis rejects what Number 02 said to keep himself together, despite knowing that all of what he said was true. "I'll have to punish you for your insolence!" He raises his hand into the air, a ball of flame forming above growing close to ten feet in diameter. He lowers his hand and the fireball flies towards us. I put up a force field protecting Number 02, Amaryll and I. The force field shatters upon contact with the ball of flames destroying it entirely and luckily absorbing the blow preventing any injuries. Earlier Mindartis almost seemed as though he had brought himself back together, but that facade quickly fell apart as his attacks grew more and more erratic. His fragile world view sliced into pieces by Number 02's sharp tongue. He throws more fireballs at us which I block with my force field. He uses authority to freeze Amaryll and me in place, running over grabbing me and holding me over the edge of the cliff.

"Alex!" Amaryll cries out, frozen in place. Number 02 slowly begins walking towards Mindartis.

"Don't move!" Mindartis yells out, "Move one more inch and your friend here will be tasting the rocks at the bottom of the cliff!"

"Friend? You must be mistaken. These people are not my friends. Please go ahead."

"Damn you Number 02!" I exclaim.

"Hmph. You're really going to abandon them here? You really are tactless Number 02."

"Abandon them? Oh no that's not what I meant." Suddenly the feeling of solid ground was beneath my feet and Number 02 was the one holding Mindartis over the edge of the cliff.

"What did you do?!"

"I did only what I said I would. I let you go ahead and dangle over the edge of the cliff Mindartis.'"

"Damn you! You know what I meant!"

"Ah, yes my synat's ability. Is that what you wanted to know? I guess you could say it has something to do with chaos."

"Chaos?"

"Yes. The chaos of everything. The chaos of the universe! Comprehension of my synat is beyond your grasp Mindartis!"

"Damn it! I won't lose here. I can't lose here!" Mindartis exclaims, squirming clawing at Number 02's hand which were holding him up by the neck.

"You reached the end of your usefulness Mindartis."

"No, you can't do this!"

"I'm done playing with you. This is where your story comes to an end." Number 02 gives Mindartis a cold dead stare letting go of his neck letting his squirming body fall down onto the rocks below. There's an audible thud as Mindartis's body hits the ground. The pressure holding me in place is released.

"Thank you for your cooperation, Alex, Amaryll. I suggest you take a look at those files back in the base. They may prove to be useful."

Number 02 holds us in place using authority as he leaves the old mining town, preventing us from following him. As soon as we're able to move we run back into the base to the room with the desk. There's a manilla file laying there on top of the desk. I pick it up and open it up. There are numerous papers inside. Taking a closer look, they're all written in,

"English?!"

"What?" Amaryll says.

"These papers they're written in English!"

"So, these papers must've been written by someone from Earth then?"

"Presumably. But who?"

"Well, what do they say?"

"At the top of the pages it says 'ATUR Discovery Unit, Scout Team 1. Date: Unknown. Journal entry 36: This is the 3rd base we have constructed since our Arrival on SOTAQT. Our goal is to continue exploration and scouting of SOTAQT. In a few days we plan to send collected information back to ONT.' It goes on but it's written in some sort of unintelligible code."

"What is ATUR and ONT, and why are the letters in Sotaqt all capitalized?"

"I don't know. Maybe they're acronyms?"

"Read the next one."

"Alright, 'ATUR Discovery Unit, Scout Team 1. Date: Unknown. Journal entry 1: We have landed in what seems to be a large mountain range near the equator. We had planned to land in the plains nearby, but our predictions about the tilt of this planet were off and so our trajectory was hastily altered causing our current predicament. We have begun fabrication and construction of the 1st base. This planet has life exactly like on Earth; the vegetation even matches species with plants back on Earth. There even seem to be humans in the early stages of civilization equivalent to 7000 bce in Earth history. The theory proposed by the head of the research departments seems to be correct. He proposed that the other universe may contain an alternate earth, but for life to be exactly the same..."'

"Landed? It's like they're talking about coming here in some sort of rocket ship and they seem to be aware of this place being another universe and based on what they said about the humans here. These must be thousands of years old! How are they still intact?"

"I have no idea, Amaryll, but these must have something to do with Kevin and the numbers. We have to get back to Tirentod, this is crucial information." I put the papers back in the file and run out onto the train en route to Kailias. *What was all that? Do these Scout team 1 people have anything to do with Kevin? I mean they can't still be around. Those papers must've been over 10,000 years old. How did they create those bases and how are they still around? Who are these people?* A few minutes later we arrived back at Kailas station. We take a carriage back to our house. Opening the door, we're greeted by an unfamiliar face.

"Who are you?" I ask.

"Oh, has the mayor not told you about me?" The mysterious man standing in front of us had piercing red eyes and long flowing white hair. He looked to be in his early twenties, but the fox ears on his head would lead me to believe he's much older.

"No, he hasn't."

"Then let me introduce myself. My name is Eris, Eris Astraea. I will be taking care of the house while you are away." He was well dressed in black slim fitting clothing, with glasses of the same color sitting on his face. "I will also be Alex's personal tutor."

"Tutor?"

"The mayor has informed me that you are illiterate. Is that correct?"

"I guess so."

"Don't worry. It's to be expected, you are from Earth after all, the languages here differ."

"But why just me? Isn't Amaryll from Earth too?"

"Oh, I can read and write in Abramonic, perfectly fine. I must've learned how while under The Assassin King's control."

"Well, I do not wish to keep you any longer. I shall be on my way now." The man walks out of the door and down the street. We walk into the house and go upstairs to the bedroom. I put the files onto the nightstand and sit down on the bed.

"Alex."

"Yeah?"

"This connection between the Earth and Sotaqt. How long has it been going on for? And what caused it?"

"I have no idea Amaryll. It's certainly something we have to look into. It might be connected to Kevin after all."

"And there were those people, the 'Scout Group 1'. If they were able to create those bases, then could they be from the earth's future?"

"I mean it's possible. I'm from 2020 and you're from 2024 so that's the future from my perspective."

"I guess you're right. But to be able to create those bases, how far in the future are they from?"

"I'm not sure, but with that kind of tech it could be hundreds of years in the future for all we know."

I turn off the gas lamp and head to sleep. *These people from the future. Did they come here by death or some other way? Are there even other ways to get here from earth?* My mind spins and spins thinking about all the new information before finally falling asleep.

"Hey Alex! Alex!" I wake to Amaryll shaking my shoulders.

"What?" I look out the window seeing that the sun has barely just risen from the horizon. "It's so early in the morning."

"I know. We have to take a steamship up the river to Tirentod today. It's a long ride we need to leave now! The ship sets off in an hour!"

"Oh!" I quickly get out of bed and we rush out to the port on the Saavon River. We hand them our tickets and board the ship and are on our way to Tirentod.

Chapter 22: Borne Back Ceaselessly

We arrive in Tirentod after a short carriage ride. We walk over to the river port to meet up with Alex and Amaryll.

"Alex! Amaryll!" I call out, waving to them. They wave back from on the ship walking out down the ramp onto the docks.

"Good to see you guys," Alex says.

"Yeah, it's been a month," Amaryll says.

"Good to know you're okay. We went to a base in the Piliverres and met Number 02 there. He mentioned that he had met you in the Western Piliverre's and I was scared that something had happened to you," Azalea says, in her usual concerned motherly way.

"He didn't give us any problems. In fact, he helped us out a little," Alex explains.

"What do you mean?"

"Well, not only did he point us in the direction of these," Alex holds up a manila folder quite like the one we found in the base in the Piliverres, "but when Holomion showed up he helped us take care of him."

"You mean Holomion's dead?" Azalea asks.

"Yeah, Number 02 dropped him right off the cliff. I heard the thump when he hit the rocks," Amaryll explains.

"Good to know that high elf bastard's dead." We arrive at the church and are greeted by Argent at the door,

"Oh you have arrived. It's good to see you all." We walk into the church and sit down at a meeting table set up in one of the rooms. CJ walks in and greets us,

"How are you guys doing? How'd the information gathering go."

"Good. We went with the EIA to a base in the Piliverres and had a little bit of a skirmish with Number 05. We even met Number 02 there, he actually ended up killing Number 05 and pointing us in the direction of this." I drop the aged manila folder onto the table.

"What's inside?" Argent asks.

"I don't know. We haven't opened it yet." I slide the folder over to where CJ was sitting. He picks up the folder and opens it, sifting through the various papers.

"What does it say?" Alex asks. CJ begins to read,

"It says 'ATUR Discovery Unit, Scout Team 1. Date: Unknown. Journal entry 67: Earlier this morning Scout leader Oliver Lucius gave a rousing speech about the future of the ███████ and the leader and ruler of earth, ███████. It was funny seeing him so enthusiastic about something, usually he's so mellow and can be such a drag sometimes, but he's still our leader and my belief in him stays strong. I hope I can get him to lighten up, his smile was so pleasant today, I sorely wish to see it again.' The rest is just them going on about this 'Oliver' person."

"Those are just like the ones we found at the Western Piliverre base!" Amaryll exclaims, "They talked about arriving here in Sotaqt thousands of years ago and being from earth. They even claimed to have built those bases themselves."

"They built the bases? If that's so, they must be from the earth's future."

"Exactly, that's what we thought too."

"But what does all this have to do with Kevin?"

"I don't know. It's possible these people are still around. Maybe they interfered with Kevin and were connected to the numbers."

"Still around?! Didn't you say these people came here thousands of years ago?!"

"It's not impossible considering that the peoples of the Kitsunes Kingdoms, Empires, and Dutchies can live for over ten thousand years and the fae can live until killed," Azalea explains.

"The Kitsune!" CJ exclaims, "That's it I remember now. Back in that base outside of Heizengaard, Kevin told me to go to the capital city of Aoimachi in the Kingdom of Aochikyuu, the blue kitsune majority country, and speak with Furui Taimā. If kitsunes live that long they might know what happened all those years ago."

"So, you think we should go to Aoimachi then?"

"Exactly."

"Before we get moving. What did you two find out?" I ask CJ.

"It was a riddle if I remember correctly 'the base below the ice and stone, where something wicked has finally grown'. We ran into a section of the remnants of The Assassin King's cult that had been formed by Number 02. Apparently, they wanted to kidnap us and bring us to this so-called 'base below the ice and stone'."

"'Below the ice and stone'..."

"What is it, Azalea?"

"That riddle sounds familiar. I wonder... Due to their old age Kitsunes are known for their historians. They might know where that base is."

"So, we definitely have to go to the Kingdom of Aochikyuu then."

"The fastest route would be to go down the river to Kailias, then take the train to Obervios, from there we'd take a carriage to the border and then walk the rest of the way. We can Probably be in Obervios by tomorrow morning if we leave now," Amaryll says.

"Well, then let's head out."

"Agreed," we all say in unison. CJ puts the papers back into the folder and hands it back to me. We walked out to the river docks and boarded a ship headed down for Kailias.

"You know there is a certain someone we know who might be of some help," Amaryll says to Alex.

"You mean!... Agreed."

We arrive in Kailias a few hours later and take a carriage over to Alex and Amaryll's house.

"Welcome home Alex, Amaryll, I didn't expect to see you so soon. Ah and the rest of you are here as well. Please come in." We take our seats at the table.

"Before we start, I will introduce myself. My name is Eris Astraea, I am currently working as the housekeeper here and Alex's Abramonic tutor. I hope to be helpful to you all."

"Nice to meet you," I say.

"Eris, our next destination is the Kingdom of Aochikyuu, so we thought that you as a kitsune might be of some help. Is it possible for you to come?" Alex asks.

"Why of course. I would be happy to help. I am fluent in the kitsune language after all. But there is one thing I have been meaning to tell you."

"What is it?"

"Well, you see, like you, I am also from earth, but when I came to this land, I was transformed into the shape you see now. From what I have gathered this is not a very common occurrence, although it is known to happen. Many years ago, when I came here, I traveled around with a group of friends not unlike all of you. Recently, I have settled down here in Kailias, but I'm still confident in my fighting ability."

"Wait, do you think it's possible we're not human anymore?" I ask.

"Of course, it's not impossible, but it is highly unlikely. Though a lot of the time people will develop traits of certain intelligent species without showing any physical differences. These traits often take time to develop, they can take months and even years. So, there's no saying for certain whether or not you have changed, but for now you seem to be regular humans."

"That's not exactly reliving, but I guess it helps to know."

"Eris if you're from earth would you mind telling us about your life there?" Alex asks.

"Why of course, I would be happy to. You see, back on earth I was quite the astronomer. I had always had an interest in the cosmos since my childhood. As it turns out this interest would lead to my demise. There was supposed to be a near earth asteroid passing by, so I grabbed my telescope and took a flight to the best viewing location. What ended up happening was that passerby ended up on a collision course with the city I was in. The asteroid struck the city right while I was viewing it through my telescope and so my life was ended abruptly. And then, I ended up here. Curious about my peculiar circumstances after my journey I set off for the Kingdom of Aochikyuu to study. This is when I found out about my transformation. I should be of some particular help as I have quite good relationships with the blue kitsune. After my time there I settled down here as I previously mentioned."

"Good to know we have someone as reliable as you Eris," Alex says, bumping Eris lightly with his elbow.

"You flatter me Alex. I merely wish to be helpful."

"Anyway, now that our greetings are complete it's about time we head to the train station."

We get up from our seats and walk out the door getting in a carriage headed to the Kailber Train Station. A few minutes into the ride a loud sound blast from the right side of the carriage causing it to violently roll over. Alex creates a force field protecting all of us and the driver from any major injury.

I claw out of the rubble having to burn some of it to successfully get out. Eris is already in a confrontation with the attacker. I stand up and get ready to attack.

"Please allow me to handle this one Ms. Cathryn."

"Oooo, as gallant as ever Eris," the attacker mocks.

"Chris? why are you here?"

"I'm here to execute a preemptive strike, you could say."

"But why, we were once friends. Could we not resolve this peacefully?"

"I'm to say, but this is what must happen. You see, my current musical employer has quite the shady connections. When he said I would be able to use my musical talent in a special manner, this is not what I had in mind. But a contract is a contract and money is money, so I'm going along with it." The attacker shrugs their shoulders. They have a mild complexion along with some fiery red hair.

"Fine then. If we cannot resolve this peacefully then so be it. Prepare for a fight." The attacker 'Chris' begins to strum their guitar creating a loud blast of sound aimed at Eris. Eris masterfully dodges them, and they end up only doing minor damage to the houses around them.

"Let's brighten this place up!" the attacker exclaims, lifting his hand in the air creating a large ball of light in the shape of the disco ball. The light is almost blinding and in conjunction with another blast of sound acts a sort of a flashbang, disorienting Eris. With another blast of sound aimed at the ground causing the earth to quake and throwing Eris off balance, While he's still on the ground the attacker sends another blast of sound directly down onto Eris. Alex swiftly responds with a force field in an attempt to protect Eris from the incoming pressure wave. The wave hits the force field shattering it and absorbing most of the blast. Eris, a little roughed up but finally back on his feet, raises his hand into the air. Within a few seconds a barrage of flaming rocks fall from the sky onto the attacker at blistering speeds. The attacker skillfully dodges most of the meteoroids except for one that grazes his leg. Now slightly injured, the attacker blasts the ground with sound, causing a large cloud of dust to form. In all the sound and dust, the attacker disappears without a trace.

"Damn, and I was going to get them too!" Eris exclaims.

"It's alright Eris as long as we're all safe it's fine," Amaryll says.

"Still though, who was that? They seemed to know you," I ask.

"Like I mentioned before, I used to be an adventurer, that was one of my traveling companions."

"If he was your friend then why did he attack us?"

"I'm not exactly sure. It seems as though it had something to do with a contract. The real problem is that if he's here it's possible that the others are nearby."

"The others?"

"My other traveling companions. They were far more morally questionable than Chris, so they were probably involved in that contract. I think it's best if we get moving."

We get up and walk the rest of the way to the station and board our train. We take our seats as Azalea heals up any minor wounds we have acquired during that skirmish. I begin to feel a little nauseous.

Chapter 23: Hubris of Holliday

I'm gonna be real, I don't quite get trains. Like, how do we know they burn coal? They've used steam in the past, so anything that produces gas could work; for all it matters they could rig up the crematorium to the ovens and everybody would be none the wiser. On that subject, I am currently on a train with my party of five and also Eris; I requested to sit by myself, hence why Eris and Argent are talking with one another about the history of Abramon in the booth in front of me. Of course, I am not ever alone these days, there is the constant weight of my guilt. Also, the ghost, Kevin; he sits beside me even now, cleaning the blood off his mask, but nothing is leaving.

"Please absolve yourself, let me go to hell," Kevin comments, not looking up from his constantly blood-stained mask.

"I'm trying," I mutter, getting up to use the restroom to avoid this specter, if just for a moment. I splash water from the sink on my face and look in the mirror, only to see my own reflection replaced by Kevin looking back at me.

"Just forgive yourself already, you're so loud in your sleep," the reflection complains, visibly annoyed.

"I can temporarily get rid of you, would you like that?" I ask.

"Yes please, purgatory and hell combined is a less tortuous fate."

"Is hell real by the way? Or is that a figure of speech?"

"I don't know, I'm a hallucination manifested from your guilt."

"Fair; begone foul spirit." I punch the mirror, shattering it before walking out of the bathroom with my blood slightly on my knuckles. *This has become way too casual.* I sit back down in my seat, looking at my reflection in a shard of the mirror. *It's become way too hard to sleep with him standing above me, those eyebags look miserable. Maybe something like this era's versions of sleep pills would do me well.*

"I-I think I need a drink." I stand up, walking to the food car. I take a seat at the bar.

"Something to help me sleep," I ask the bartender.

"How long?" the small fellow asks, green skin and pointed ears, eyes that close vertically instead of horizontally. *A goblin, I think.*

"Until we arrive."

"How fast you want out?"

"How fast can I?"

"Here." the bartender pours me a glass of mead before pulling out a brown medicine-like bottle and adding half a shot of that.

"What's that?" I ask.

"Codeine."

"Huh," I shrug, taking a chug before slamming it down. Naturally, I don't want to pay, so I say, "tastes like piss."

"Oh, that's a shame, have some complementary snuff." The goblin hands me a fancy box.

"Huh, not much of a fan of opium, but thanks." I begin walking away, but before I walk through the door to the other car, I hear someone in there say 'Let us out! Help us!' followed by a thud. I turn around to tell the barkeep, but they've already stood up.

"Sorry, can't let you do that," the goblin says as the metal of the door molds itself shut, trapping me in with the goblin and the other fellow at the bar, a green kitsune.

"Oh, are you one of the people responsible? If so, what is going on and who are you contracted to?" I ask.

"Robbery, and we're freelance. Thanks for asking." the kitsune smirks, standing up. He looks about my height, with black hair and a green stripe on both of his tails. He has a semi-muscular build, with deep olive eyes. I think he's a bit under the influence of some kind of drug. His hands look dexterous, and he's wearing a robe with some chains on the waist.

"Both of you? This is very well orchestrated. I'd guess there's five of you?"

"H-how did you know?" The goblin is taken aback, visibly surprised.

"Simple; there are two of you in here, and the luggage car is that way. You probably have two in the other car to keep the people on the train from trying anything, and probably hostages too. Finally, one person in the engine room, as a last resort you can threaten everyone. Two, two, one, that makes five. Your reaction just confirmed that for me." I smirk back at the kitsune, to assert dominance.

"Huh, this isn't good." The goblin moves his hand in order to create a wall of metal between us. I almost immediately shatter the metal by using my synat to make it as proportionally fragile as glass before punching it. Immediately after I grab the goblin by the throat, looking at the kitsune and saying,

"Step back or your friend is gonna be dust," naturally, I'm bluffing, but with my synat boosting my charisma I know he won't know that.

"He's using a mind-" I shut the goblin up with my hand, knowing what he was about to say. *He must not be affected.*

"So? Kill the little bastard, see if I care?" the kitsune calls my bluff, either that or he doesn't care.

"Huh, didn't expect that," I throw the goblin against the floor, knocking him out and making him look dead.

"The name is Kinobashi, remember who defeated you when you reach the gates of death," the kitsune mocks.

"And I am Clark Julius La Démence, but you may tell the warden it was CJ who caught you," I retort.

"You the fellow who killed The Assassin King?" he asks.

"Yes."

"Okay, if this fight doesn't go my way I will run away." Kino starts producing what looks like toxic gas from his hands, similar to that lady who was mind controlled by the cult leader fellow.

"I can't make your gas fragile, that goblin bastard told you about my mind affecting abilities, and the gas doesn't care if you can see me or not," I think out loud intentionally, "your synat by all means beats mine."

"Are you surrendering?" he asks.

"No." I pull out my six-shooter again, sending a warning shot through the metal and leaving a hole.

"Oh, my synat can't defend against that; may our paths cross again, you look kind of cute in a threatening way; you can find me in the Midorochi

Kingdom from time to time." Kino runs out of the train car, I chase him but stop when I see him jump out of the moving train. *Am I that scary?* My next move is to shatter the door between me and the passenger car, only to see that everyone has already passed out, one of which is a sleepwalking grey orc.

"I thought there were two people in this car?" I mutter before seeing said orc running at me. Even for an orc, her speed is extreme, same as her strength in throwing an entire bench at me.

"I don't have time for this!" I exclaim, shooting at her, only for her to dodge the bullet. I fire another, this one she catches. I examine my choices and empty the last 3 bullets into her, only one connecting with her eye.

"Now where is that other guy?" I ponder, looking at the unconscious bodies to see if any move, "oh, by the way. I killed The Assassin King, if you reveal yourself now, I will have mercy, if you do not you will die." I play that card, knowing the consequence that Kevin will appear again as a side effect.

"Oh, hell no! I'm out!" one of the bodies stands up and runs into the engine room, a lunar elf.

"Huh, that sort of worked." I crouch down, shaking as many of my allies awake as possible, but only getting Argent and Eris.

"Eris, do you know a man by the name of Kinobashi?" I ask.

"Y-yes, he was one of my friends, though he already had a criminal past. I also saw Septimus in this car."

"Tell me everything you can about Septimus."

"His synat is 'Inebriated Combustion'. He can create alcohol at will, ignite flammable inorganic objects, and he has a passive aura of intoxication around him. He is a 6'4" lunar elf and is skilled in psionics. He is both greedy and cowardly. He is a slight pyromaniac. He carries a small crossbow. His big weakness is that he is always drunk. Do you need to know anything else?"

"No. Come with me." I begin walking towards the conductor's car.

"Psionics, huh? That's mind magic basically, and you're already on the cusp," Kevin's ghost chuckles. I ignore him as I open the door to what I thought was the conductor's car, but it actually is an empty room that seems like it may have been mid-renovation when the train departed. Standing at the end of the room and blocking the door is Septimus himself, his greyish-white skin and solid eyes of a slightly bluer shade making him appear monolithic.

"You know, there's three types of people who can't hold their liquor; priests," suddenly Argent falls over, "scholars" Eris falls just the same, "and annoying bastards like you." I feel a bit weakened but am mostly unaffected.

"See, when your childhood sucks, alcohol kind of helps, y'know?" I explain myself to Sept before realizing I don't need to explain to him.

"That sucks. I guess we got to fight, boss man is kind of upset. Two questions though; first, is Kino okay or? Because we kind of had a thing and-" I cut him off.

"He jumped out the train, he's probably okay."

"Thanks. Two, so like you do know I can see him, right?" he points at Kevin.

"Me? I'm a hallucination you idiot- CJ, call him an idiot for me."

"Psionics you moron, I can see his hallucination. I can also do this." suddenly Kevin starts to dance, clearly not of his own will, before saying,

"Septimus is the best! Such a genius!"

"You're stalling, aren't you?" I ask.

"Yep, you may notice your clothes are soaked in alcohol." Sept snaps his fingers and my clothes ignite. I manage to turn invisible and take them off, running behind him while wearing just my leggings and scarf as my shirt, pants, and cloak burn.

"I win! Book One is over!" Septimus exclaims. *He thinks I'm dead.*

"Almost. I did theatre, I know how to change clothes fast." I grab him in a headlock from behind, pulling him backwards and tossing him out the train, "your boyfriend should be a few miles back, give or take." I begin walking into the engine car, having only my leggings, scarf, and an empty gun. Inside the room is a man who appears to be a crossbreed of man and raccoon. The man is evidently an ex-convict, as he is quite literally still wearing his black and white prison uniform as well as a metal collar and broken chain dangling from it. His outfit is a bit ripped, but not from combat, probably from age. His hair is white and eyes black with large bags around them. His skin was somewhat tan, like that fake wood in cheap desks when you look at it from the side.

"Oh, I assume you defeated everyone else? I'll be honest, I did not expect that. Also, where is your shirt?" he asks.

"Sept burnt it."

"Ah, gotcha, he did like them pale."

"Huh, he was trying to kill me, but I didn't take him for that type. Regardless, you going to surrender or?"

"Nah, if I die the train might crash."

"I'm not gonna kill you, I need info." I run at him and hit him with the handle of my gun, only to see Kevin's ghost fall to his knees.

"What's going on?" I ask.

"Ah, feeling it? My synat makes you feel more pain in relation to the more you think, that is one power of Tortured Genius. It also makes me smarter and gives me a faster reaction time," the racoon boasts.

"I'm pure thought you moron! It's focusing on me!" Kevin screams, his tears disappearing before they hit the ground.

"Ah, that's why I'm immune." I hit the man again.

"What, because you're a moron?"

"No, I'm the smart one, I'm just mentally ill." I smirk intentionally, punching him so hard this time that when he hits the wall it leaves a tiny dent.

"Damn, so I assume it'll just be hand to hand combat?"

"Nope, notice the dent in the wall? Metal is malleable, so how come this isn't?" I punch a pipe next to me, shattering it with my synat. The pipe above falls as a result, hitting him and shattering the floor below him in the process. If it weren't for his reaction time he'd be dead, but instead he's just injured by the pipe.

"Huh, you are smart." he stands back up.

"If you tell me who you work for this can all be over." he dodges my punch.

"Uhh, I'm the one running this operation. I have no relation to that terrorist near the station you moron." he returns an even stronger punch to my gut.

"Really? He and two of your men were old friends." I aim another blow at his neck.

"Really? News to me." he suddenly grabs me by the throat.

"Small world-" I gasp as he picks me up by his hold, dangling me over the hole I made.

"Any last words?" he smirks up at me due to how he's holding me.

"N-" I fail to get my snide remark out, swinging my legs up and shifting into a choke hold.

"G-get-" and so the roles are reversed.

"I know what you're thinking, CJ. torturing him for info is fruitless, he's too casual about the info to be lying, and everyone else referred to him as boss." Kevin watches over my shoulder.

"What, are you trying to be my conscience or something?" I snap back.

"Yeah moron, that's what your brain made me for." I pause for a moment before sighing, telling the man "be honest, do you really not know about the contract? If you lie, I'm going to send you there" I point at the furnace.

"I-I'm not! I don- don't know! M-maybe old Assassin K-king agents?" he theories, seeming honest.

"Well, your synat is genius, and you seem to be telling the truth." I choke him until he passes out before throwing him out of the train, sparing him.

With the whole robbery thing over with, the rest of the trip was boring by comparison, and over fast. I slept through most of it, though I will need to replace my clothes in the Aoimachi.

Chapter 24: DB Cooper's Captive.

Ugh... I put my hand to my forehead. There's a dull pulsing pain in my head.

"What happened?" I think of what the cause of my current suffering could be.

"Oh Alex! You're awake. Oh..." Cat is standing over me. I'm presumably lying down on one of the train seats.

"What's the problem?" I ask.

"Well, you look so pale. I guess you have a low tolerance." Cat laughs, "Azalea could you come over here."

"Huh? Sure." Azalea walks over from her seat, "Oh... Don't worry I got this." A familiar pale blue glow hovers over my body. Soon my headache dissipates.

"What happened?" I repeat.

"Well, you see..." Azalea trails off letting CJ cut in,

"There were enemies on the train, one of them happened to be an old friend of Eris, who had the ability of making anyone within a certain distance of himself drunk."

"I see... That explains it then. So, I assume you took him out?"

"Certainly, I threw him out of the train."

"Is he dead?" CJ shrugs his shoulders. "What about the others you mentioned?"

"One of them is dead, another one hopped off the train and the other two are unconscious."

"Alright, so how close are we to Obervios?" I ask. A voice comes over the speaker,

"Arriving at Obervios Station."

"Seems I spoke too soon." We get off the train and onto the platform quickly finding a long-distance carriage and hopping in. Argent hands a set of coins over to the driver.

"So, where are you headed?" The driver asks.

"To the border with the Kingdom of Aochikyuu," Argent replies.

"Alright then." A few hours pass and the sun is beginning to set. I begin to doze off, but before I fall asleep the carriage comes to a sudden stop waking me up.

"This is the border. You'll have to make the rest of the way on foot." We hop out of the carriage and begin our walk through the dense evergreen forest. The setting sun casting long shadows of the trees. After a few minutes of walking I notice movement around us in the corner of my eye. *Maybe it's just an illusion. It's starting to get dark out after all.* Again, I see some sort of movement in the brush around us. *There's definitely something there!*

"Guys I think someone's following us."

"What? Are you sure?" Cat asks.

"No, I'm sure. I saw it earlier and then again just recently." We stand in a circle facing outwards. The movement continues, this time the whole group is aware. Soon enough the sun had fully set behind the horizon and its light no longer reached the depths of the forest we were in. Suddenly I hear footsteps rushing towards us, but I'm unable to see anything, and then immediately after I'm unconscious. I slowly regain my consciousness, My hearing muffled and vision blurry. I attempt to move my arms only to find that they are tightly bound. I begin to panic. I try to kick my feet around with no success. I'm completely immobile. I scream out for help, but no sound leaves my throat. My vision finally clears up and I take a look around. The room is relatively small, completely bland and featureless, most likely made from concrete or something similar. The only notable things in the room are the singular candle hanging from the ceiling, illuminating the room, and the reinforced metal door. I'm up against the back wall, strapped to some sort of chair. I look around looking for anything else in the room only to find disappointment. I try to think of a way out of this situation, but my inability to move hinders any sort of plan I could think of. *What happened? Was I kidnapped?* I remember what had just happened in the forest. *Is it possible that it's part of The Assassin King cult? It can't be one of the numbers, Cat said that Azalea's dad killed the rest of them, the only one who's still alive is Number 02, but...* The sound of the reinforced door creaking quickly interrupts my stream of thought.

"Ah, I see you have arrived," says a voice coming from behind the door. *Arrived? Is he not the one who brought me here?* The door fully opens and the man behind the voice enters the room. He seems to be a blue kitsune with shoulder length straight black hair. His tails furling out from behind him, their tips blue in color. He wore a form-fitting jet-black suit with the sleeves rolled up, revealing a strange pattern of circular scars on his forearms.

"It's good to know that they successfully delivered you here. Of course, they failed to capture the others; Do they have no faith? If they were true believers our goals would be carried out perfectly through his divine grace!" The man mumbles to himself.

"Oh my, I forgot to introduce myself! You may refer to me as Number 10." *Number 10! But he's supposed to be dead! Azalea's dad killed him!*

"Killed me? He did no such thing. He merely brought me to the brink of death and was too lazy to check whether or not I was alive. These scars are a mark of my survival." *Is he reading my mind?!*

"Exactly. One of the many benefits of being a blue kitsune is proficiency in psionics." *Psionics?*

"Yes, psionics, the science of the mind. The study of analyzing, observing and otherwise augmenting the mind. It's a perfect match with my synat, False Memory. You see, as a child and even now I am so heavily interested in the subject of memory. My synat allows me to implant false memories for a certain amount of time. I will be using psionics to 'amplify' this ability." *Amplify?*

"Yes, I will use psionics to amplify these implanted memories and cause them to repeat over and over again. Enough talk, let us begin." A familiar scene begins to play in my head. Kevin gets crushed by the brick wall and we're fighting that first assassin. The vision gets to the point where he was about to explode, but unlike what I remember he doesn't get vaporized by Cat and he explodes killing us all. Our blood splattering on Argents face who had just walked out of the church. The scene replays over and over again in my head. *No! That's not what happened!*

"Oh, but it is what happened. It's your failure that led to this." *No! It can't be true!* My denial's resistance can only last so much longer. Suddenly, I'm brought back to reality and the false memory disappears.

"How was that? Did you enjoy seeing your friends getting killed over and over?" *Damn you!*

"Let's continue." Reality fades away as another memorable scene plays out in my head. I hear the explosions above; dust and small bits of rock begin to fall from the ceiling of the large cavern. The pieces of the ceiling falling to the ground continue getting larger and larger. And almost as if it was in slow motion the entire ceiling falls to the ground, crushing everyone except me as I create a force field to protect only myself. *No.* I dig myself out from the rubble and come out into a dark cavern. I dig through the rocks, grasping at some thin string of hope, praying to whatever god will listen that they're still alive. *No. No.* The only thing I find is their bloodied and mangled bodies in pieces strewn throughout the rubble. The rocks caused an indentation in CJ's chest and torso which had been separated from the rest of his body. Cat's skin being shredded off in multiple places exposing the red stained pink flesh underneath. *This can't be happening!* I keep digging, finding CJ and Cat's lifeless and lacerated faces. Their heads detached from their body's. The light clearly long gone from their foggy and clouded eyes. *No. Cat. CJ. I failed you... You were my best friends... I only thought for myself...* Tears stream down my face, but I don't make a sound. Staring blankly in the darkness of the cave. I look up to see a large piece of rubble falling straight down upon me. The last thing I think before my life comes to a close being, *please put an end to this putrid existence. A failure as a person and a friend...* This horrid vision repeats in my head. Over and over their bruised, scratched, and soulless faces etch themselves into my mind. *Over and over and over and over and over and over and over and over and over... IT WON'T STOP!* I can almost feel my sanity slipping away slowly as my grasp on my mind continues to loosen. Absolute desolation. I completely failed as a human being. Their deaths haunt my endless and soulless repeating life. Wishing for this meaningless life of mine to end only for it to replay the same tragedy over and over again in my head, unable to change anything and unable to escape. The light has left my side. I travel through an empty void with no one. No light to guide me. I lay in the darkness's cold embrace, sinking deeper and deeper into madness. My thought process begins to end. I feel my presence in this world beginning to fade away.

"Alex."

"Alex."

"Alex!" I'm thrown back into reality to the sight of Amaryll releasing me from the restraints. "Alex are you okay?" I see Number 10's corpse on the floor. As soon as I'm freed, almost as if it was instinctual, I hold onto Amaryll. Gripping her tightly.

"Alex! Hey! What are you..." She looks down to see tears silently streaming down my face. I continue to hold on tightly as she picks me up and carries me out of that room. I look up at her face, her beautiful features standing out more than before. A shining star in the vast empty darkness that had enveloped me. A light at the end of the tunnel. My vision begins to go black and my consciousness fades away. When I come to, I seem to be laying down on a floor mattress futon.

I look to my left seeing Amaryll passed out next to me grabbing onto my hand. I push the mattress aside and slowly get up walking out of the room. The floor's in the building are made of tatami mats. I walk down the hallway searching for someone else. I bump into Cat while walking through. I apologize, but when I look up all I can see is her face in that vision. Those clouded and soulless eyes and that cold grey skin. That face from that horrid vision carved into my mind and my soul. I immediately fall to the floor.

"Alex! Are you alright?" Cat looks down at me. All I can see is that face, that cold dead face.

"No! Not again!" I run down the hallway past Cat. I keep running and running until I bump into CJ.

"Hey Alex. You Okay?" I look up at him only to see eyes fogged over and shattered glasses upon a distorted and disembodied face.

"I'm so sorry CJ. So sorry." I start sobbing my head to the ground.

"Wha- Alex I... What happened?"

"It's all my fault CJ. It's all my fault."

"What's your fault? What happened?"

"I let you and Cat down. I'm a failure as a friend and as a human being."

"Alex. We're both fine. What are you talking about?"

"It's all my fault. I let you all die. I let my friends die. All because I thought only about myself."

"Die? Alex I'm right here. I am alive, my heart's still beating. Cat's still alive," CJ puts his hand on my shoulders and looks me straight in the face, "Alex I don't what that bastard showed you, but it's all fake. None of it was real." That dead face fades away and

I'm able to see CJ again. CJ walks me back to the room where I woke up and they sit me down to explain what happened.

"We were standing in a circle when we were ambushed by the same sect of The Assassin King Cult that had kidnapped me and Argent. They had been founded by Number 02, but apparently, he had little involvement in the cult's activity, and it was actually run by Number 10. Their whole goal was to get revenge on us for 'killing' The Assassin King by kidnapping us and bringing us to the 'base under the ice and stone' and exact their revenge there."

"So, then what happened to me?"

"Well, when we were ambushed one of the cult members knocked you out and brought you to an underground base they had recently constructed. It was not created by those 'Scout Group 1' people. As soon as we had fought off all the cultists, we headed for the base breaking in. We took out all the grunts while Amaryll went to find you. She ended up killing Number 10 and bringing you here. She said something was 'off' about you and stayed with you throughout the night."

"I'm pretty confused about how Number 10 was still alive. Julius told us that he killed the remaining numbers. Did he say anything to you Alex?"

"Yeah, actually I think he did. Something along the lines of, 'I was at the brink of death and he was too lazy to check whether or not I was alive'."

"That makes sense. Dad was pretty badly injured when we found him. Whatever happened I can't imagine he would have time to check. Did he say anything else?"

"Yeah he had these weird circular scars all over his forearms. He said they were a 'mark of his survival'."

"That sounds like my dad's work. His synat is the ability to take the moisture out of the air and shoot it at high speeds. That's usually the type of wound he'd leave behind."

"So, one more thing; where exactly is here?"

"This is the closed palace in Aoimachi. We explained the situation and told them our identities and they let us stay in this house. We got here last night after we rescued you."

"So, did you talk to them about the riddle yet?"

"No, we didn't really have the time. We'll have to talk to them about it today."

"Then it's a plan."

Chapter 25: A History of Heresy

I look up, noticing CJ's new outfit.

"What's with wardrobe change?" I ask.

"Oh this?" CJ tugs on his robes, "Well, during the fight with Septimus my clothes burned off and I kind of need new ones. Luckily Argent had a spare set of robes that happened to be a good fit."

There was a white underlayer which came to a point just above his ankles. The outer layer is mostly black with white trim. The only thing remaining from his original clothing being his striped scarf and glasses. We all walk out of the room and walk out of the house. The fragrance of pine trees wafting from the open door. Small houses surrounding a temple at the center encased by a dense forest of tall evergreens. We enter the temple to see a kitsune sitting upon what appeared to be a throne. Her eyes, a piercing deep blue, with pupils of a fox. Several tails unfurl out from behind her, their tips golden in color.

"So, you have finally come to see me?"

"You were expecting us?" I ask.

"Yes. I think you should already know why. Your friend told you to come see me. Did he not?"

"You mean Kevin?" CJ asks.

"Yes, that one."

"You knew Kevin? How?"

"It must've been ten or eleven years ago he came to me. He asked about the origins of this world and so I told him. Once I was finished, he asked me that if a group of five humans and an elf were to show up here, I should tell them the same. I was surprised by his knowledge of the future. I have my own ability to predict the outcome of events. In fact, I saw a vision of you coming here just before your friend showed up. That is why I humored his question."

"That does make sense..." CJ mumbles to himself, "So, what was the story you told him?"

"It's a tale telling the origins of civilization here on Sotaqt. I shall now begin. 10,000 years at the dawn of civilization. A bright streak of light crosses the sky. The start of the Great Invasion. Then, only a few days later a group of individuals wearing strange clothing and carrying strange devices. They attempted to reason with the native population of the world, but to no avail, for their goals were too vast; A plan to take hold of and control the population of the world. In their frustration they released a deadly plague upon the land, slaughtering most of the world's peoples. The ones who survived were blessed with the power now known as synats. These select few are the ancestors of all living People in this world. The people who released this plague disappeared, never to be seen again. Then, something strange began to happen to the humans left alive; they had their forms changed, some became the elves, others became multitudes of crossbreeds, and even the Kitsune themselves. Though some stayed human. This event is known as the Great Transformation. From there civilization continued to develop into its current form."

"Those people... The 'invaders' they couldn't be..." Alex stammers at a loss for words.

"Alex, you think it could be those people? The ones from the journal entries?" CJ asks.

"It all makes sense. If they're the ones responsible, then..."

"I understand this information may be very shocking to you, but there is one that you wanted to ask me about. Isn't there?"

"You're right. The riddle. Below the ice and stone, where something wicked has finally grown." CJ recites.

"That riddle!" Furui exclaims.

"What? What does it mean?"

"I thought that riddle had been lost to history. Even I had forgotten it until now. Where did you hear it?"

"It was when we were fighting a sect of The Assassin King cult. They said they want to 'bring us to the base below the ice and stone, where something wicked has finally grown'. But what does that mean?"

"It's an ancient riddle. It refers to a rumor that the place the great invaders had gone to after their disappearance was in the southernmost tip of Saezia, underneath the mountains and glaciers. It's currently part of the Kobolda Empire, the goblin majority country."

"Then that's where we're going," CJ nods.

"It won't be easy. Not many people have gone that close to the south pole, and even less have come back."

"Well, there's no point in coming this far just to turn back," CJ looks over his shoulder at nothing, "For Kevin's sake."

"Well, if you're going to go, I might as well assist you in your journey. The best thing to do would be taking a ship from Obervios to the outer circles of the Capital of the Kingdom of Yavolia, Cocytus. From there you can take a train to the southern Kingdom of Yavolia, but from there you're on your own. The goblins aren't exactly friendly to outsiders, so don't expect any help from them. I wish you the best of luck."

"Thank you." We bow to show our appreciation. We are given a carriage ride out to the border with the USP and begin walking to the closest village to catch another ride back to Obervios.

"So, Alex, you were about to say something earlier, but Furui cut you off. What was it?" I ask.

"Well, the thing is. If those people from the Earth's future somehow had or created that virus that killed all those people, and then the ones who were immune gained the power of synats and transformed, It all brings up a question; What are synats and how are they related to this virus?"

"Honestly, I have no idea."

"Oh, that was a rhetorical question. I mean how could a virus cause such change to the human form? Is it really even a virus? It doesn't make sense."

"Well, I don't know any of the answers to your questions, I do know that a lot of this doesn't make sense. I mean we are in another universe and we all have these superhuman abilities. What makes sense about that?"

"You're right Cat, Maybe I shouldn't think about it too much."

"Yeah, you need to relax a little Alex; You're gonna stress yourself out," Amaryll says.

"I know, I know, It's probably for the best if I clear my head." Alex looks out into the distance. We arrive in a nearby town after a few more minutes of walking. After walking around a little we find a carriage service and order a trip.

"Oh, I just had an idea!" Azalea exclaims.

"What?"

"Well, the western portion of the Kingdom of Yavolia is famous for its natural hot springs, nestled right in the Azael Mountains. I think it would be a good opportunity to relax."

"That sounds great!" I exclaim.

"But that would slow us down. We have to get to those scout group people. I have to know what happened. For Kevin's sake I... I..." CJ trails off.

"Look I understand where you're coming from CJ. If these people are connected to what happened with Kevin, then they'd be responsible for my brother's death. I understand that you want to know what happened, I do too, but I think it would be for the best if we take some time to clear our heads. We can't confront these people if we aren't in the right headspace. We can't have any more unnecessary deaths."

"Maybe you're right. If we can approach this situation with clear heads, then maybe... just maybe... we can get to the bottom of this mystery."

"Then it's settled then. After we head out of the outer circle of Cocytus, we'll go to the hot springs." A few hours later we finally arrived back in Obervios.

"It seems It's time for me to take my leave then," Eris waves awkwardly.

"You're not coming with us?" Amaryll asks.

"Yes, of course I would like to come with you, but I must leave for Kailias. I got some urgent news from the mayor while we were in the Kingdom of Aochikyuu."

"Urgent news?"

"Ah, don't worry, it's urgent, but it's nothing for you to worry about. It has something to do with city affairs; I can't really go into more detail."

"Alright, well as long as you're not keeping anything important from us then it's fine."

"Of course, if it was something relevant to your current endeavor then of course I would share it with you."

"Thank you, Eris, you really did help earlier."

"You flatter me Ms. Chaleur. I'll be leaving now." Eris walks off towards the train station as we all walk over to the docks. I think about all the stuff Argent was saying about the city while we were on our way here. *The buildings here are some of the oldest in the world, as Obervios was the first of the seven core cities of the USP. There are old churches with intricate stonework and beautiful stained-glass windows. The town hall is made from marble with designs carved into the walls. The town hall was based in a building created almost two thousand years ago. Most of the houses are at least several hundred years old most of them being built back when Obervios was still an independent city state, though the city does still have a great degree of autonomy. It's also known as the democratic haven of the world, being one of the freest cities in the world. The citizens here have a great deal of control over what happens in the city. For the rest of the USP it's practically the shining city on a hill, and a beacon of hope for the rest of the world.* We finally arrive at the docks, walking up to the ticket stand.

"We need 6 tickets for a trip to the outer circles of Cocytus," I say.

"Cocytus! Wait... Oh! I understand. Please go right ahead." *Well, that was strange.* We walk up the ramp and onto the ship.

"You know, Cat..." Azalea says.

"Yeah?"

"A Lot of half elves and mixed elves like me come to seek refuge here. Especially when having children. They don't want their kids to suffer the same fate as them. I'm lucky; I'm treated well because of my father, and my appearance doesn't really give away my wood elf heritage, So I tried to help as many people as I could. That's why I became a nurse. A lot of migrants from the UEF come through Tirentod, so I thought that if I worked there then I could help people who weren't as fortunate as myself. I'm glad I was born with my synat, one that can heal people; It made me feel as though I was made for the job. I met a lot of others like myself, people created for government experiments, most of them not as fortunate as myself."

"Really? I guess I sort of understand."

"You know the thing I'm most glad about though?"

"What?"

"Meeting you."

"Huh?!" I'm taken aback, not really sure what to say.

"Well, if I hadn't met you, I wouldn't even be alive to do anything I set out to do. Thanks to you I'm able to avenge my brother's death instead of being part of the tragedy. I wouldn't know what to do without you. After my brother died my goals became blurred and my life unsure. When I found out you were the one that saved me it brought it all back. I reaffirmed my previous goals and set out to reach for new ones."

Azalea's brilliant pale blue hair flutters in the wind as the ship sails towards the horizon, "Thank you Cat, if it weren't for you I wouldn't be standing here today. My life is yours." I didn't have the words to respond. The shining scarlet sun slowly set below the horizon casting beams of light from below, the clouds illuminated a pale pink by the sinking sun, the dark of night creeping up from behind, slowly encasing the sky in a deep violet.

Chapter 26: Iscariot's Mercy

The boat appears to be steam powered, boiling the water by using flame-based synats of the crew members. The sky is black by this point, but that long rest after the scuffle on the train has hindered my sleep schedule, which I am fixing in small increments. As a result, everyone else is asleep, except of course-

"CJ, mind eating an apple real quick? You don't remember the taste of them, and I can't get one here unless you do," Kevin requests, having become much more casual despite his somewhat gruesome appearance and dark origin.

"You can see my memories, I hate apples, they taste like cardboard."

"Oh, come on! Just a bite, then I'll leave you be." Kevin floats over, levitating on the opposite side of the guard rail.

"Think of it as an act of repentance, making up for the incident." He's clearly guilt-tripping me, but to be fair there is a lot of guilt to trip me on.

"Fine, if it'll get you to shut up," I sigh, going to the mess hall area and picking up one of the apples from breakfast. As I am doing so, I hear one of the employees talking with another. *I assumed only the necessary crew were still awake.*

"Eavesdropping is rude, you know," Kevin comments, floating behind me as if lounging on some invisible chair.

"Bold words from you. Plus, if I'm doing something while listening then it's just overhearing," I mutter, listening to the conversation.

"Once we reach The Kingdom of Yavolia, you lay low for a bit before going to The Midorochi Kingdom, I wait a week before catching up with you, and we wait until the heat dies down." The voice sounds familiar, but I can't put my finger on where it's from.

"Is that one of your buddies?" Kevin jokes.

"Shut it, they might hear-"

"Hey, you made sure nobody followed us, right?" a second voice asks.

"Yeah, why?" the first replies.

"I just heard something over there." I hear footsteps coming in my direction and instinctively hide under the table before remembering I can just turn invisible.

"Seems like nobody was here." The first person chuckles, appearing to be a lunar elf in the sailor's uniform of the ship's staff, yet it's too dark to see their face.

"Seems so." The second appears to be a green kitsune, a bit shorter than the first, in the uniform of the kitchen staff.

"Oh, and if you're hiding, we will let you go if you reveal yourself." the first says, seeming to look right at me, or maybe a bit to my left where Kevin is.

"There's nobody here, even if they did hide, I'd smell them." *Normal invisibility wouldn't have worked here, but thankfully my synat is a bit more complex. It doesn't make me invisible, it makes it so I'm not perceived by others.* The two begin to walk away, and naturally, I follow.

"This is kind of creepy of you, not gonna lie." Kevin floats alongside me.

"These guys might be Assassin King Agents; it's called being safe."

"Listen, my memories are just your estimations and guesses about me, but I don't think I hired them."

"Does the CEO hire each fry cook? No." The two open a door to one of the rooms, using the proper key to get in, "Do you think they killed the actual patron?"

"No? That's you being paranoid." Kevin simply phases through the closed door after I rush to get through before the two close it.

"So, what are you gonna do as a free man?" the first asks the second, neither turning on the lights.

"Probably get a place for us to stay, get it prepped and stuff, then after stuff cools down, I'll go back to the usual. What about you?"

"I'm gonna spend my money and get one of those fancy combustion engine carriages, they're like one-man-trains."

"Where would you drive it? There aren't paths big enough for that in the woods, and the city is too small to warrant its use."

"It's not about using it, it's about having it, with my synat I'd probably crash it." By this point I've heard enough, I draw my pistol before revealing myself.

"I've heard everything, you're agents of The Assassin King, aren't you?" I ask, pistol pointed at the first one.

"No! Please, put the gun down, I can trade you some of my loot for your silence about what you heard." the first one offers. I turn on the light, finally realizing why these two are familiar; they're Septimus and Kinobashi.

"You two? What are you doing here?"

"Us? Why are you following us? Are you working with the police or something?" Kinobashi asks.

"No, I thought you were following us."

"What would we gain from that?" Septimus questions.

"It was the only explanation I had, though I'd prefer now if you told me the real reason you're here." I slowly lower my revolver.

"Oh, we're escaping the feds, and because there's no extradition deal with The Kingdom of Yavolia, we're camping out there to cover our trail." Kino explains.

"Is robbing a train that serious a crime? Why? Nobody even died," I say.

"Oh, that's not what we're wanted for. That robbery was in exchange for the boss getting us out of here in the stolen train. I'm wanted for arson in several countries and anarchist affiliations." Sept gestures as he speaks.

"And I'm wanted for a string of large robberies and cons." Kino adds.

"And I should let you violent criminals go for what reason?" I ask, wanting a definitive reason for or against it.

"As if you're any better," Kevin scoffs.

"There are no victims, for either of us. We aren't violent, hell, we're only criminals against the state, we have no crimes against the gods," Sept pleads.

"The arsonist and robber have no victims? Explain," I instruct, curious.

"He burned down government buildings when nobody was inside, I stole from large businesses, the only victims were numbers in leather books," Kino replies. For a moment I consider their stories, and weigh them with my own crimes, against the state and against god.

"Not only will I keep this secret between us, I'll help you out some. With my synat I can make myself more trustable and charismatic, I can impart some of that onto you so nobody questions you. There is one condition, however."

"What is that?" Kino asks, looking terrified.

"If you go back to that anarchist business, consider calling me up if you need an alibi, or an accomplice." I smile at the two, prompting a small chuckle. There was a secondary benefit of my choice as well, for the rest of the trip I got extra breakfast thanks to Kinobashi. From there the rest of the voyage was as calm as a puddle in a bank safe. The outermost wall of The Kingdom of Yavolia, separating the first circle from the outside, is much bigger in person. Each wall from there got bigger, to a nigh-comical point.

"Hey, is he staring at you?" Kevin asks me, pointing at a Demon with an odd looking set of grey horns.

"Most likely, I don't see any humans." I accidently say out loud.

"Most likely what?" Alex asks.

"That people are staring, there aren't that many humans here."

"Of course, here in the Kingdom of Yavolia, there are rules for who is allowed within which walls. We are the first non-demons to ever come this far in." Argent explains.

"I see, so it's a bit of a culture shock?" Cat clarifies.

"I suppose, yes." Argent looks down at the map, "we're in the eighth circle, pride. This place has some of the best high-quality crafts and smiths in the country. One of my favorite thespians lives here when not on tour, Asmodus Stolz. Considering we're here, we ought to buy some fancy weapons for our journey, considering how lazy SOMEONE was." Argent is very passive-aggressive in that last line, referring to how the cleaning person either lost or accidentally threw away my pistol.

"None of us can read Yavolian, right?" Alex asks, to which everyone shakes their head.

"Though, I do know some Russian, and this language also seems to have cyrilic root words and characters. Like akter, krasnyy, korol, and lyubovnik," I comment.

"So, do you know where the blacksmith is?" Amaryll asks.

"That sign says zheleno, that one says bronya, iron and armor respectively, so I'd wager both are."

"Let's go to the one that says armor, armor smiths and weaponsmiths do very different jobs." Argent begins walking towards the shop with the 'Iron' sign, along with the rest of us. The shopkeeper is a somewhat burly woman, with growths similar to the material of that man's horns coming out of her right hand in the shape of a hammer, and her left in the shape of a vice. She's currently hammering away at something blade-like as she asks

"Aye, you here for the strongest metalwork in the bleedin' kingdom?"

"Yes, we were hoping to purchase some weapons-" Argent begins.

"Aye, speak up laddie, I cannae hear ye."

"We need some weapons for each of us!" Argent repeats.

"Need some weapons? What kind?"

"Your pick, you're the expert-"

"A bit louder laddie, yer as soft as a kitted deer!"

"You pick, you're the expert!" Argent near-shouts.

"Aye, don't raise your voice at me, bleedin' priest!" This sends Argent into a religious fervor of him attempting to spread the word of Azathoth to the smith, who either cannot hear or is ignoring him.

"Aye, a weapon to each of ye's tastes. I eyeballed ye' to get a rough shot of ye soul. For the strong lassie, a flail as strong as thunder. For th' loud lad, a rapier as sharp as a sunbeam. For the impish lad, a set of throwing knives as quick as a thought. For the recluse, a scythe as pure as the first frost. For the socialite, a broadsword as strong as God's will. And for the skeleton, a double-bladed dagger as stealthy as a shadow." she says, giving the weapons to, in order: Amaryll, Argent, Alex, Azalea, Cat, and myself.

"Huh, fits me perfectly." Amaryll picks up her flail, the weapon having something like a basketball of solid steel on it's chain.

"I used to practice swordsmanship as a boy." Argent picks up his blade.

"This may take some practice," Alex comments.

"A bit gothic," Azalea adds.

"Kinda heavy," Cat comments. I look down at my dagger, not saying anything.

"They've got you pegged as a killer. You've got an assassin's weapon, and I should know," Kevin whispers in my ear from behind me.

"Aye, and it'll be yours for 500 Royal Credits," the blacksmith says.

"This is equivalent." Argent hands her a handful of platinum and gold pieces. For a moment the blacksmith looks at the coins before throwing them at Argent.

"Ye disrespect me, ye disrespect th' art, and now you dirty foreigners try ta pay me in ya dirty forigen coins!" the blacksmith hops over her anvil and forge, slamming the hand with a hammer-like growth into Argent's face. Almost immediately after a few royal guards rush over, separating us to stop the fight early.

"Wait, are you Mr. La Démence? And Ms. Perpetua, Ms. Leitner, Father Veau, Ms. Chaleur and Mr. Ścianicz! You guys are always welcome in the hall of the king. Here, we can escort you into the palace," the guards say, seeming in awe of us as they bring us over a bridge and into the ninth circle, inner Cocytus, the royal palace. The blacksmith still seems to be angry as she's dragged off. We are brought, mostly of our own will, to the door to the king's chambers, a door made of mahogany with gold and jade trim.

Chapter 27: Regicide of Romanova

The magnificent and grand doors slowly open exposing the palace's innermost chamber. A large bed with curtains made of some sort of translucent fabric a delicate seafoam green. The light of the midday sun beaming in through the large windows on either side of the room. The walls made out of large finely polished marble bricks with jade etchings, the floor covered in a rug with an intricate pattern, and from the ceiling hung a delicate looking glass chandelier. The covers on the bed of matching colors to the curtains looked to be made of silk, made noticeable by their shining in the bright sunlight. The pillows seemingly made of a similar material and in a similar color with white frills traveling around the circumference. There was a person sitting at the end of the bed, their skin smooth, grey in color with fleshy undertones giving it a slight red hue. Their hair, a shining platinum in sharp contrast to their dark grey skin, with a slight waviness flowing down over their shoulders almost reaching their hips. Their ears come to a point at the top. Small dark ram-like horns protruded from the side of their head. A silver crown sat atop their head, exemplified by a jewel of a vibrant and deep emerald hue. Their eyes a distinct red, creating a contrast with the jewel atop their head. They wore clothing of striking white with accents of a dark jade green. It looked to be an almost gaudy military uniform with gold frills on the shoulders, a large white sash going from the right shoulder across to the waist and decorated in several pins and medals. A sword lay sheathed at their hip. They looked to be about a year or so younger than myself. This person...their appearance so flamboyantly feminine, *did we walk into the wrong room? I thought we were to have an audience with the king.*

"Um excuse me, guards I think this is the wrong room..." I look behind me to see that the doors have already closed, and the guards long gone.

"No, please do not be mistaken Mr. Ścianicz, this is indeed the correct room." *With a feminine enough voice to match their appearance, this person couldn't be the king, Could they?*

"But I thought we were going to see the king. No?"

"Indeed, he is right here."

"Wha-"

"I understand your confusion, but the king and myself happen to be the same person, that is to say, I am the king of this land, The Lord of The Eternal Wheel, Nikolae Romanova. You may refer to me as Niko, however."

"Oh! I'm so sorry I had no idea!"

"Please, there's no issue. I understand that appearances can be deceiving. Also, your last name... Ścianicz. Do you happen to have any Demonic ancestry?"

"Demonic ancestry? No, as far as I know I'm completely human."

"I see... Never mind then."

"So... Niko, why exactly are we here?"

"Well, you see, back a few years there was a 'friend' of mine who was killed by an agent of The Assassin King. So, when I heard the people who were responsible for his death were coming here to the Kingdom of Yavolia I went to go see you. What struck me the most was your uncanny similarity in appearance to my 'friend', so I decided to bring you here. As for my appearance. I have always had feminine features, so I decided to embrace it. It helped in my rise to the throne. People thought I was weak, due to my frail appearance. They were sorely mistaken. Anyway, there was something I wanted to do, but since your friends are here, I guess it will have to wait. So, why did you come to my fine land?"

"We are looking to go to the Southernmost point on the continent and planned to take the train through the Kingdom of Yavolia and figure it out from there."

"The Southernmost point! You know no human has gone there and came back right? If you're going to go, you'll need someone to help you. I could go with you, but I won't be available for a few days. I'll have to meet up with you along the way, are you stopping anywhere?"

"Wait, you're saying you'd come with us? But what will happen in the meantime? Don't you have to run the country?"

"Don't worry I can have that all sorted out. So, where can I meet you?"

"Well, we were planning to go to one of the hot springs up in the mountains," Azalea chimes in.

"The hot springs! That's a great idea! I have my own private hot spring in the mountains. You can take the palace line to get there. I'll make sure you're treated well. They know you're coming so don't worry about money, passes, or anything like that."

"That's great."

"Hmm let's see... Well I have some time before I have to go, so why don't I tell you a little about myself. That alright with you Alex?"

"Uhh... sure."

"Well, the best place to start would be how this country works. The way you become king is simple, You just have to kill a certain amount of Demon depending on your rank in society. The lower down the more you have to kill in order to go up the ranks. I was born fairly well off, but I had larger goals, hence why I joined the military and quickly rose through the ranks during a large skirmish with the Kobolda Empire on our southern border. At that point I was a war hero, but it just wasn't enough, So, I killed one of the top generals, then one of the archdukes, and then finally the queen at the time. That's how I ascended to the throne. This is how it's always been in the Kingdom of Yavolia. Only the strong can get to the top, but don't worry, despite all this killing it rarely results in bad blood. You see, when a Demon is born, they are sent off to the 5th circle, a place partially for childcare. Once they are deemed ready, they are released into the world, so us Demons don't really have parents in the traditional sense. The only time when grudges are held is when an outsider gets involved, like The Assassin King... Anyways I do really have to thank you. In killing The Assassin King, you brought peace not only to my country, but to the rest of the world, though the latter was never my concern. Believe me, internal affairs were a mess when he was still around. Sorry for going on and on like this."

"Oh, no it's fine. It's just..."

"What?"

"Oh, it's nothing..." *Back when we arrived in Tirentod from Heizengaard we decided that the fact of The Assassin King being controlled by someone else and him also being our friend was to be on a need to know basis.*

"Also I must apologize for not talking to any of you, I was so fixated talking to Alex that I simply forgot you were there," he chuckles, "On a more serious note, I do have to thank all of you. It would be short sighted of me not to. I do realize that all of you played a part, So, as the ruler of the Kingdom of Yavolia I must offer up my gratitude, we are truly in your debt."

"Oh, there's no need to worry, we already received the bounties about a month ago," Cat remarks.

"That's different, regardless... Don't move."

"Wha-"

"Shhh! Someone's here; Stay out of it." We all step back further into the room, Niko moving in front of us closer to the door of the bedroom. Suddenly, the chandelier falls from the ceiling, hitting Niko. It shatters, sending glass shards across the room.

"Ugh, what a pain." Niko gets out of the broken chandelier looking relatively unscathed, brushing the glass dust off his uniform which had been torn in multiple places. "I just got this uniform. Seriously, interrupting my meeting with Alex too." Niko looks annoyed that his clothes were wrecked, and his chandelier destroyed, but his annoyed look soon turned to one of arrogant confidence. "Trying to take the throne is quite the bold move." Niko looks around the room, a cool air surrounding him. "To try such a thing only a year after I assumed the throne," he shakes his head, "You would think to end my rule so soon? It's unfeasible. My rule will certainly end tragically, but only after a long and peaceful amount of time." His confidence is almost infectious, to the point that my worry almost disappears. I look up to notice a hole has formed in the ceiling where the chandelier once hung. A figure in a dark cloak drops down from the hole. They land on the ground lowering their hood revealing their dark hair and pale red skin. Smooth pointed horns stick out from just above their forehead with a slight upward curve. "So, you've finally decided to come out of hiding and reveal yourself."

"I'll shall be taking that crown off your head, Nikolae Romanova. Let me give you the courtesy of knowing the future ruler of this country's name. Yakov Yurovsky." Niko points his finger at Yakov, and a small ball of metal begins to form in the air. Yakov's face goes pale. The ball of metal zips towards him and just manages to miss his head by a fraction of an inch, hitting the door behind him shredding it into pieces. Niko stands there with a smug look on his face as the shrapnel from the door bounces off him hitting Yakov. He seems to be relatively unharmed by the shrapnel. Again, Niko points his finger out at Yakov, a set of even smaller metal balls form. They zoom towards Yakov's face at an unimaginable speed. Just before impact Yakov sticks his hand out in front of himself. The projectiles drop down to the ground just before they make contact with his body.

"Hmm, seems this may take slightly longer than anticipated. Let's see, maybe three minutes now?" The comment regarding the fight seemed to have slightly angered Yakov.

"I have been planning this my entire life. I won't have it cut short here."

"Your entire life, huh? That means nothing. You could try for hundreds of lifetimes and you still wouldn't even be close to achieving what I have. People such as yourself have no chance at ascending to the throne. I was able to do what I have done, only because it was destined to happen. Aazari holds out their torch, shining the reflected light from the flames of war upon me. You will never bask in such a glorious glow, for your fate has already been decided, and for Aazari's torch burns cold for thee."

"Silence! I will go against fate and light the torch myself!" Suddenly, Niko crashes into the ground, shattering the smooth marble that makes up the floor. Niko is pinned to the ground by some invisible force, unable to move an inch.

"You see it now don't you? That gleaming light. For I hath rekindled the flames of Aazari's torch. Now that your fate has been sealed, your torch begins to cool, and the flames wither. You shall not become one with Aazari." Niko looks smugly up at Yakov. "Why? Why do you smile? Your fate has been sealed. Do you not see? Why would you smile? Could it be?... No!" Niko slowly raises his arm pointing his finger at Yakov. "But how? You shouldn't be able to move." Yakov slowly backs away from Niko.

"You know, the more you doubt yourself the weaker your ability to hold me in place will get."

"How did you know?!"

"It was just a guess, but that pretty much confirms it." Yakov backs up into the wall, unable to move back any further. Niko stands up, brushing the dust off his uniform, walking over towards Yakov. He slouches down to the ground, cowering from Niko.

"May your soul enter the void." Niko puts his index finger on Yakov's forehead creating a ball of metal right on it. He sends the projectile straight through Yakov's head. The force of which causes it to explode, painting the pure white marble wall a brilliant crimson. Niko sighs, "I'll have to get this mess cleaned up. Please let me lead you to the royal station." We get up from the back of the room a bit shocked and begin walking through the palace to the station inside.

"Who was that guy?" I ask.

"He was one of my top military generals. It's a shame too, he was a great tactician, but he can be replaced. There are many fighting for his spot." We get on and are greeted by a luxurious cabin with golden and jade decorations. The train spirals down the palace before leaving the city, headed south for the mountains. The view of the city from the top of the palace was particularly spectacular.

Chapter 28: Ash on the Ashtabula River

Azalea and I were escorted into a private cabin, just the two of us. It's well furnished and has large windows perfect for looking out at the scenery. Will be passing through the Pazuzu Desert and then into a large evergreen forest and after that we'll be in the Azael Mountains where the hot springs are. An awkward silence persists for several minutes. Azalea attempts to break the quiet,

"So, Cat?"

"Yeah?"

"Have you thought about it?"

"Thought about what?"

"You know, what I said back on the ship."

"Uh, yeah. I don't know, Azalea it's just... I don't really have an answer yet. I just need more time to think."

"It's fine, I totally understand. It's going to be a long ride after all." The silence returns and persists for another few hours. *I'm just not sure what to think. What she said on the ship... It was certainly full of strong feelings. I'm still kind of in shock. I'm just not sure what to make of it. To think that I'm that important to another person...* Suddenly, my stream of thought is interrupted by a large bump shaking the train. *Is something going on? There's not going to be another train crash is there?* I look out the window to the front of the train. There's a bright flash, my vision completely whites out. Then there's a blast wave that travels back along the train, my hearing going out too. The train car flies up into the air, I feel weightless in the short moment before the train car hits the ground. I fall unconscious. I open my eyes, my vision still blurry. Brilliant reds, vibrant oranges, and bright yellows; The colors I can see are reminiscent of the trees in autumn. It reminds me of home, a place I left a long time ago. I think back to my time on earth, while it was certainly peaceful it was purposeless. Until I came here, I wasn't really sure what I was meant to do in life. I'm glad to be here with my friends from earth and with the ones I met along the way. My ears ring, engulfing me in only silence. The colors continue to dance in front of my eyes, a sight I remember well. My vision begins to clear as my hearing begins to return. The sound of fire crackling and the sight of smoke rising into the deep and dark night sky, twinkling with the light of thousands of stars and countless embers. The twisted metal wreckage of the train all around me. The fire has already spread to the nearby trees and the locomotive is completely gone, most likely destroyed in the explosion. I attempt to stand, but find I'm unable to move or feel my legs. I'm still able to move my arms. I crawl dragging my useless legs behind me. *No! I have to find them!* I continue to pull myself through the wreckage inch by inch. *I left my life on Earth behind so I could save them!*

"Cat, is that you?" A whisper, almost completely silent; Undoubtedly it was Alex. I crawl over to him, he looks up at me, his face covered in burns and lacerations from the wreckage, almost unrecognizable.

"No. Cat... Not again... I let this happen again..." Tears silently stream down Alex's distorted face. *If they die... Then it's all in vain...* I look up to see that brilliant pale blue. That unforgettable hue. I slowly pull myself over to her.

"Azalea... No..." I try to say, but no sound comes from my throat. I feel as though I'm crying, but whether or not there are tears I'm unable to tell. The pain keeps getting worse and worse, my vision begins to blur again, and my ears start ringing. Within a few seconds my vision blacks out and I'm unconscious again. I regain consciousness to the sight of the warm orange glow of the sunrise and the pale blue glow of Azalea's synat.

"Cat! You're awake!" As soon as I sit up Azalea wraps her arms around me. "I wasn't sure if you'd make it."

"What happened?"

"Well, we think there was some sort of bomb or spell that blew up the train and we all woke up uninjured, but when we found you, you burnt to the point you were almost unrecognizable. I wasn't even sure if you were still alive, but luckily, I was able to heal you back up. It took me all night."

"Uninjured? But when I woke up... That must be it."

"What Cat?" CJ asks.

"Remember when I came back for you all in the factory and we were going up the elevator. I mentioned that I got a third word for my synat, Martyrdom. Burning Song of Martyrdom; that's what I call it. I'd never used it until now. In fact, I even forgot about it for a while"

"So, what does it do?"

"If any of you were to sustain any major injuries, they would all get transferred to me healing you all. Not something I can really use often."

"You're saying, you decided to save all of us at the expense of your own life?"

"Pretty much."

"I'm in debt to you once again Cat."

"What do you mean? If you hadn't healed me, I'd be dead and who knows whether or not I would have been able to come back. I'm alive thanks to you Azalea."

"But still you've already saved me more than once. I'm still in your debt."

"I... How's Alex?"

"He's... Well, you should see for yourself..." CJ replies. He's sitting down against a tree rocking back and forth slowly, his arms wrapped around his knees, tears silently running down his face. Amaryll sitting next to him, her arm on his shoulders. He's mumbling something,

"No... Cat... CJ... I let you down..."

"What happened?"

"I think when he saw your injured face it may have triggered memories of whatever he saw in those visions from Number 10. He just needs some time."

"How are we going to get to the hot springs now?"

"There's probably another train on its way here. The one with the Yavolian King should arrive in a few hours."

"So, we just have to wait until then?"

"Yeah." I walk back over to Azalea.

"You think this was another assassination attempt?"

"On the Yavolian King? No. I think it was someone who's after us."

"Like who?"

"Not sure. Remnants of The Assassin King Cult, Number 02, maybe even those 'Scout group 1' people."

"Do you think they're still nearby?"

"It's not unlikely. We'll keep a lookout and if they come to fight, we'll deal with them." Azalea puts her right fist into her left hand in a confident gesture.

"Well, we certainly aren't at full capacity."

"Yeah, Alex is out of the picture at least for the rest of the day and Amaryll will probably be defending him in case of an attack. Though you and I do pack a decent amount of firepower all by ourselves. No?" Azalea says.

"Yeah, literally."

"Hmm?"

"It's nothing." *Does that not translate well or something? I guess she didn't get it.* "I mean come on, that was pretty funny. Right CJ?"

"Sure Cat. Sure..." *Is my sense of humor really that dry? Oh well guess I'll have to try next-*

"Do you hear that?" I ask.

"Hear what?"

"I heard a rustling behind us in the woods."

"It could be the people who bombed the train. Stay on your guard." A man slowly walks out of the woods.

"Who are you?"

"I'm the head of the Kingdom of Yavolia branch of The Assassin King Cult... Not ringing any bells? Maybe you'll recognize me in my original form." The man slowly transforms into a woman. Her hair is short and black, her skin a sort of maroon, crimson. Argent exclaims,

"Wait! Your Asmodus Stolz!"

"Who?"

"She's that actress I mentioned earlier. She's the most well renowned thespian in the Kingdom of Yavolia. I must say it's a pleasure to meet you. I've been a fan of your work for... well as long as I can remember and-"

"Argent this is the enemy we're talking about here," CJ says.

"But Master CJ..."

"It's alright just let him be a fanboy for a little."

"Master CJ can I-"

"No."

"But..."

"No."

"Now that that has been dealt with. Let the show begin." Her arm morphs into a sort of a blade, the edges turning a little shade and gaining a crystalline appearance. She runs straight for me, her blade arm raised in the air ready to strike. I pull out my broadsword and parry her arm with ease. *Did I learn how to sword fight and then forgot about it?* I started to vocalize and the flames which I had learned how to control wrapped themselves around the blade of my sword, forming a thin fast-moving stream of flames. *What is going on?*

"Oh, a synat weapon, how crafty." She runs at me again, but this time her arm has transformed into a large hammer. She hits my flaming sword with her hammer hand; the blade vibrates in my hand, stunning me for a moment. While I'm stunned, she morphs her hand back into a blade and slashes at me. I'm partially able to deflect the blow, but she hits my right arm, leaving a large gash. *Damn, she's good.* Azalea steps in front of me saying,

"Let me handle her."

"Oh, my how bold. Defending your cute little friend." Azalea removes her scythe from her back. She lunges at Asmodus with her scythe but is narrowly blocked by her blade arm. They hold there for a second, trying to push through each other's defenses. Azalea's scythe begins to dig into Asmodus's flesh.

"Hmph, this means nothing. A small injury will not secure your victory."

"Agreed." Azalea's scythe begins to glow a familiar pale blue.

"Your glowing scythe will help you none."

"Oh, really?" Azalea pushes some extra force through the scythe shattering Asmodus's morphed hand.

"Wha-"

"Surprised? As soon as my scythe dug into your hand it began to freeze, but because it was already crystalized you failed to notice. Then just a little more force and your hand was no more."

"I still have another hand. Your victory is not assured." Azalea runs at Asmodus this time aiming for her head. Seconds before the scythe slices Asmodus's head in half she transforms into an exact copy of myself. In shock, Azalea's aim is thrown off, narrowly missing her.

"You wouldn't hit your precious little friend, would you?"

"You... you bastard."

"What?"

"You bastard! How dare you use Cat's body! I'll kill you!" *Pretty sure that was the plan, but... Rock on Azalea!* Azalea readjusts her aim and drives her scythe straight towards Asmodus's head. She quickly raises up her left arm transforming it into a blade to parry Azalea's strike. While she succeeds in preventing her head from being split like a log, it only saves her a few seconds as Azalea quickly freezes and shatters her only remaining arm. She jumps back just in time saying her own life, but Azalea quickly follows up freezing her. She taps her with the end of her scythe shattering here into countless pieces. *I'm sure Argent's crying inside.*

"Thanks for that Azalea."

"No problem Cat."

"You think there's anybody else around?"

"Probably not, especially after seeing that." Azalea points to the shattered pieces of Asmodus. After we cleared the train tracks, we waited around for an hour or two until the train with the Yavolian King arrives. We get onto the train and sit in the cabin with the Yavolian King.

"Alex! Are you okay?" the Yavolian King exclaims.

"He won't be able to talk for a little while. They'll explain. I'm bringing him into another cabin," Amaryll explains.

"What happened to him?"

"Well, after the train exploded, I was severely injured, and I think when Alex saw my face it may have triggered memories of the visions, he was shown by Number 10."

"Those damn Assassin King Cult bastards! Wait, did you say the train exploded?" We explain to the Yavolian King what had just transpired.

"Asmodus huh... I never would have thought; and you say there might be others in the military? I'll have to look into it. Anyways, you all should relax now, we'll be at the hot springs soon after all."

Chapter 29: The Truth of Theseus

The hot springs, like a light halfway down a tunnel that allows you to see the end. It's a good bit of relaxation before we plunge ourselves into the frost anyway. The water is a bit colder than my tastes, but it'll work.

"So... this is meant to be a way to cool our nerves, right? Before I start, is this cooling our nerves in a partying and drugs way or in a therapy way?" I ask, trying to be funny.

"We don't have drugs, so therapy," Alex laughs awkwardly.

"I've got a snuff box." I stand up and pull it from the pocket of my cloak, making sure my towel doesn't fall.

"Snuff box?" Alex asks.

"Opium." Niko answers.

"I'll pass. If it will be easier for you, I can start on the group therapy thing" Argent suggests.

"I'll take some." Niko reaches a hand to me. I give each of us some of the powder, but not too much. Niko uses alchemy to turn a branch into a pipe to smoke with. *Alchemy exists. Judging from the glow, I think there is a philosopher's stone in Niko's earring. My knowledge of this world's magic is limited, but I read in the church's library that there are four forms of magic: racial magic, the magic of the blood. Psionics, the magic of the mind. Alchemy, the magic of the body, and synats, the magic of the soul. Psionics is the focus of my studies.*

"I don't have any reason to conceal my stuff, my 'friend' died, he looked like Alex, hence the wish to replace him. I killed several people, and I collected their fingers." Niko confesses.

"Why the fingers?" I ask.

"Trophy." Niko answers. *Weird guy.*

"Well, I did say I would go next. If I go then that will set the counterclockwise precedent. My life story is also one of success, but I never harmed anyone. After I was left at the steps of the church as an infant, I was raised in the light of Azathoth by Father McKenzie. Naturally, when he told me about the nature of how I arrived at the church, I fell into a depression, and I heard the voices and saw the faces of the Dark Spider tempting me. This got worse when the father died from a bad batch of bread in the passing, but through prayer and the miracles of Azathoth I was cured. Since then I have presided over the church, and I have not strayed from Azathoth's path." Argent explains. *So, he was delusional, and his delusions lasted during the time of Father McKenzie's death; could he have been involved?*

"A killer and a zealot, yet you're even worse." Kevin taunts. *Bold words.*

"Did you kill the old man?" Niko laughs. *Better he asks than me.*

"No! I am a man of Azathoth, not some sinner!" Argent denies. Even now he's refusing to be clad in just a towel and has worn his ryasa into the spring, so he doesn't exactly seem to be a sinner.

"You saw him kill a man," Kevin comments. *Listen, I doubt he killed one of his own. He's a zealot, and that's the best proof of innocence there is.*

"Well, I suppose I'm next," Alex looks down for a moment, evidently gathering his senses, "During the time I was held captive by Number 10, he forced me to live out false memories where everyone I cared about died. I know it's fake now, but I just can't shake away my fear of how that could happen. I've had nightmares, and during that crash I saw the memories again. That's my secret."

"What a dunce! You've got good cause to be the delusional freak you are, and Argent was an orphan, but he's just a loser who had a nightmare!" Kevin tells me, sitting next to me in the water. *That's a legitimately awful thing to say.*

"CJ, you're up next." Niko points at me. For a moment I consider how much I should say, as well as how much I *can* say with Niko here.

"Well, if this is gonna be some bad group therapy, I guess I've got a lot to get out. How much do you want to hear?" I ask.

"As much as you feel comfortable-" Argent is cut off

"All of it, kid. My favorite actress just died," Niko jokes.

"You should kill him," Kevin suggests.

"Okay then; so, when I was little, my father took me to visit my grandma every Sunday, thing is, she wasn't all there mentally. She never knew who I was, but she often would think I was my father. I hated her, I hated visiting her, and yet when she died, she wasn't the person I was mad at. I was 13 when she died, and I was relieved; she was better off dead, you catch me? Nah, the person I was mad at was my younger cousin, she was loud, and kept on saying stuff like 'why are we burying nanna?' or 'I hate this dress', and that in combination with how much I hated those awful tight fancy shoes, I was ready and willing to throw that little bastard into the grave with Grandma's coffin." I let it all out, from the beginning.

"They're judging you," Kevin whispers into my ear, "better stop now, before they figure out how much of a monster you are under that skin of yours." In all honesty he's not wrong on that first clause, Argent is praying, Niko is smiling, and Alex, he's hard to read, it's either concern or judgement.

"Pity or judgement you mean," Kevin chuckles, "they hate you; they're just being nice."

"So, that night, I went home, and I thought back on how I felt. It's miserable, thinking that the way you feel is wrong; that night I tried to drink away the feeling of being sad that I wasn't sad before, and since then I've had issues with alcohol, usually to deal with stress from school or expectations, y'know? I thought I kicked it about a year ago, but recently it came back," I continue.

"There's still a chance to keep me a secret, keep that last shred of respect from all of them. Keep your true self hidden under your skin, and nobody will hate you." Kevin is trying to intimidate me, but if I know one thing, it's my friends, past tense included; Kevin's left eye twitches under two circumstances, when he's scared, or when he's lying, and right now I think both apply.

"The incident with Kevin?" Alex asks. *Damn, that pause did seem unnatural.*

"In a way. When I killed The Assassin King, under his mask, his face looked just like an old friend of mine he killed named Kevin. I did all the stuff I did since getting here to avenge Kevin, but when I killed The Assassin King, I felt a twinge of guilt." I lie a bit due to Niko being here, "Since then, I've developed this hallucination of him. When on the train to the Kingdom of Aochikyuu, I ended up fighting a Psion named Septimus who could see my hallucination. I've come up with a plan to learn Psionics, so that Kevin may live vicariously through me, almost like a ghost. Either that or I will forgive myself and he will escape the purgatory of my mind," I confess, and in their eyes, I see no judgement.

"Y-you really did it, huh? They're gonna try and get a Psion to get rid of me, you just killed me." Kevin sounds scared, no, terrified.

"Is this specter your friend or The Assassin King" Niko asks, unaware that they are one in the same.

"Some of both," I answer.

"Mr. La Demente, I hold the utmost respect for you, both for the courage in telling me that, and for your prowess in battle, and I would like to make one request. If I kill you to finally banish that monster, please do not hold a grudge in the afterlife." Niko looks into my eyes with both respect and rage.

"I was right!" Kevin exclaims

"Under one condition, don't be mad if I kill you first."

"Deal." Niko extends his left hand to shake mine, and I shake back. I can see that Alex is vaguely concerned, and Argent is now praying even more than before.

"Also, call me CJ," I add.

"So...is this all for our bonding experience?" Alex asks.

"May I recite a quick prayer first?" Argent requests. Niko and Kevin visibly roll their eyes, though I avoid doing so.

"I'll take that as a yes." Argent clears his throat and closes his eyes, putting his hands in a state of reverence. "Blessed be the broken, the vagabonds, and the damned, for they shall enter the second dreaming garden of Azathoth. Blessed be the seers, the blind, the crippled and the failed, for eyes and arms are not needed for prayer. We all find light in Azathoth, blessed be," Argent recites, and while he's speaking, I actually believe that I am blessed by Azathoth. This is his synat, of course, but I still feel compelled to say,

"Blessed be."

"Prayer cured my curse, young master, perhaps you can be cured too" he adds.

"Thank you Argent." The rest of the time in the hot springs is spent talking about all the stuff you'd expect a group of unsupervised teenagers with mental illnesses, magic powers, and a lack of supervision to talk about; women, dudes, a heated debate about politics, the future, philosophy, and dumb things that can be done with Niko's alchemy, some of which we actually did. Also it turns out I can use my synat to make people perceive me as another person under the same clause as invisibility; I discovered this by accident while mocking something Niko said, and while doing so everyone saw my face and body contort some to look like Niko. After leaving a firework-sized hole in the wall and some silver statues of random ideas we found funny, we left and got ready for our train south. Due to Niko's wealth and status, we were able to get one of those first-class rich people trains. I spent most of the trip in the library car, reading by candlelight about psionics and how I could use that to give new life to the hallucination of Kevin. I found what I was looking for, but it wasn't what I wanted to find. The theoretical method necessary to give life to something like Kevin was proposed almost 200 years ago, but never tested. The first problem is that it would require a mix of both alchemy and psionics, which is an even bigger challenge than expected. The second problem is the components; to perform this, I would need a superperfect philosopher's stone with an alchemical karat of 200, which to produce would require 60,000 units of life energy, or roughly 60,000 human souls, though using some other races could decrease that amount. What I would need to do is implant that philosopher's stone into a homunculus with a Mental Cognition Rate of 100, with the last bit of life force in the stone coming from the hallucination of Kevin himself. Naturally, it would be both wrong and nigh-impossible to kill that many living things just to give life to one, but perhaps there is a less dangerous way. Regardless, I began minor preparation for this plan. *Perhaps I could convert some other form of energy into life energy, like electricity to heat?* By the time the sun began to rise, I had read every page of every book in that library about alchemy, and from a couple of mice in the kitchen car, I created a philosopher's stone with an Alchemical Transference Rate of 6.67%. *If the other people attack me first and I kill in self-defense, then it's perfectly fine to put their life into the stone.* By the time it was complete, my candle had burned all the way down to it's base, and the grandfather clock behind me had rung seven times to signal it was seven in the morning.

Chapter 30: Mechanical Monstrosity

We leave the hot springs lobby walking out onto the platform before getting onto the royal train.

"Don't worry about the train. It shouldn't crash again," Niko says.

"You would hope so," CJ jokes.

"As I was saying, there's extra security and I don't think there will be any more attacks from those remaining cultists."

"What makes you say that?" Azalea asks.

"Well, you killed their leader, so right now they have no central leadership and we are currently on a hunt for remaining cult members. I would think most of them are in hiding at the moment."

"You're probably right. It would be pretty risky for them to attempt any sort of attack now."

"Unless they set one up in advance," CJ suggests.

"That's pretty unlikely in my opinion. They're pretty confident and without The Assassin King's cautious style of doing things, I would seriously doubt that they would do something like that. They're just too arrogant," Azalea explains.

"Yes, so you all have nothing to worry about," Niko says, before guiding Amaryll and mc to an empty cabin.

"What is it Nikolae?" Amaryll asks.

"Oh, I just thought you two might want to be alone. After all that happened."

"Your oddly considerate Nikolae."

"Exactly what kind of impression of me do you have? Anyway, there's no need for formality, just call me Niko. You've helped Alex out enough. I can see you two are quite close."

"Quite close?!... I'm not so sure of that." Amaryll seemed flustered by Niko's comment.

"Well, I wouldn't want to bother you two. I'll be leaving now."

"Hey wait! Niko..." She pauses before mumbling to herself, "What does he think he realized?" She looks over at me looking more flustered than before.

"You know Alex you're being awfully quiet."

"I..." I'm not really sure what I should say.

"I'm sorry that was kind of insensitive." Amaryll stairs at the floor. A tense silence persists between the two of us. *She's saved me more than once and I can't even muster up the words to say anything. If it weren't for her... I could be dead or even worse my mind could have been totally broken.* I accidentally whisper something,

"Thank you Amaryll."

"Did you say something Alex?"

"Ah, no I was just... Thinking out loud."

"Oh... Alright then." *Damn! I'm such a coward. I had the opportunity and I missed it.* Niko pokes his head into the train car.

"We'll be in Vencies soon." He leaves quickly before I can say anything. *If I remember correctly Vencies is on the Sea of Sezzin coast. Niko did mention earlier that we'd be stopping there along the way.* After a few short minutes the train stops, and we walk out onto the station platform. *It's supposedly one of the most populated cities in the Kingdom of Yavolia.*

"So, what are we stopping for?" Amaryll asks.

"I Thought it would be good if we spent some time off the train, as an attack in the city would be less dangerous and I thought it would be good to stretch our legs. Also, as Vencies is one of the historic and cultural centers of the Kingdom of Yavolia, I would be a failure of a King if I didn't show off one of it's most beautiful cities." The whole city seems to be built upon a slope leading down to the black sand beaches on the brilliant cerulean waters sparkling in the sunlight. The houses here are a pale off white and have tiled salmon colored roofs. There are small trees all along the black stone brick road. Picturesque is how I would describe it. *There were so many places I wanted to go back on Earth, but being able to travel all over this world... It certainly helps satiate the desire for exploration. If I had the option to go back, I'm not sure I would take it. I do miss earth to a degree, but with the life I found here I don't think I could go back... Especially if it meant abandoning my friends.*

"So, where should we go first Alex?" Amaryll asks.

"Huh? Uh... I-" Niko cuts in.

"Actually, there's a really nice Patisserie nearby. They have the best sweets in the Kingdom. Their right down the street; Jeanlian Patisserie, and don't worry about money, they know you're here with me." Niko points us in the right direction and we're on our way. I look behind us to see that everyone else is gone.

"Where is everybody?"

"Oh, they went to other places. Niko thought we should have some time together." *Not really sure what Niko is getting at...*

"Oh alright." The sign in front of the shop is a pale green with white lettering. Presumably it says 'Jeanlian Patisserie', but as I can't read the script, I'm not sure.

The shop is surprisingly modern with large glass windows and colorful decoration. We find the shop relatively empty and walk up to the display of sweets and pastries.

"What would you like?" The clerk at the register asks.

"I think I'll have a strawberry parfait. What about you Alex?"

"Me...? I guess I'll have the same." The clerk quickly puts it together and puts them out on the counter for us. His hair is a dark brown and his eyes a bright blue. His ears coming to a point at the end.

"I have to ask, are you from the UEF?" Amaryll asks.

"No, actually I was born here. I'm a half elf you see. My mother was a moon elf and my father a human. They moved here right before they had me."

"Really, why'd they move?"

"Well, half elves aren't exactly well liked in the UEF so to speak. They decided to move here so I wouldn't face any discrimination and also partially because of the location. I'm quite proud of my parents. I'm Jeanlian the owner of this shop."

"Oh, nice to meet you."

"The pleasure is mine. You are some of the peace bringers after all."

"Yeah... Well, thank you for the parfaits."

"Of course, I wish you the best." We walk out of the shop and sit down at the tables they had set up outside.

"You know this kind of reminds me of something."

"Hmm?"

"I remember back on earth going to this new shop that had just opened and my parents ordered me a parfait just like this one. It's one of the few memories from back then. I was just a kid after all..."

"Yeah, I guess that makes sense. I don't have too many memories from when I was younger either."

"Sometimes I wonder what would have happened if I had stayed on earth. I've grown up but with almost no memory of it. I have no idea why I am the way I am. All that time is lost to me... almost ten years. I'm not sure if I want my memories back either though. I mean what happened when I was under The Assassin King's control. Do I really want to know what happened? If I got those memories back would it help or hurt me? I don't know." Amaryll is staring into the sky, deep in thought. I try to think of a response, but fall short of finding any words to say. *Damn! I can't even say anything! She obviously is having some internal issues, but I'm too much of a coward to even speak!* It's a perfectly clear day, an endless expanse of blue. It's just the right temperature and there's a cool breeze coming from the shore. People walking up and down the streets nearby. It's almost disconnected from my current reality. Everything seems to fade away, only for it quickly to come back. Despite the clear day it seemed as though there were dark clouds on the horizon. "Anyway, Alex. I do have to say that I am happy with things as they are now."

"Huh?"

"Surprised? While I can't say these are the best of circumstances, it could be a whole lot worse. If you didn't show up, I would still be under The Assassin King's control, doing whatever horrible things they ordered me to do. I got vengeance for my old friends, made some new ones and I met you Alex. So, I'd say things are looking up for Amaryll Chaleur!"

"I..."

"Don't worry Alex, you don't have to say anything. I understand." *But I should say something...* We finish our parfaits and start walking towards the center of the town to meet back up with Niko. We get to the center of town where there's a large fountain with a large statue of a person in the middle.

"So, how'd it go?" Niko asks.

"I'd say it went well," Amaryll replies.

"That's good to hear."

"So, who's the statues of?"

"It's the first Yavolian King, Emperor Lucifer. The founder of the Kingdom of Yavolia. It was built in the city on the thousandth anniversary of the founding, though that was quite a while ago. It is the most famous and important sights in the city." It's quite the grandiose statue. The first Yavolian king is riding on a horse with his sword thrusted up into the air. Niko leans in and whispers something to us, "There's somebody watching us. They're wearing a black cloak and are behind us. Don't look, just act natural. I'll monitor their movements." We both nod in response. I create a preemptive force field to protect us from any ranged attacks. I can see them out of the corner of my eye. Their head slowly turns towards us and then,

"Brrrrrrrrrrt." A hail of bullets comes straight for us mowing down anything in the way. My force field is able to block the bullets, but quickly dematerializes afterwards. *That sound! A mini gun?!* I quickly put another force field back up. The cloak is removed and underneath it is no human, but a robot. It has a sleek metal body, a large camera in the head, and instead of legs there are tracks akin to a tank's.

"It's just like what they describe in the Book of Demonic Prophecy."

"Book of Demonic Prophecy?" Amaryll asks.

"It's an encyclopedia of future events in the Kingdom of Yavolia written by the Second Empress Lilith; it has yet to fail to correctly predict the future." Amaryll pricks her finger with a needle pointing out towards the automaton sending a high-pressure beam of boiling blood it's way. It makes no attempt to dodge, treating it as if it was no threat. The stream hits the robot turning into a fine red mist, but doing no damage. Niko then points his finger out creating a bullet shaped object out of metal before launching it at the robot. It ricochets off doing minimal damage.

"That's never happened before," Niko says

"Well, how fast do your projectiles go?" I ask.

"The maximum speed is 10,000 mph." *Mph? I assume that's part of the automatic translation.*

"10,000 mph... That's like Mach 13 and It didn't go through!"

"Exactly!"

"I have an Idea. You two stay here and I'll handle this. Niko can you make my body a bullet mirror? Just in case my force field breaks."

"Yes. I'll make sure no civilians get hurt either." I walk up to the robot slowly, my force field still up. It fires again,

"Brrrrrrrrt." My force field blocks all the shots, but then breaks again. I quickly put up another.

"Niko, I want you to shoot continuous fire at my force field."

"Why?"

"Just do it. You can control the ricochet so they will bounce right off me if my force field breaks."

"Fine." Niko shoots at the forcefield and it blocks the hit, but breaks immediately after. This happens a few more times until I'm right in front of the robot. It fires again but all of the bullets bounce off me either going into the ground or shooting up into the sky and then landing into the sea. I squat down and uppercut the robot hitting it on the space between the tracks. It goes flying way up into the sky. It shrinks and shrinks until I'm unable to see it. Niko and Amaryll run up to me.

"What did you do?" Amaryll asks.

"Well, I stored all the energy from the bullets it shot at me and the projectiles from Niko and released it all in one punch. It probably sent that thing to space."

"So, the reason you asked me to shoot the force field was so that you could build up more energy?"

"Exactly." The rest of the group shows up after a few minutes.

"What happened?" Azalea asks, seeing all the bullet holes in the ground.

"Well, we were attacked by a robot with a minigun."

"Robot? Minigun?" I explain to Azalea what a robot and a mini gun are.

"With that kind of tech, who could have sent that thing after us?" Cat asks.

"Maybe it's those 'Scout group 1' people. They're supposedly from the Earth's future," CJ suggests.

"It's possible. We'll have to keep our eyes out there could be more. It's probably best if we get moving." I say.

"Agreed." We all leave for the train station boarding the royal train after just a few minutes of waiting. We take our seats. Now we're on the track towards the southernmost border with the Kobolda Empire one step away from 'the base below the ice and stone'.

Chapter 31: Buccaneer O' The Bootstrap

A few hours had passed since the train had departed from Vencies and we're almost at the border with the Kobolda Empire. I slept through most of it. *Things have gotten better with Azalea, after the train crash and all. It's not as awkward as right after what happened on the ship, but that awkwardness hasn't just disappeared. I'm still not sure where I stand on the whole thing. So, until I figure it all out for myself, this awkwardness will continue to be a standout feature of my relationship with Azalea.* The train comes to a stop and we go out onto the platform. We seem to be in some sort of evergreen forest. The trees are large and tall, in fact they're probably the tallest trees I've ever seen. There's a large stone brick wall visible in the distance.

"So, where exactly are we?" I ask.

"Well, we're not too far from the border with the Kobolda Empire. That wall you can see in the distance is the border." Nikolae explains.

"How exactly are we going to cross?"

"Well, the Kingdom of Yavolia and the Kobolda Empire aren't exactly on good terms at the moment. We'll be crossing stealthily with my help." Suddenly looking around I can barely see anybody as all our bodies turn into mirror-like surfaces.

"What did you do?"

"Well, my synat is 'shot *vanity*' after all. So, I turned all your bodies and clothes into mirrors. It should make us harder to spot." We walk over to the stone brick wall. It looks to be about fifteen, maybe twenty feet high.

"So, how do you plan to get over this thing?"

"CJ," Nikolae says.

"Yeah?"

"Do it." CJ places his hand on the wall and then taps it with his finger. Part of the wall shatters leaving a hole just large enough to walk through.

"That works." We walk for another few minutes before a carriage pulls up in front of us. Our mirrored bodies return to normal.

"You're late," Nikolae says.

"I'm deeply sorry your highness."

"It's no matter. Come on everybody get it." We all get into the carriage not exactly sure what's going on.

"I had this all set up in advance. These are special operatives. I obviously can't have military personnel out in another country, especially the Kobolda Empire without causing issues. I'd rather not be known as the Yavolian King who started another war with the Kobolda Empire. They're bringing us to a large cabin on the edge of the tundra. It has all the supplies we'll need. We'll stay there for the night and then head out." The ride is relatively quiet until a few hours later when we arrive at the cabin. The sun is almost totally set, and the stars are starting to show. I head inside and Azalea and I pick a room. *I almost would rather have a separate room, but I guess it's just not the way it was organized. Obviously, I have nothing against Azalea but...* I'm quite tired after traveling all day. With little dialogue I get ready and then hop into bed Azalea soon getting into hers. *At least there are separate beds.* I turn out the lamp and quickly fall asleep. I hear some rustling which wakes me up. I look to my side seeing that Azalea is nowhere to be seen. Unsure of what's going on I get out of bed. Looking out the window, the moon is out and the sky is still dark, it was the middle of the night. I open up the door to hear a relatively loud crunch akin to the sound of someone biting into an apple. I walk out into the Hallway to Azalea standing there leaning against the wall. She had lit one of the candles on the wall to illuminate the hallway. In her right hand was what looked like an onion with... a bite in it? *Did she seriously just take a bite out of an onion like it was an apple?! I mean I know she can be a little eccentric sometimes, like how she's a little clingy with her uncle, but this... I'm not sure what to say.*

"What is it? Cat, couldn't sleep?" *Does she not realize that what she's doing is weird?*

"Uh... no I just heard you getting out of bed and it woke me up. I wanted to know what was going on."

"Oh alright." She raises the onion up to her mouth taking a bite with an audible crunch. *She did it again! Right in front of me! How can she not know? Was she sheltered as a kid? She seriously just took a bite out of a whole onion... I...*

"I'm going back to bed."

"Alright Cat, goodnight. See you in the morning." I walk back down the hallway and into the room. *What did I just witness?* I try not to think about it too much. I wake up again, but this time the sun is already above the horizon. The light is streaming into the room. Azalea is now in the room, though she's already awake.

"Oh, Cat! I was just about to wake you up. Today's an important day after all I can't have you sleeping in."

"Azalea, so about last night."

"What Cat?"

"You know the thing with... the onion."

"Onion?" *Wait? Does she seriously not know? Does she not remember? Does she want me to ignore the whole thing? Is that why she was so nonchalant about it? Was it all a dream? Maybe it's better if I don't ask...*

"Uh... never mind. Forget I even asked."

"Alright." We walk out the bedroom and out into the main room of the cabin. It's made out of large logs and has a faint scent of pine. There is a fire set in the stone fireplace at the back of the room. Everyone is putting on what looks like heavy snow gear. Thick jacket, snow pants, boots, and even goggles.

"Oh, you two are finally awake. Get your gear on, we're heading out. I actually have a surprise for you all."

"Wait Niko." Amaryll says.

"Yeah?"

"Why aren't you wearing any gear?"

"Oh, well I'm a Demon, our bodies adapt to the environment. We have a particular resistance to the cold."

"That's interesting." We put on our gear and walked out of the cabin. It's utterly frigid. The cold wind mixed with snow stings my face. It's snowing very hard. Probably, a blizzard.

"So, what's this surprise you mentioned?" Amaryll asks.

"Hold on, I'll go get it." Azalea's standing pretty close to me. I can see her breath. Suddenly I smell something. *That smell... onion! I can't be.* The scent quickly fades. *It's gone? Was that really her breath? Maybe it was just my brain messing with me. Yeah, that's probably it.* I look over at Azalea, maybe in an attempt to provoke some sort of reaction. She looks at me with a slightly confused and inquisitive face.

"What is it, Cat?"

"Nothing."

"You sure? You've been acting weird all morning. Are you sure you're not sick or something?" *I've been acting weird? Did all that really happen?*

"No, I'm fine. I must have just tuned out for a moment there."

"Alright. If you think anything's wrong you can always come to me. Okay?"

"Yeah, of course." Nikolae walks around the cabin and a minute or two later he comes back around with a large wooden sled, with a capacity for maybe six, seven or maybe even eight people if you tried hard enough. I looked to be well crafted and sturdy. The sled was not the center of attention as with the sled came a group of six sled dogs, which looked to be what you'd call on earth a Siberian husky, though I'm sure they're called something different.

"Aww, they're so cute!" Azalea exclaims, running over to pet them. "I used to have a dog when I was younger. That was a while ago though. What breed are they?"

"They're Khuitenian." Everybody else looked visibly happy, especially Alex. I remember he had dogs back on earth. It certainly brightened up the mood. I'm glad to see Alex happy, he's certainly had a rough time lately. We get on the sled, Nikolae is on the reigns and we head off.

"So, you've done this before?" Amaryll asks.

"Yes, actually. I participated in dog sledding competitions when I was younger. They were near here actually. There was a land exchange a few years ago with the Kobolda Empire. One I'm not particularly happy about, but I would prefer not to start another war." It gets a little quiet, except for the sound of the wind and the dogs running. "Anyway, I did that for a couple years. It has been a while since, but it's not a competition so we should be fine." Nikolae laughs. "Just, hold tight, we should be near the base in a few hours." It seems to just be endless fields of snow. It's already been an hour or two since we left, the forest gradually turned into fields of snow, the occasional bush or small tree. Almost completely devoid of life. I hear a familiar sound. A distinct sound that seems out of place in this world. That sound, the sound of a piston engine. I see it in the distance, the plume of black smoke coming from the exhaust. It has a large metal hull painted black. It looks to be on tracks.

"What the hell is that thing?"

"It's one of those tracked exploration vehicles designed by the dwarves for traversing the northern ice sheets. I heard about some goblin pirates getting their hands on one, but I thought it was just a rumor until now."

"Pirates? Aren't we pretty far inland?" I ask.

"They're land pirates. There are train lines that run through here and the occasional dog sled. They must be using that thing to get around in the colder climate. Wait... It looks like they mounted a cannon on that thing." Boom. They fire the first shot. The cannonball wizzes towards us. Alex puts a force field which shatters upon impact, but succeeds in stopping in it's tracks. Now that it's closer you can easily hear the sound of the tracks clinking as they turn. The cannon gets pulled back into the vehicle to reload.

"Guys I have a plan."

"What is it?"

"Alright so Azalea you can freeze the thing in place, then Nikolae will shoot a hole in it, and that's when I send a thin stream of fire into the thing."

"Got it." We circle around the vehicle and Azalea freezes the tracks in places preventing it from moving. They move the cannon to another gun port and fire. The cannonball hits Alex's force field, but this time it bounces off.

"I wasn't sure if it would work but I made Alex's force field into a bullet mirror." Nikolae brings the dog sled to a stop, forming a bullet shaped piece of metal in front of his finger shooting it out at hypersonic speeds towards the vehicle putting a small hole in the hull. I quickly follow up by sending a thin stream of fire into the hole filling the entire inside with fire. Fire shoots out of the gun ports followed up by an explosion caused by the fire igniting the remaining fuel and gunpowder. My plan had worked. Nikolae pulls on the reins and we're back on our way to the base. There are mountains out in the distance.

"I had a feeling something like this might happen," Nikolae says, "Though to be fair I thought it would have been border guards, but..."

"Well, it was what you'd call a chance encounter," Amaryll says.

"Yeah, you're right. I'm pretty lucky it wasn't border guards. That would have unprecedented consequences for the Demonic peoples. The border guards would also have been harder to deal with. They are specially picked for combat oriented synats and good ones at that. Though when you think about it maybe them being in the military would lead to death synat that's good for fighting. So, these people are predestined to join the military."

"It's a bootstrap paradox," Alex says.

"Bootstrap paradox? I've never heard that term before."

"Well, it's related to time travel, but in this case with synats having some way to perfectly predict one's death. If them dying in the military in the future is what causes them to have a good combat synat and so they get picked to join the military they join and then they fight and die. Them dying in the future caused them to be in the military and die. There's no beginning for the information; it is a causal loop. The question is, does dying in the future cause them to get a good synat leading to said death or is being born with a good synat what leads them to join the military and to die? Is it the death that causes the synat or the synat that causes the death?"

"That's a good question, but not really one you can answer. Oh, and by the map we should be right around where the base is." There are mountains right in front of us. We climb up and after only a few minutes we find the entrance. There are large, reinforced metal doors. I try blasting fire at them for them to melt the door but to no avail.

"Don't worry I got this," Nikolae says. Nikolae forms a metal ball in front of his finger and sends it flying at the door. The force alone blasted the doors open destroying whatever was keeping it shut. There's a long staircase leading deep down into the mountain. A familiar sight. Hopefully the ending to this journey won't be a familiar one.

Chapter 32: The Penultimate Battle

It feels weird to be at this stage of progress; the awkward stage of being almost there. Too early to celebrate, too late to get cold feet. Not that I have cold feet, just theoretically, y'know? Unlike the prior bases, this one appears to have an elevator. Functional lights too, and signs of use. My name is Clark Julius La Demente, and my goal is within my grasp.

"You really do think highly of yourself. Thinking like a megalomaniac, it'd be cute if not so terrifying," Kevin comments. There are eight people in this elevator, that means seven living people, five humans, five earthlings, four from the crash, or two alchemists, yet there is only one me.

"Shut it, at least I exist," I retort.

"That's not a comeback, moron."

"Speaking of coming back, what's the deal of you getting revived three times and still ending up dead? Couldn't use a comeback if it, I don't know, T-boned you?" In hindsight, I should not have said that, because now everyone is looking at me funny.

"You made this problem, you'll suffer from it," Kevin begins to vanish.

"You know, I don't think you ever did tell us how you died. Car crash, huh?" Amaryll comments.

"Because somebody couldn't drive." I jokingly tease Cat.

"It was 100% the other driver's fault."

"Yeah, fair." The elevator door opens, and most of the area seems to have been evacuated recently. There is one guard, a woman, who hasn't noticed us yet. *I recognize that woman, she wrote the journal entries in those files! Her photo matches perfectly.*

"I got this, stay quiet" I say. I use my synat to make myself appear as the Scout Group Leader from the file and walk towards her.

"Oh! Sir, I didn't realize you were there, I thought you were-" I cut her off, moving closer to her. *Unrequited love, how sad, yet so useful.*

"I have some...personal business...to attend to here. Wait for me in my office, I'll fill your shift here. Sound good sweetheart?" I internally cringe from my own behavior, but to her it seems like her unrequited lover is flirting.

"Are you sure? You specifically told me not to leave my post, no matter what."

"That was then, this is now. If you want to stay here and guard, I won't stop you-"

"It's no problem sir, I'll wait in your office!" the woman cuts me off, sounding excited. She briskly walks in the direction of the Scout Leader's office. Once she's gone, I return to being CJ and gesture for the others to follow me.

"How'd you know it was her?" Alex asks

"I saw her in the file."

"And how'd you know that would work?"

"I didn't." We continue down the hall. Suddenly, from behind the corner, I feel a gun against my temple.

"I knew you were a doppelganger, but I couldn't shoot you then because you might have been real. Now I know you're fake, and I'll get a promotion." the guard from before sounds mad.

"Ah, that's your mistake," I turn into the Scout Leader again, "you should have shot first and talked later." I intentionally laugh to piss her off.

"What, you think I'll fall for that twice?"

"Not in the slightest. The thing is, my synat ability isn't shapeshifting, it makes you perceive me as the person I become. Even if you know it's me, your subconscious thinks it's him, and thus won't shoot," I smirk, wanting her mad, "now, hand me the gun."

"Uhh, no?" the guard refuses, but I see her hesitate.

"Are you sure?"

"Yeah." She hesitates again, but now her answer doesn't matter. I've touched the wall with my hand, and thus can make part of it fragile, allowing me to drop a chunk of the ceiling on her head.

"Tragic," I pick up the gun and become CJ again.

"Well then, that went well," Nikolae chuckles.

"Agreed." A voice from behind us chimes in, saying

"A truly marvelous show. You should go into theatre, the spot of Argent's favorite actress opened recently," I recognize that voice. After all, who could forget someone like Number 02. *Or I guess technically Number 01 now.*

"You again? You're the only recurring antagonist here," Amaryll sighs.

"And not even directly," Azalea adds.

"Listen, I'm all for building up a rapport, but I'm the funny one," Number 02 smiles.

"You really aren't," I comment.

"Oh really? Fine then" suddenly, reality begins to change, and there is now a table blocking the hallway.

"That's neither comedy nor a hindrance." I decide to start running, gesturing for the others to follow. I slide over the table, and suddenly, the table is gone.

"But that sure was funny!" he begins to laugh.

"And you bought three seconds." Nikolae shoots at him and continues to run. I hadn't gotten up yet when the table returned, cutting off Nikolae's legs.

"Ah! Damnit!" Nikolae bites his lip, writhing in pain.

"I can fix this, just distract him!" Azalea begins to form new legs for him, but it'll take a while.

"I got this!" Cat shoots a ball of fire at him, but he manages to evade it somehow.

"Honestly, I'm kind of just messing with you," he throws an apple at Cat, hitting her in the head. It does nothing. I notice a sign up ahead that's in English, reading 'Power'. I get an idea, running over to that room. I see a device labeled 'power converter', and place the Philosopher's Stone in it. *I'm past the awkward stage of being an arm's reach from success. I have won, without a drop of blood being spilled.* Once it charges, I start breaking as much as possible. The lights, vents, and heat are now broken. Once I return to see the fight, I see that Cat's fire is the main source of light now, and Alex is unconscious. I think that he's been hit with something blunt.

"Oh, someone has been causing issues; did you know that, until the backup generator starts, there's only a day's worth of air?" Number 02 smiles.

"I see. Say, do you believe in magnetism? The idea of opposite polarity things being drawn together, as similar ones are repelled?" I ask.

"Oh! The dramatic monologue with a question to engage the listener! I use that gimmick! And yes, I believe in magnetism," Number 02 replies. Argent starts sneaking behind him.

"You and I are very similar. We both believe in chaos and freedom as the path to a better world, for this reason you and I repel. You and hell are very different, as hell is the ultimate form of order, and as a result you are being pulled into hell," I dramatically monologue.

"Oh! That's a good one, kid. If this is what we're doing, do you mind if I use a gimmick line like that?" Number 02 asks.

"It's only fair, do you want constructive criticism?"

"Sure," he clears his throat, "there are many forms of chains in this world, but there are three I would like to emphasize; the chains of the slave, the chains of the master, and the chains of the bystander. No living thing is truly free right now. The slave is the most obvious. The bystander is bound by inaction or consequence. Finally, the master, chained by their own responsibility to the slave. Some are freer than others though. No living being is free unless all others are free. I will destroy all chains," Number 02 monologues.

"Hmm, a bit wordy, but I like it, and I agree. Want another one?" I offer, needing to buy Argent more time.

"Sure."

"Thank you," I smile, "in this world, all living things inevitably die; that is the most basic rule of all things. There is a loophole there, nothing forbids the return of the dead. I have become Prometheus; I have charged a philosopher stone to the needed degree for my ultimate plan to revive Kev-The Assassin King."

"Hmm, the stutter at the end kind of messed it up for me. Otherwise, I like it"

"Thank you. Naturally, I assume you know why I'm saying this, right?" I ask.

"Buying time?" Number 02 sighs.

"Yep." Argent breaks the water pipes, causing two effects; water is slowly flooding the area, and one of the chunks of metal flies at Number 02. Finally, the first successful hit on Number 02, a combo of myself and Argent.

"Damn. Smart move with the pipe, but what's the deal with the water? Or is that just collateral?" Number 02 asks.

"Well, there is one thing I should emphasize: water has not only covered the floor, but the walls and ceiling too." I point at him theatrically.

"Cut to the chase"

"Fine. Azalea!" Just as planned, Azalea manages to catch her cue, freezing the water just well enough to freeze him in place but not harm anyone else. *Hit Number 02*.

"Okay, this one I can give you props on."

"Thank you. Next up, Cat, transfer your wounds to Amaryll, then start creating steam under Number 02!" I shout. Cat's injuries mostly vanish and instead appear on Amaryll. Cat then starts creating steam under Number 02.

"Is this meant to burn me? Because it just stings," Number 02 asks.

"Nope. Your synat needs you to be able to know where a target is, thus-" Amaryll jumps up and lunges for Number 02 her fist less than an inch from his face when suddenly Number 02 appears a few feet to the left of where he just was almost as if he had teleported. Amaryll, still in the air, flies into the floor, falling unconscious.

"You people really are funny." Number 02 begins to laugh, "Did you seriously think you could harm me? My synat is the embodiment of chaos. You are not at fault for being unable to touch a being like me. I am just on a more elevated plane of existence."

"That's very arrogant of you-"

"Not like you're one to talk," Kevin remarks. I decide to ignore him for now.

"Embodiment of chaos? How can it be true chaos if you can control it?"

"That is what you may think, yes, but as I myself am the harbinger of chaos my control over my synat is just chaos creating more chaos. Therefore, it is even more chaotic in nature just like a double pendulum."

"A good retort."

"You have amused me, but now that amusement has faded. I'm sure the role of the dice will bring us together once again." Then without any sign of movement Number 02 disappears. Once Azalea manages to heal all of us including waking up Amaryll, we continue down the halls of this building. "It's weird thinking I might live again," Kevin comments.

"Yeah," Alex agrees. For a moment I don't realize what's wrong with that.

"Alex, what are you saying 'Yeah' to?" I ask.

"Kevin-" Alex realizes what he heard and said.

"You can hear him?!?"

"I can see him too…" There is a moment of silence among all eight of us. Alex looks down at the floor. He looks up, tears slowly moving down his face.

"Kevin… your back." He rushes over to hold Kevin in a tight embrace, but Alex runs straight through him.

"I… uh…" Kevin looks shocked, confused, and somewhat flustered, "I am still a hallucination you know."

"This is gonna be something to talk about later. For now, we have more important concerns." I smile.

"I'm sorry to leave when something important is about to happen, but something's happening back in the kingdom. I'll be back by the time you guys are done and if I'm not I'll have someone to help you back," Niko says.

"Alright Niko. See you," Alex says.

"Goodbye Alex. See you soon." Niko runs back down the hallway towards the entrance. Before us lays a door made of metal, but slightly fancier metal. It has, as an engraving in the door, the name "Scout Leader Oliver Lucius." *We are at the edge of victory. Months of work, all for this. I think I turn seventeen tomorrow; I can't remember the dates well. If I've lost track, I suppose I get to choose; tomorrow I will be a new man, for I will have won, and so tomorrow is my seventeenth birthday. I miss my mom and dad.*

"So, this is it, isn't it?" Cat asks.

"Yes, it is," a voice says from behind us, an unfamiliar voice, but I can hazard a guess that he's Scout Leader Lucius.

Chapter 33: Progressus Ultimum

I hear a sigh from the assumed Scout Leader Lucius as I open the door. Strangely enough, looking to the side of the room there seems to be another door into the room. "What a bother." He turns around to face us in the office chair he's sitting in, standing up. He looks up from the clipboard in his hands, adjusting his rectangular glasses. He tries to fix up his messy dark brown hair. He puts the clipboard down on the desk taking his two hands and straightening out the unbuttoned white lab coat he's wearing. "Did that girl Leal not stop you on your way?"

"Leal? Oh, you must mean that guard we ran into earlier," CJ says, walking through the doorway into the dim room only lit by the blue glow of computer screens, "She's currently out of commission."

His eyes widen in surprise for a second, a hint of concern visible on his face just for a moment. "Out of commission? You don't mean..." Despite the thoughts surely going through his head at the moment he shows little to no emotion on his face.

"Don't worry, she's still alive, just unconscious," I say, out of some sense of humanity. CJ looks at me with a look of disappointment almost. *This person they're responsible for everything... Kevin's deaths, Amaryll's lost memories, Azalea's lost brother, and the deaths of thousands. So why...? Why would I show any humanity to such a person? I'm not sure...*

"Well, it's good to know she'll still be of some use. Anyway, who exactly are you people?"

"Huh?" CJ looks shocked.

"We're Kevin's friends! The person you turned into The Assassin King to do your bidding!" CJ is visibly fuming.

"I'm not sure what your... Oh! Actually, I do remember Number 02 saying something about Number 01. I never actually met him of course."

"You never met him...? You're lying! Number 02 even said he was under your orders 'father'." CJ exclaims, putting his hand on the wall in an attempt to make the ceiling fall down onto the Scout Leader.

"'Father'? I guess he would refer to me that way, but no I haven't had contact with him in years. Fine, since you're being such nuisances, I guess I'll indulge in your petty violence." Suddenly, we're back in the hallway, Number 02 right in front of us. *Huh...? What? But we were just...* I put my hand to my head which starts to ache, and my mind clouds up.

"You have amused me, but now that amusement has faded. I'm sure the roll of the dice will bring us together once again." Then without any sign of movement Number 02 disappears... again? Azalea heals us all before we begin walking down the hallway.

"It's weird thinking I might live again," Kevin comments. *Wait, this has all happened before.*

"It is weird isn't it?" I ask, looking over at CJ.

"Alex, wait, you can hear him? You don't look surprised. Wait... This... It's already happened. What's going on?!"

"Calm down CJ. I'm not sure what's happening, but this is probably the synat of the Scout Leader."

"You're probably right. It's almost like time has rewound."

"Yeah... We should probably go back to that room." We run down the hallways back to the room we met him in. I open up the door, the blue glow of computers coming from the doorway, but the Scout Leader is nowhere to be seen.

"He must've gone somewhere else." Suddenly I feel my weight leave me. Looking down there's a square hole in the floor about 6 feet in size. The hole goes down maybe 15-20 feet before it goes into a large open room. I prepare to dampen the force of the fall. I put up a force field. As soon as we hit the floor the force field absorbs the impact from the fall preventing any injuries. The room looks to be some sort of command center. There's a huge screen on the back wall displaying what I would assume to be a map of this world. Lining the back of the room are smaller computers at desks that are all linked together with their displays showing several different technical programs, most likely related to the facilities at the base. There he is standing in the middle of the room. He adjusts his glasses again.

"This place used to be a lot livelier, but now it's just the two of us. We lost most of them during the search for the numbers. Though that was a long time ago now. I assume you're not here to talk."

"What exactly would there be to talk about?! You're responsible for the deaths of thousands and maybe millions! And especially... and especially... Kevin's," CJ exclaims.

"I see you're not in the mood to hear me out." *I have my hesitations about this guy. If he really is responsible for all that he sure doesn't act like it. Honestly, I would like to hear what he has to say for himself, but even if he has the purest intentions, we can't take the risk. If Niko was here, I could be a little more confident, but...* I put up a force field in case of any attacks. "I wish you would stop bugging me and interrupting my work and I would like to resolve this peacefully, but it seems that is no longer an option."

"CJ I don't know if this guy-" Kevin is cut off by CJ, "I'm doing this for you okay. So, stay out of it."

"I..."

"What no snarky come back?" Kevin stays silent. There's been something I'd wanted to try ever since I got those throwing Knives back in Cocytus. *Luckily, I have some stored energy from that fall earlier.* I take out one of the throwing knives hidden on my belt. I point it at the Scout Leader and send it flying at him with the stored energy. He puts his hand out and an area of about 6 cubic feet in front of him including the knife shrinks down to an infinitesimally small point before disappearing with a bright flash of blue light. *Huh?* It must've created a vacuum as I feel air rushing from behind me towards the point at which the knife disappeared.

"You know It's taken a long time to perfect this ability. You are very interesting. Being able to have such good control over your synat in such a short time." CJ turns himself invisible, only to the Scout Leader though, and rushes towards him with his dagger. Just moments before the knife plunges into him he looks down at his watch. "Ah, times up." That same strange feeling again. The scene swiftly changes as we're right in front of that small room in the hallway with the plaque that reads Scout Leader Oliver Lucius. *It happened again! Time rewound!* I open up the door to see that same office chair and computer screens, but Lucius is gone. We run out of the room in search of a staircase or an elevator. After a minute or so of searching, we find an elevator that goes down. It opens up and we walk inside right before it starts to move down. There's a display inside that says we're going down to BF10. The elevator stops and we all get out. We walked down a short hallway and into the command room, but he was not there.

"Where is that bastard?" CJ asks.

"He could've gone back to his room while we were searching for a way down here," I suggested. We take the elevator back up and run back to his room. We burst through the door and just like I thought he's sitting there in his chair.

"You all figured that out quite quickly. There's really not enough room to use that in here... Is there?" He looks down at his watch and sighs, "I guess that's it for me then." CJ rushes towards him with his dagger, but at the same time someone bursts through the door on the side of the room placing themselves in front of Lucius, their arms put up to shield him. CJ continuing his movement stabs the dagger right through their left arm but fails to kill them or Lucius.

"You... You're that girl from earlier. Leal!"

"Wait, just let him explain. We didn't know anything about 'The Assassin King' or 'Kevin'. He has no idea what you were even talking about. If you just let him talk, you'll understand." She's barely able to get the words out through the pain.

"There's nothing for him to say." CJ pulls the knife out and moves it back ready to stab Lucius. Leal falls to the floor clutching her arm.

"CJ stop!" I grab CJ's wrist preventing him from killing Lucius.

"Alex... Why? This man he's responsible for everything. He's the scourge of this world!"

"CJ, I think we should at least hear what he has to say. If he knows something, we need him alive to tell us otherwise questions go unanswered. I mean what if he's not responsible? Are you okay with just killing an innocent man? Is that what Kevin would have wanted?"

"It would just be another body on top of the pile I've already made and besides how would you know 'what Kevin would have wanted' I knew him better than you did!" Tears begin to form in CJ's eyes.

"CJ... I..." I'm at a loss for words. *This person... Is this really the same CJ from before? What happened to the CJ that would go and hang out with us? We'd crack jokes, laugh, and talk about what was really important to us. He's the closest friend I've ever had, yet right now he feels so distant. Where? Where did that CJ go?* Tears begin to form in my eyes.

"Let go Alex." CJ says sternly.

"I can't CJ. I can't let this go on. Why CJ? If you keep going, I feel... I feel like you won't be able to come back."

"Let go!"

"Stop this Young master CJ."

"Argent? You too?"

"I don't want this for you Master CJ. Please just listen to what he has to say. If he truly has done what you think he's done you can kill him, but only after you hear him out."

"Argent. Do you really think it's possible that he's not responsible?"

"I do Master CJ."

"Alright. I'll hear him out, but by the end of his explanation if I don't believe him, he's dead."

"Thank you for seeing reason, CJ." I wipe the tears from my face. I'm relieved. *I thought I had just lost a friend, but it seems as though he's almost found. The light is travelling beside him.*

"Thank you for giving me a chance, but please heal Leal first."

"Right!" Azalea says, immediately going over to heal her.

"Well, to begin I will state that I had no knowledge of 'The Assassin King' nor any involvement with him or his actions. If you don't mind me asking, how exactly did you find this place?"

"He's telling the truth master CJ."

"If you say so Argent then I'll believe him and to answer your question it was a combination of a riddle and the journal entries we found at your other bases."

"Journal entries? I'm not aware of any such-" Leal cuts him off.

"You read the Journal entries?!" She looks as though she might faint, whether or not that's because of us reading the journal entries or the stab wound in her left arm I'm not sure.

"Yeah, is that a problem?" CJ asks.

"It certainly is..." she says meekly and looking quite embarrassed.

"Regardless of that we need to ask you some questions."

"Please, ask."

"Alright, who are you, where are you from, how did you get here, and what is your relationship with Number 02?"

"Well, to start I am Oliver Lucius the leader of this scout group and this is my assistant and secretary Leal Reine we work for ATUR."

"ATUR?"

"It stands for Alliance of Trans-Universal Research."

"Trans-Universal Research?" *I do remember Kevin saying something about this world being an alternate universe.*

"Well, as you may or may not already know, we are from the Earth, specifically the year 2267. ATUR was founded to find a way to another universe capable of human habitation."

"You're saying you're from the future!?" I exclaim.

Chapter 34: Postultimum

"The Future? I guess from your perspective it would be the future. You see ATUR wasn't founded for some reason like expanding the knowledge of humans, rather it was created to deal with a problem. Let me tell you a little history. So, in 2036 the physicist Dr. Mark Pendrick theorized about an object called a Pendrick gate, a stable space time structure that could allow for travel to other universes via Kerr black. Years later in 2084 his son Elijah Pendrick was able to create a Pendrick gate and the first human expedition through began. Unknown at the time the Pendrick gate they created was unstable and unable to be traversed, still being unaware they attempted to send two people through. Elijah Pendrick's daughter Elise Pendrick and her longtime friend Orion D'arcy who were 18 at the time. When they attempted to go through, they were pushed back out of the gate as it collapsed leaving them in a coma for nearly two years. Strangely enough when they awoke, they reported having a shared comatose dream, to this day the reason this occurred is unknown. Inspired by his time working in the scientific field early in life Orion became a scientist himself. He was a staunch safety advocate to prevent such an occurrence from happening again. He was well renowned in the field of nano technologies and in the year 2097 he founded Orion Nano Technologies widely known as ONT. He found great success in his advances in nano medical technology and his company quickly became one of the most profitable in the world. Then, in the year 2135 he created his magnum opus, a nanobot that could rearrange subatomic particles; they quickly gained the nickname The Alchemist due to their ability to rearrange subatomic particles they could literally turn lead into gold. Their extreme abilities lead to quick terraforming of and colonization of Venus and Mars. This also eventually led to nano bots that were able to extend people's life spans far beyond their previous limits. By extending the telomeres on people's chromosomes they were able to stop aging entirely and theoretically give someone an infinite life span. While this was hailed as the greatest medical discovery of all time it led to problems later on. ONT was the most powerful company in the world with a CEO that had the reputation as the man that discovered immortality. People lived prosperous lives as most issues humanity faced had disappeared, poverty, hunger, disease, and war were things of the past. For almost a century humanity thrived, but as time went on a problem began to arise, Overpopulation. People weren't dying so the population went up and up and even with all the room on other planets conditions began to become cramped. By 2250 the average population density of the planets was over 200 people per square mile. The human population had outgrown its bounds. So as a way to deal with it ATUR was founded as a daughter company to ONT by Orion's lifelong partner and spouse Elise Pendrick. Within only a few years they were successfully able to find a way to create a stable Pendrick Gate, but it would not be easy. They would have to send an expedition to a nearby blackhole to harness its energy to create one. This is where we come in. In 2276 we left earth, headed for the nearest

Kerr black hole to earth V616 Mon, 858 parsecs away. With the most recent development in space travel faster than light engines via Alcubierre drives were now commonplace which could achieve up to 300 times light speed. Within a little bit less than a year we had reached the nearest black hole and successfully created a Pendrick Gate and travelled through. When we got through the other side, we saw a planet with an appearance almost exactly like Earth's. Something strange we observed is that relative to Earth, time here moved backwards and the relative rate varied as well. We landed on the plains just north of the Piliverre mountains."

"Wait, you're saying you're the great invaders?" Alex asks.

"Yes, I think that is the colloquial term for us. We named this world Sotaqt meaning reverse time world, a little literal. We then found tribes of humans nearby and we attempted to communicate with them, but to no avail. Our surveying showed that this was most likely an alternate version of the Earth and would be perfect for habitation, but the population of humans was far too high and would cause issues. We weren't sure what to do, but then something unexpected happened. There was a hidden protocol built into our ship that we had no knowledge of. It was to release a nanobot virus to thin out the population of another world if the readings were too high. So, as soon as those readings were recorded it activated. This nanobot virus is known as Synthetic Nano Autoimmune Transmitters or SyNAT."

"Wait, SyNAT you mean like the powers all the people including us have here on Sotaqt?" I ask.

"I'll get to that in a moment. So, this virus ended up killing over 90% of the human population on Sotaqt. I was horrified. I was totally unaware of this protocol if I had known I would have tried to stop it. We began to notice something strange in the living population. The virus caused them to gain strange powers, these are now known as synats."

"So, synats are actually the work of nanobots?"

"Yes, these nanobots in their extremely advanced abilities are able to give people these powers, though we are unsure how. To continue, another strange thing began happening, certain groups of the survivors began to mutate and change into the multitudes of races you see now such as, Elves, Kitsune, Demons, etc. This is known as the great transformation."

"Alright, that explains a lot, but how exactly do you know Number 02?" CJ asks.

"Well, about a thousand years ago we got orders from Orion D'arcy himself to find him a new body among the population here. We were unsure of why, but we began the search for ten candidates; most of our members died during this campaign leaving just me and Leal. Number 02 was the second most qualified candidate."

"So, what happened to Number 01?"

"Well, the original Number 01 was actually Number 02's biological brother and we raised them together, but he died in an accident at the base. After that point we began to see less and less of Number 02 as he would leave the base often and not come back for long periods of time. Soon the other numbers followed him. I think he was searching for a new Number 01.

That's probably how he ended up finding your friend Kevin, but why he would make him The Assassin King and control him I'm unsure. I hadn't seen Number 02 in over a hundred years until just before you got here, he came to visit me and he mentioned this Assassin King briefly, but he didn't go into detail."

"So, you're saying that Number 02 was the one orchestrating all of it the entire time? He killed Kevin?"

"Based on what I know, that seems to be the most likely scenario. I assume he killed him when he got out of his control. He probably had some sort of device implanted into him so he could kill him at the click of the button."

"So, we've been chasing the wrong people this whole time?" I ask.

"I guess so."

"So, then what about ONT and Orion? You came here to scout for colonization, correct? So, will there be more of you?"

"It's highly likely I'm just not sure when. I was appalled by the actions that led to the deaths and personally I don't want to work for him anymore and now seeing you all standing up and defying the odds, I think if we work together, we can stop another atrocity from happening."

"I think you're right. If it will help us get revenge for Kevin and track down Number 02 then I'm willing to cooperate," CJ says. *A lot of this is going over my head. I'm sure Azalea, Argent, and Amaryll feel the same way, but this alliance does seem like a good idea.* "Alex what do you think?"

"I agree. I think if we work together, we can accomplish our goals." Alex shakes hands with Lucius.

"Well, now that we'll be working together, I should know your names. I've already told you, but I'm Oliver Lucius or just Oliver works." We introduce ourselves before moving to a meeting room.

"Alright, one more question for you Oliver. Why are we here?" Alex asks.

"What do you mean?"

"Well, we're from earth at least some of us, specifically the early 2020s. We died in a car crash so why are we here on Sotaqt and not dead."

"Ah, you're talking about the Postmortem Earth Sotaqt Habitation initiative or the PMESH initiative for short. It takes the minds of people who died in non-natural ways back on earth and brings their mind into a replicated version of their body onto Sotaqt. This was a way to start a population of Sotaqt and propagate Earth-like culture to make things go smoother with the remaining natives."

"Alright so how exactly does that work?"

"Well, we send nanobots back into the past via a Pendrick gate and create a digital copy of someone's mind just before death as well as a copy of their body and clothes. The criteria include any person who died in between the years 1940 and 2150. They have to die from non-natural causes other than disease or aging. Things like getting murdered, suicide, getting into a car accident, dying in a hurricane, etc. all ways one would be selected for the program. Only a small number of these people are chosen however so as to not overwhelm the local population. Only 0.1% of these people are selected. As a sort of a fluke of the algorithm that picked these people, all of the people who died in the bombing of Hiroshima and Nagasaki were transported to right before the SyNAT virus was released. Their descendants are now known as the Multitudes of Kitsune countries that live in northwestern Azaronia. So, the reason you are here is because you were selected for said program and brought to Sotaqt. Another part of this program was to study the power that came from SyNAT and so if a person who came here from earth were to die there is another 0.1% chance they would be transferred via Pendrick gate to a slightly different earth than the one they died in and if they were to die again they would be transferred back to Sotaqt, but due to the opposing directions of the flow of time in our two universes they would be sent into the past of Sotaqt relative to when they first arrived."

"So, that's the reason I have the three-word synat?" I ask.

"Exactly, it's also the reason you were sent two years in the past. This was all to study the development of these powers. It has been what I've been studying these past few thousand years."

"So, all the weird phenomena in this world were caused either directly or indirectly by you?" CJ asks.

"Yes. As much as I dislike him it would be wrong not to recognize the genius of Orion D'arcy. The Alchemist is the pinnacle of human achievement. It led to immortality, cross universal travel, faster than light travel, colonization of other planets. I think the power must've gotten to him. I mean the world is in the palm of his hand. I've never met him personally, but I hear he was quite the good person when he was younger. He's solved all of humanity's problems, but what he's done and what he's trying to do now... I can't vouch for that."

"Agreed, but on another note is it possible you could move to a base closer to Tirentod. Coming down this far south is quite the chore," CJ says.

"There's no need. There's an advanced rail system called the Super High-Speed Tube Rail also known as SHSTR sometimes pronounced Shuh-ster that connects all the bases. You can go between bases within minutes. There should be one nearby Tirentod that you can go to. Here's a map of the lines." I take the maps handing one to CJ and one to Cat, pocketing the third.

"Really? That must be how Number 02 got around so quick," Alex says.

"Most likely. Anyways, I'll take you to the SHSTR station. It should only take about 20 minutes to get to the base near Tirentod. They're hypersonic after all." Oliver leads us to the elevator where we go all the way down to BF20. It's a relatively small room with a tube with an opening in the wall which is about 10 feet in diameter. A pod comes up to the opening and a door opens up.

"When you need to come back to talk, come through this." We get in and the door as well as the opening on the tube shut. The inside is similar to a small airplane with well-furnished seats, but no windows. We sit down and within 20 minutes it stops. We get to a familiar sight, a base just like the others. We find our way out and go to the church.

"Welcome home Master CJ, Father Veau."

"Ah, you haven't met her yet, this is Sister Rubral," CJ explains. We go and sit down at one of the tables in the room.

"So, what do we do now?" I ask.

"Maybe it's best if we split up again. We could cover more ground and see what we can do to find Number 02, but the incursion isn't really something we can deal with at the moment."

"I agree with Alex," Azalea says, "I'm sure with help from the EIA we can find Number 02 a lot faster."

"Agreed. I hope this goes well and we catch that bastard. Good luck ," CJ gives a nod of assurance, though there is an odd, dark light behind his eyes.

Chapter 35: The Zealot and The China shop Bull

Light is a myth invented by the beast of mankind. Darkness is the true nature of life, just as much as light; the balance of night and day, dark and light, is what gives both meaning. However, light is only natural to us; the true natural state of all things is darkness, the absence of light. There is a darkness inside me, one that will never be lit; eating candles is weird, yet I am hungry. As a result, my only choice is cheese and bread.

"We're almost out of that, should I purchase more?" Argent asks.

"Not today, we should buy more this weekend." As it turns out, the calendar is different in this world, as it is now Faleeve, the 11th day of the 11th month, a perfect birthday. Previously, my date of birth was April 18th, and my date of death the 15th of March, but that doesn't carry over well, and I decided yesterday that today is my birthday. Here I am, celebrating with bread, cheese, candles, and a bible.

"You know, you should have decided your birthday earlier, that way I could have prepared," Argent jokes.

"Perhaps I ought to have chosen a better day to be reborn, but what is better than the eleventh day of the eleventh month?"

"Seven and seven, to be reborn on such a holy day would be an honor."

"Eleven is twice one, because I was a man of god then and a man of god now; one then, and a new one now."

"I see. So, perhaps we should discuss some of yesterday's...ramifications. For purposes of my next sermon, of course." there is a solemn look on Argent's face.

"Ramifications for your sermon? How so?"

"Azathoth gave us synats, the great spider formed the plague from its 6th leg, yet now they are one in the same. I suppose my point is..." Argent pauses, swallowing "is god a lie?" *How do I answer that? Odds are, if Argent is suspect, he's using his truth zone.* I realize what I need to do, and alter my own perception of myself, and thus reality.

"Of course not. Azathoth cares for his creation, it is simply that from time to time he uses metaphors, like us." I say, speaking truth.

"And tests?"

"And tests." Argent suddenly embraces me in a hug, and I feel his tears stain my scarf.

"Thank you, oh thank you," he says, barely coherent.

"Us two, and those of our holy discipline, are the sole anointed ones in God's path. We are the highest in the world, we are foremost, we are the best; this is the penultimate birth, and the dreaming gardens await." I comfort him in his delusions, which are temporarily also mine.

"Through the heavens and earth, we alone are honored," he continues the verse.

"And from the womb to the tomb, we anointed ones follow the path foretold upon us," we speak in unison.

"Thank you, young master. My faith was subconsciously wavering. I-I heard the voices, the same ones from when Father Makenzie died. I-I'm scared, young master." Argent looks genuinely terrified.

"We all need help to stay upon the holy path at times. You know, maybe it's best we are so close; after all, we both have that same issue, though mine are born independent of faith," I chuckle.

"Yeah, it's guilt, idiot." Kevin smiles, clearly joking. *Alex can see him now. Once we hang out again, after the next stage of invasion, we might be able to get back to normal. Especially once I-* my thoughts are cut off.

"Oh, and one other thing. Follow me." Argent stands up, starting to walk to the bell tower. *Couldn't he have stayed that close a bit longer?* Along the way, I notice the name on the urn that lives above the fireplace, 'Makenzie'. Up the ladder, we enter the bell tower, and at the last second, Argent covers my eyes from behind.

"Argent, if you cover my eyes, I can't see the surprise"

"Are you ready?" he asks

"Of course. Unless this is a wedding proposal; that's not my style, y'know?" I tease. Argent uncovers my eyes and reveals a special bouquet of flowers and a custom-made necklace with the symbol of Azathoth, the eye of the star, as its centerpiece. *Cross necklaces exist in every universe, huh?*

"Oh god, Argent, I-" at that moment, my actions are without thought. Before I realize what, I am doing, Argent and I have entered a deep kiss.

"Young master- the ladder hole-"

"I'm not gonna fall." I smile, continuing to show my appreciation.

"Sir, that isn't the issue." There is a moment of silence before I look backwards to see what he means; the ladder is one that folds itself upwards, and somehow it became folded.

"Oh. Is there another way out?" I ask.

"We can either wait for help or climb down the outside." Argent looks vaguely lovestruck. *Or maybe that's your optimism.*

"Oh...so, if we're stuck, can we kiss again?" I ask, flirting. Argent sighs,

"Once, and make it short." Obviously, I take any chance I can get. A noise interrupts us.

"Hey, lovebirds, I'm stuck here too." Kevin glares.

"Okay third-wheel, buzz off back to my subconscious then," I tell Kevin, before seeing Argent's confused expression and explaining with the single word of "Kevin."

"One, I can't do that freely, we both know that. Two, your subconscious is scary. Deal with your relationship with authority first." Kevin taunts.

"Were you not a phantom of my mind, I would beat your ass."

"Not agreeing with him?" Argent asks.

"Naturally," I smile, "regardless, I figured out the best way to get down."

"Oh really? How?"

"I did some gardening earlier." I hop out the window of the bell tower, landing in the hibiscus bushes and ending up unharmed.

"I think I'll miss!" Argent shouts down.

"Then I'll catch you!" I shout back. Argent jumps down, as planned, I catch him in my arms, bridal style.

I try to give him another kiss, but he blocks my lips with his hand,

"Let's keep that special, lest they lose their meaning." he smiles warmly up at me.

"Then I'll settle for this." I kiss his hand, feeling warm internally. *Do I have a fever or is this love?* The day of festivities was long in the past tense yet short in the present. As it turns out, we both had the same general idea of a gift for one another; he got me a copy of *The Books of Abramon*, I got him my journals from during this long journey.

"This is my journal. Everything that's happened so far is in here, each thought, idea, and event. I even got some photos of the places we went, I kept some of the train tickets, and I even got a newspaper clipping about The Assassin King's defeat. All of it is in here." I hand him my journal, a red book with the words "A Journal of a New World" written on it.

"Oh my- thank you! This is one of the best gifts I have ever received!" he exclaims, holding it close to his chest.

"There is a drawback, however," I sigh, preparing myself to break the news.

"Oh? And that is?"

"I'm going to be going on a...business trip. I don't know how long I'll be gone, but I can't bring you with me." The words are hard to say as I see Argent's eyes darken.

"When do you leave?" he asks.

"About a month from today, don't worry. I still need to pack." I feel the sadness radiate off of him.

"Should I help?" Argent asks.

"If possible, yeah." Packing takes about an hour for me to get all the bags ready. There is my special bag, which I need to keep iced. After all that work, sleep comes easy, as do dreams. In the dream, I was a giant man with an ember hidden inside a radish. I use the embers to start a fire for some of the smaller people.

"Oh, thank you, thank you," the small people say.

"It is my duty," I say, helping more fires be lit. After a certain point, I'm called over to one of the larger fires. I see several other beings the same size as me lower themselves from the clouds.

"You have given fire to man. For this crime, you are condemned. Stingy Jack, your punishment is to be eaten by the eagles upon mount Vesuvius. Two of these people, one with bronze skin and a gold helmet, the other wielding a spear, drag me away. Upon reaching the mountain, I am chained up.

"Wait! I have done no wrong!" I exclaim, but the two have left. I look over, and next to me I see Kevin pushing a boulder up the mountain. Upon reaching the top, it falls, and he starts again.

"What's your sin?" I ask him.

"Trickery. You?"

"Brought fire to man." The dream went on for a long time, the feeling of the eagle consuming me was unbearable. At one point, the boulder shoved by Keven ends up rolling down and crushing my arm. At the end of the dream, I feel a wave of heat and a flash of light flow over me before I wake up. Evidently Argent had kicked away the blankets onto me in his sleep, and the light started to shine through the window. *Damn.*

One month passes, a night with the same dream as one month prior. I grab my bags and start running, needing to make my appointment in time. I reach the train station, then stop. *Wait, what?* I try to remember what I was doing, confused. Then, I wake up, actually this time.

"Dear, you said you needed to be out by sunrise," Argent says.

"Oh, yeah. I had the wildest dream-" I start to explain.

"Sweetheart, there isn't time. I got you bread, a candle, and a cloak." Argent gestures to some bread and clothes on the desk next to me.

"Thank you, you ought to receive your first letter from me in a month or so," I smile as Argent gets ready to go back to bed. I put on my cloak, the dark fabric flowing in the breeze from the window. *No hiding our faith wearing this, I look like a missionary.* The cloak is covered in Azathoth's eyes. The candle is much more neutral, being a simple red candle holder with a handle and a dish at the bottom. The bread is simply bread, and that is all. I exit into the darkness of the dusk, venturing onwards. The lack of light makes things...difficult. I almost get hit by a carriage along the way but manage to jump out of the way. I put my knowledge of this world to good use, shouting as many swears and obscenities at him as possible.

"You want to say that again?" The man gets out of the carriage and walks towards me.

"Yes, I do!" I pull back my hood, revealing myself to be myself, the man who killed The Assassin King.

"Oh, Mr. La Demente, my apologies-" he starts.

"You have ten seconds to run, shortie." I glare down at him, reaching for my knife to scare him. The man runs, as expected. He dropped a few pieces of silver, which I pick up for myself. *Easy money. Not that I need it, but bastards like that ought to look where they're going at night. Honestly, the next bad driver like that is gonna lose a pearl necklace and a finger.* I joke to myself as I walk.

"Thinking like that is bad," Kevin chuckles.

"Do you endorse those kinds of drivers?"

"Nah, threats are wrong though, especially when you're famous."

"They deserve it." I laugh. In the distance, the sun is starting to rise, though I'm facing the other way. The sun rises behind me, a shadow forms before me, and so the world is right again. Two and two is four, four and four is eight, the world is as it should be. I am with sin, a repentant man, but on the winding path of heaven.

Chapter 36: Heartache of a Sanguine Amaryllis

It's been a week but... I can't ignore what happened. How was he there? Kevin... What was that? Is he really back or...? It wasn't just me; CJ was able to see him too, but no one else could. He even acted like he'd been talking to him for a while. I was ecstatic at the time, but I would like to know what's going on. Next time I see CJ, I'll ask.

"Alex. Alex?"

"Huh! What?"

"You were spacing out. We're here." Finally, after a long ship ride down the river we arrived in Kailias. Getting off the dock and finally back onto solid ground, I notice something. *Are those...*

"Cable cars?" *I don't remember seeing those last time we were here.*

"Oh, so that's what they look like," Amaryll comments, "I remember my dad talking about cable cars after he came home from a business trip in San Francisco."

"Did they really put these in while we were gone?"

"Of course not. Don't you remember they started construction on these about 6 months before we moved here. They must have just finished while we were gone."

"Hmm... I don't really remember that."

"Well, that would make sense as they started construction on the opposite side of the city from where we live. I saw it in the newspaper, so since you rarely looked it makes sense."

"Well, there was kind of a lot going on. I didn't really have the time."

"Yeah, we should probably get on, it'd be faster than a carriage. Pretty sure there were plans for a station nearby where we live." We get on and take our seats. *Luckily it was pretty early in the morning, so it wasn't too crowded.* It's a nostalgic feeling riding in a cable car. *I remember when I was younger going on a trip to San Francisco. Though it had been such a long time ago I barely remember it. I haven't thought much about my life back on earth, not since I got here. It's been almost six months.* Amaryll is looking at the map of the cable car routes.

"How about that, there's a station right within walking distance of our house. That's some good luck if you ask me," Amaryll says.

"Guess we just picked a good spot." After a few minutes we finally arrived at our stop. We walk back to the house and open the door.

"Welcome back, Alex, Amaryll," Eris greets us. We walk in and sit down at the table. "How did your mission go?" *Hmm... Eris is already pretty well informed on the situation, so I guess I should tell him.*

"Well, it wouldn't feel right to say it went well, but I wouldn't say it went bad either..."

"What happened?"

"It's kind of a long story, so I guess I'll start with the end result; As it turns out the Scout Group people are still alive, but they had almost nothing to do with the creation of The Assassin King."

"Do you know who is responsible?" Eris asks.

"It turns out it was Number 02 the whole time."

"Number 02!" Eris exclaims.

"You know about him? I didn't mention him 'cause public knowledge is pretty limited on the numbers, in fact you wouldn't be wrong in saying it's non-existence."

"Oh, I don't know anything about him. I was just surprised by the name."

"Oh..." *The way he reacted... Does he know something I don't? Maybe it's best to save the questions for later.* "I personally don't get him. Number 02 I mean. One minute he's trying to kill us the next he's helping us? What's his deal anyway? And the whole time he's just orchestrating everything? The Assassin King while he was alive and then the remaining cult members after words. He obviously wanted us alive, but why? Assuming that, how did he know Cat would come back to save us? If he didn't know, none of it makes any sense. Was it all just a game to him? Was everything we've done up until this point all the result of the whim of one man? Was there a reason for any of it at all?" *Eris seems uncomfortable with me continuing on the same subject.*

"I don't know Alex. Maybe there is a reason and we just can't see it yet?" Magnolia replies.

"That must be it."

"Ahem, anything else important happen?" Eris asks.

"Actually yes, we met with the Yavolian King or more he wanted to meet with us," Amaryll explains.

"The Yavolian King! But how? Why would he wish to speak with you?"

"Well, I said us, but really it seemed like he just wanted to talk to Alex."

"Yeah, he mentioned something about a friend of his who was killed by The Assassin King looking similar to me. He saw us when we went to the Yavolian capital for the celebration."

"He should be here pretty soon actually. I sent him a telegram earlier," Amaryll says.

"He's coming here!"

"Yeah, is something wrong?"

"No... never mind." *Is he nervous about meeting him or something? I mean he is the ruler of one of the more important countries in the world, but... He's always been so casual around me I never really thought about it.* I hear someone knocking on the door.

"I'll get it," I say. I open up the door and there Niko is.

"Oh, Alex, good to see you."

"Good to see you too. Come in, we were just talking about you."

"Really? You know what they say..." Niko jokes.

"Speak of the devil? Right?" We sat back down at the table.

"Exactly." Niko walks in and closes the door. "Oh, who's this?"

"Oh, this is Eris, he takes care of the house and he helped us get to the Kingdom of Aochikyuu."

"Ah, another one of Alex's friends." Niko extends out his hand. Eris in response freezes up.

"Don't worry, a friend of Alex is a friend of mine. Call me Niko." Eris meekly grabs Niko's hand.

"N-nice to meet you."

"Sorry I had to leave right before something important."

"Don't worry about it Niko. I am curious about what happened though."

"Well, one of the archdukes attempted to take the throne by claiming I had died. They even went as far to create fake military reports from the Kobolda Empire confirming my death. Then he was able to convince enough people and was crowned the 902nd Yavolian King. You see, as the Yavolian king I have the capability to telepathically communicate with anyone in the Demonic race. I can only hear what someone is thinking if they intend for me to hear it of course. So, one of my followers alerted me of the situation just before the coronation in hopes that I was still alive. So, I immediately left to deal with the situation. As soon as I arrived at the palace, I took out the false king and retook the throne. I was recrowned as the 903rd king, as despite the false pretense for the 902nd king's coronation it was still an official coronation. With the long history of the Kingdom of Yavolia this is not the first time something like this has happened. There is something I'm worried about though."

"Well, what is it?"

"You see in the Yavolia book of prophecy it says, '...and thus under the reign of the 903rd emperor The Beasts of the Black Sun shall return; creatures with metal where they should have flesh, and the great invaders shall invade once again, a second strike upon this land.' I think you know what this means."

"The second invasion and you mean those robots too... With what the scout group said."

"Yes, I think that those secondary invasion forces will be here sometime during my reign. Whether that will be days or years from now I do not know, but with my position and a death word like mine any idea of a peaceful end to my life is but a pipe dream."

"The only thing we can do is prepare, but with Number 02 around... I do think it's best we deal with him first."

"One thing I do have to say is I feel bad about my earlier judgment of CJ. I didn't know the whole story."

"It's fine Niko. It's my fault for not telling you about everything earlier." Eris looks down at his watch.

"Oh! I'm going to be late. Sorry Alex, I have to leave. The mayor needs me."

"Nice meeting you Eris."

"N-nice meeting you too..." Eris pauses for a moment at the door, his face going red, "Niko." He closes the door. *What was that?! I can't tell if he's nervous, embarrassed, or scared!*

"Sorry to be so brief, but it seems I have to go as well. I'd love to spend time with you again sometime Alex, but it's goodbye for now."

"Come see us as soon as you can." I wave goodbye as he walks out the door. I start laughing.

"What is it Alex?"

"It's just... Did you see Eris's face?"

"You're right, what was he so flushed for?" Amaryll laughs as well.

"Ahem, anyway, is there anywhere you want to go today?"

"Actually, I heard there's this really nice park at the foot of the mountains. It's about an hour by train if I remember correctly."

"It sounds nice. It's still pretty early, we should be able to make it out and back before dark. Let's go."

"I'd love to." We get ready and head to the station on a cable car. We get on the train and take our seats.

The city passes by as the train car moves on out into the forests. The time passes by quickly, the scenery swiftly moving by as the forest continues to get more and more alpine. The loud screech of the train coming to a stop snaps me out of my dream like trance.

"Alex, we're here." We walk out onto and then off the platform. We walk down a gravel trail. The air was fresh and crisp as you would expect being at the foot of a mountain. The tall slender evergreens numerous and dense around the trail. The scent of the pine sap wafts through the cool air. The winding corridor of trees finally gives way to a large atrium in the forest. There in the center a rotary pavilion coated with vines meandering down its sides in a particular way avoiding the entrances. Around the pavilion are four large patches of vibrant sanguine. Six petals ordered into the shape of a trumpet, thin red stamen sloping down and out ended by a clump of red-orange pollen. These flowers were undoubtedly...

"Amaryllis."

"You know your flowers pretty well Alex. I'm surprised."

"Well, I wouldn't want to be uninformed about..." *the name of someone close to me.*

"About what?"

"Never mind."

"Actually, Alex there's something I need to tell you."

"What is it?" *She's not gonna...*

"What I said early..."

"Yeah?" *Maybe not.*

"I lied. Sorry." *Definitely was not 'that'.*

"Lied? About what?"

"Well, earlier I said I heard about this place, but that's not exactly true."

"Then how..."

"You see, I'm starting to get my memories back..." She pauses looking out onto the flower beds. "It's pretty isn't it?" I'm not sure if I should respond, "I remember now. This place... it held a special importance to me." She looks down at her feet moving them around, walking around the flowers. "What I did here... what if I... It's pretty isn't it... the flowers that I share a name with." She kneels down to caress the outside of the flower in front of her. "Deep red, like blood... Isn't it funny? For me to be named after these flowers, to end up with the powers I did. Maybe my parents were able to see the future?" She laughs looking up at me with a pained smile. We walk in and sit down in the pavilion.

"Your memories... You mean from when you were under The Assassin Kings control. These memories... how many have come back?"

"They're very faint and not very numerous, but..." She looks up at me, tears forming in her eyes, "I'm scared Alex. I'm scared. What I did during that time... It terrifies me. If they all come back... How will I be able to live with myself? If they come back Alex... if they come back... I think... I think I'll fall apart." In an almost instinctual motion, I pull her into a tight embrace, before pulling back. Amaryll looks up at me, her eyes wide open.

"There's no need to worry Amaryll."

"But I... but... " She struggles to get the words out through her tears. "My memories of my time on earth... they're so faint... if... if I remember everything that happened. I'm worried I won't even be the same person anymore..."

"I'll be here for you. Always. It doesn't matter what you become, I'll stay with you regardless." Amaryll begins to laugh through her tears,

"You're such an idiot, worrying about me... when you have it worse off."

"Oh, come on, Amaryll, you know there's no point in comparing things like that."

"Your right Alex." She wipes the tears off her face, the pain leaving her smile leaving something more beautiful behind. We stand up. I see it again CJ, Cat their grim, gray and lifeless faces. *No! Why? Not again! Not again!* My brain begins to ache. My skull feels like it's being pushed in from all sides. I feel my consciousness begin to slip away. I begin to fall to the floor.

"Alex? Alex! Ale-" my hearing gets more and more muffled before cutting out entirely, my vision blurring before fading to black. I wake up inhaling sharply. I look around to see that I'm back in our bed at home. I look to my side, Amaryll's sitting down looking at me, her stress clearly displayed on her face.

"Alex! You're awake!" She drops onto the bed wrapping her arms around me. I slowly sit up.

"What happened?"

"I'm not sure. You just suddenly dropped to the ground." *I remember her saying, 'Your right Alex', but anything after that is gone.* "I grabbed you, ran back to the train station as fast as I could and got you back here in bed."

"How long was I out?"

"Well, it's the morning after we left, so it's been sixteen, maybe eighteen hours."

"Sorry for worrying you like that."

"There's no need to apologize. It's not your fault." *Why? What happened to me? Could it have been those memories? No I... it can't be. It's probably best if I don't think about it. I'd rather enjoy my time... with Amaryll.*

Chapter 37: ...So Below

Ah, it's been two and a half years... since I left earth. That car crash. It all feels so far away now. I wonder what things would be like if I had stayed? I guess there's no point in thinking about such a depressing alternative to the current reality. We had just arrived back at the house. Azalea leans back in the recliner we bought a few days back.

"It's interesting, you know?" She says.

"What's interesting?"

"Well, I never thought nanobots would be behind everything." *I doubt she ever thought nanobots were even a possibility.* "I mean my entire existence. I'm an elf and if these nanobots weren't here I would just be a normal human. I would have probably been dead by now."

"Your hair wouldn't be blue either."

"My hair?"

"Well, remember how when we first met, I was surprised when you told me that your hair was naturally blue."

"Yeah, I do remember that. What about it?"

"Well, blue isn't exactly a naturally occurring hair color in humans."

"I guess you're right. I mean it is kind of an exclusive trait of moon elves and I don't think I've ever seen a human with blue hair." *I mean I have, but it wasn't natural, and it definitely wasn't here on Sotaqt.* "And now that I think about it, I guess those UEF scientists were right! There is a connection between elven magic and all other unique race related abilities. In fact, they are all caused by the same thing. Though

I'm not sure how I feel about my entire existence being caused by an accident..."

"Wait, Azalea you do know that people can- Actually never mind."

"Oh, anyway, we should probably get going."

"Why?" I ask.

"Well, my parents asked if I could come over now."

"Oh, alright." We get up and walk over to Azalea's parent's house.

"Oh! Cat, Azalea you're here. Good to see you."

"Mom, we were just here earlier today."

"You're right. Actually, I have a bit of a surprise for you."

"Really what is it?" Azalea asks.

"You'll never guess who's here." *I think I have a pretty good idea, but...* We walk into the house.

"Azalea?" A familiar voice says.

"Uncle Adran!" Azalea rushes over to him wrapping her arms around him. "I haven't seen you since we arrived back in Merizon."

"You're right It's been about four months. Cat good to see you too. How are things going with you two? I hope you're treating Azalea well." *This guy acts more like Azalea's dad than Julius does, and Julius is her actual dad! I guess that's why she likes her uncle so much then. Though honestly, I'm still not sure what to think of it.*

"Things are going..." *I still haven't thought up a proper response to Azalea's 'proclamation' on the ship. It's been around a month. If I don't say anything, the distance between us will continue to grow.*

"Ah, I see. Well, I'm sure you'll be able to pull through. So, what have you guys been doing these past four months?"

"Well, after all the bounty money we got we decided to buy a house here in Sycarro."

"Ah, I did hear about that." We explain all about The Assassin King's true identity and our search for the people responsible.

"Are you really sure I should be privy to all this information? I mean I'm just your uncle."

"It's not a problem as long as it doesn't get out."

"Still though I can't believe that Number 02 bastard was behind all of this."

"The EIA is currently looking into his whereabouts, but there are currently no leads. We believe he has given up using the bases built by the Scout Group now that we have ready access to them as well as a map of all their locations. We plan to meet soon with the Scout group to see what information we can get out of them. Hopefully we'll get a lead," Julius explains.

"Still it's hard to believe all that stuff about the nano-bots and the Earth."

"Well, I had a pretty hard time coming to terms with it myself, but it does line up with the current scientific research regarding synats and racial abilities," Azalea says.

"Exactly, we also want to see how much of this technology we can harness. This is another reason we want to talk with the Scout Group. Assuming their cooperation this could be very beneficial to the UEF."

"Well, I'll tell you this I'd be willing to help you in your search for Number 02 so if you ever need help, I'm here."

"Thank you Uncle Adran."

"There is one thing that could be a problem," Julius says.

"What?"

"Well, how would we communicate with them? If they are from earth wouldn't they be speaking some earthen language?

"Well, like I explained earlier, the auto translation and speech that people who come here from earth have was something developed by the Scout Group. So, it won't be a problem," Azalea explains.

"Good to know."

"On another note there's something I think I can do to deal with the other issue at hand." Adran whispers something to Azalea.

"You're right, that's a good Idea! I'm sorry to be leaving so soon, but there's something important we need to do."

"Alright, we'll come back sometime soon," Mrs. Leitner says.

"Of course, we live right around the corner after all." We leave the house and walk out for a few minutes till we're outside of town. We finally reach the spot Azalea had in mind and we lay down next to each other. *All that time spent alone in the forest... wondering whether or not I would be able to save them. That hard work to save them. It was all worth it for this.* The breeze flows around me, brushing across my face. It moves the chartreuse leaves illuminated by the afternoon sun, the light filtering down onto the grass. The smooth pale bark above me and the soft cushy moss as a cushion below. The odd chirping of a bird, the rustling of the leaves and the whisper of the soft breeze. It's enough to just make one's worries drift away in the wind. I turn my gaze to my right to a pale iridescent blue; a cold color to most, but a warm one to me. I lightly grab onto her hand.

"Cat?!" she exclaims.

"Azalea."

"Yes?"

"I think I have an answer to your proclamation."

"You mean the one from the ship?"

"Yes. You know back on earth I always felt a little distant. I had Alex, CJ, and other people too. It always felt like I was drifting aimlessly through life without any direction or goals, but now... now that I'm here I feel like I've been set on a path. To a goal I'm sure of and a grueling hike to the peak. It hasn't been easy, but I feel all of it was worth it in the end. I don't know, maybe it's all some elaborate delusion I've created to deal with my responsibility for the crash, but I'd rather not think of it that way. I mean obviously right. Despite all the hardship these truly have been the best few months of my life. I think Alex and CJ might find that insulting, but it's true. I think you understand, no?" She nods in agreement. "Basically, what I'm trying to say is you've made this time spent here worthwhile and without you not only would I still be drifting around, but sunk to the bottom. I think I'd rather sail right to the edge of the world especially if it was you." I look back up at the leaves waiting for a response. As silence persists the tension grows higher and butterflies begin to fly around in my stomach. My face starts going red. *Wait, did I really just say that? Out loud! I mean at least I meant to this time but... Oh man I bet she thinks I'm stupid now if she didn't already. I'm such an idiot... Huh?* Azalea's looking at me with her eyes wide open.

"Aze-Azalea?"

"Sorry, I just didn't expect an answer like that."

"What did you expect me to say?"

"Maybe something along the lines of 'I understand your feelings, but I'd rather things stay the way they are' or 'it's not like I don't like hanging out with you, but I just don't feel the same way' something like that."

"You thought I would just flat out reject you?"

"Pretty much. I was totally mentally and emotionally prepared for that moment, so when I got an unexpected response, I guess I couldn't do anything but freeze. Sorry for the silence."

"And here I thought I was the idiot. It's not like I ended my own life to save you twice or anything," I joke.

"Well, it's not like I was the only one you were saving... Wait, end your own life?"

"Wait, did I not tell you? I figured the only way to get back to Sotaqt from earth was to do that. So, I may or may not have burnt myself alive."

"Wait, seriously Cat? Why didn't you tell me?! You do know the effect that can have on someone right?"

I'm pretty sure I did tell her, but...

"Of course, I experienced it myself."

"I guess I'm not the only idiot then," Azalea says. I laugh.

"I guess you're right. Should we go now?"

"We can, but is it okay if I tell you a story?"

"Sure, I don't mind."

"I've known about this place ever since I was little. I used to come here all the time and just sit under this tree staring at the sky through the leaves. Uncle Adran introduced me to this spot. I'd always come here when things weren't exactly going well to relax. It certainly helped. My childhood wasn't exactly rosy, but I do have Uncle Adran to thank for some of the better moments. You see I kind of stuck out like a sore thumb with my blue hair and all. I didn't really get along with anyone," *Well she is pretty headstrong,* "It didn't help that I wasn't at school very often."

"Why?" *I am a little curious how long school would last. I mean she's 119 and she said physically she's around seventeen. So, how long are they in school for? I can't imagine it's that entire time.*

"Well, remember how I told you I was part of a government program studying the effects of interbreeding between elven races. So, a lot of the time they would take me out of school to conduct tests. It wasn't anything bad, mostly questionnaires and physical examination as well as multiple attempts to bring out my elven magic. The only problem was that it separated me from the rest of the kids at school because I was away so often." *I think I'm starting to get why Azalea's so attached to her uncle. Anyone who helped her out through that must have been like a saint to her.* "So, you can't believe how excited I was when I heard I was going to have a brother. It was obviously a while before I could talk with him, but once he was old enough, he was really the only other kid I had a real friendship with. He had a few friends himself that I had a certain level of relationship with, but it wasn't the same. If he hadn't been there, I'm not sure what would have happened to me. He gave me a reason to keep on going. He was there with me in the experiments and through school. So, when he... when he..." Tears start to form in Azalea's eyes. "When he died I-I..." She suddenly grabs onto me.

"Azalea!" I slowly put my arms around her. She looks up at me.

"Do you think you could have saved him?"

"Azalea... Obviously if I could have, I would have Azalea, but I don't think I would have been able to. By the time I got there he was already gone." She continues to cry.

"I'm sorry Cat. I'm trying to blame you, it's just..."

"I understand... I understand."

Epilogue: The Hardest of Hearts...

My name is Elias Mensonge. My goal is bicameral, in that wish for both retribution and recompense.

"Mr. Mensonge, we have your space ready, though there are a few last-minute clarifications we need to ask about," the Ticketmaster asks, her hair in a professional bun. *Almost Cliche.*

"Oh? I thought my letter was detailed enough," I reply, with no real meaning behind my words.

"Well, for starters, there's your special baggage; you requested the bag to be kept in the freezer car, and we have policies about transporting produce-"

"It is not produce."

"I see. Also, you have one ticket to go, but four to return. Is this a mistake?"

"No. I intend to bring someone back."

"Well then, with that clarified, welcome aboard Blitz Transportation, the best train company in the northern world." The train door is opened, allowing me into my specialized deluxe room. *Produce implies intent to be consumed, this meat is not for that. Eating him would be a waste, I suppose.* Within my own personal train car, there was a bed, couch, several books, an ice bucket for drinks, a snuff box, plenty of candles, and a bell for service as needed, plus the most important aspect, the room will be cleaned immediately after I leave in order to leave no fingerprints or DNA evidence. I produce a map from the pocket of my white peacoat, placing it upon the table. Two X's are on the map, one in the Midorochi Kingdom, the other at the Merizon Museum of History. *Accomplices and primary target.* The other symbol was a double-looped O in Tirentod, *the home of my secondary target, the bastard that set my plans back by over a year. I'll kill him. Naturally, I need to be strategic about all this. First, a list of threats to my plan.*

'CJ and company. The government. ATUR. Number 02. Other interested parties' these were the groups and individuals listed under the 'threats' category. *Next, I need to figure out weaknesses.* "For CJ and company, the best way to deal with them will be through mind-games and a pre-emptive attack. Should that fail, employ individual weaknesses. CJ and Argent are vulnerable to ranged attacks, Amaryll, Azalea, and Alex all need to be able to see me, which is no problem, and Alex, who can be manipulated by threatening Amaryll; the priority is to kill CJ and then leave. The government is limited by international law, and thus can be avoided by staying in neutral nations. ATUR is unfamiliar with this world, giving me a territorial advantage. No known weaknesses with Number 02, research further," I write. Four days of time during this voyage, four days to plan and think of a weakness for Number 02, yet I find nothing. Upon reaching Obervios, I take a ship to the northern part of the Kitsune kingdoms. From there, a few hours on horseback gets me to the Midorochi Kingdom. My allies reside in a home extremely different from the others, a log cabin with a yellow buggy in front of it. I walk closer and knock on the door, from inside a voice says,

"Identify yourself." I smile, looking up and replying,

"Hanzai Yokotawaru, Alcool Voleuse, I have returned to collect the favor you both owe me." In the reflection of the buggy's headlights, I see my reflection. Black hair down to my shoulders, gold-rimmed fullmoon glasses, a red button up, and a white tie to match my peacoat.

"His name is Sea-I mean, Elias Mensonge." I hear Alcool explaining to Hanzai behind the door. *Two years have been leading up to this, two long, bloody years.* The door opens, and Hanzai steps out,

"Elias, come in, we will talk inside." He looks scared of me, I understand why. *Mercy does help in the end. My name is Elias Mensonge, and I will have recompense.*

Afterword: G

Hello this is the author speaking, G. A. Duarte, to be specific. This was a project started between me and my co-author more than a year ago in early May of 2020. It was originally just a way to take up time. In the beginning I didn't plan on finishing it and the tone was much different. I ended up re-writing several of the chapters because of this. Around when I finished chapter seven is when I realized that this was a project worth continuing. It was not an easy process and there were several times when I thought that the project would fail and that it would just be that one thing I did for fun during quarantine and nothing more. I'm glad I was wrong. This project helped me realize that I had it in me to push forward and complete big goals like this. It was good to know that I had it in me to be resilient and not give up as I have on other projects. There were certainly a lot of qualms along the way between me and my co-author trying to decide where the plot should go, what a character's synat should be, how a certain character arc would go, or even the lore of the world itself, but in the end, we always pulled through and came to compromise. It was a lot of fun writing this book; it will be my first, but certainly not my last. I hope to add to this series in the future. Look forward to the rest of the trilogy.

Afterword: S

I'm not gonna take myself as seriously as my partner, but please give me money and follow me on Instagram, @s.wentzell_author. The current pfp is me and my cat, Macbeth (AKA lil Maccy D).